ALSO BY KIERAN SCOTT

She's So Dead to Us
He's So Not Worth It
This Is So Not Happening

Only Everything

A TRUE LOVE NOVEL
BY KIERAN SCOTT

SIMON & SCHUSTER BFYR

NEW YORK   LONDON   TORONTO   SYDNEY   NEW DELHI

SIMON & SCHUSTER BFYR
An imprint of Simon & Schuster Children's Publishing Division
1230 Avenue of the Americas, New York, New York 10020

For information about special discounts for bulk purchases,
please contact Simon & Schuster Special Sales at 1-866-506-1949
or business@simonandschuster.com.
The Simon & Schuster Speakers Bureau can bring authors to your live event.
For more information or to book an event, contact the Simon & Schuster Speakers Bureau
at 1-866-248-3049 or visit our website at www.simonspeakers.com.
Also available in a SIMON & SCHUSTER BFYR paperback edition
Jacket design by Chloë Foglia
Interior design by Hilary Zarycky
The text for this book is set in Granjon.
Manufactured in the United States of America
2 4 6 8 10 9 7 5 3
Library of Congress Cataloging-in-Publication Data
Scott, Kieran, 1974–
Only everything / Kieran Scott.
pages cm. — (A true love novel ; [1])
Summary: "Eros (aka Cupid) is sent to earth after disobeying the gods and required to
match three couples without her powers"—Provided by publisher.
ISBN 978-1-4424-7718-6 (hardcover) — ISBN 978-1-4424-7716-2 (pbk.) —
ISBN 978-1-4424-7719-3 (eBook)
1. Eros (Greek deity)—Juvenile fiction. [1. Eros (Greek deity)—Fiction. 2. Goddesses,
Greek—Fiction. 3. Mythology, Greek—Fiction. 4. Dating (Social customs)—Fiction.
5. Love—Fiction. 6. High schools—Fiction. 7. Schools—Fiction.] I. Title.
PZ7.S42643On 2014
[Fic]—dc23
2013019388

For anyone who's ever felt they needed

a little help finding love

ACKNOWLEDGMENTS

True would not exist without the sage advice of my power duo—agent Sarah Burnes and editor Zareen Jaffery—who pushed me to find "the hook." That hook ended up being the coolest, quirkiest character I've ever written, so I thank them endlessly for that inspiration. Huge thanks to Justin Chanda for continuing to believe in me and my ideas, and to Paul Crichton for setting up the events that allow me to go talk to anyone who will listen about how much I love what I do. Thank you to my undying champion, Logan Garrison, who has more patience than anyone I know, and to Julia Maguire, who lets nothing slip by—in a good way. Thank you also to Valerie Shea for her extraordinary attention to detail.

Thank you to the amazing librarians, bookstore owners, bloggers, and fans I've met over the past year. You've made me laugh, cry, and feel good about my work in a way that I sorely needed. You have no idea how much it has meant to me.

On a more personal note, I must thank my husband, Matt, and our two crazy boys for making my every day brighter, and my mom, who still inspires me each day, even though she's no longer—technically—here.

Finally, I want to thank the following authors who have been a tremendous help to me without their knowing. Reading their books (some for the second or third time) helped me get through a recent creative crisis, reminding me that our writing can be simple, strong, funny, meaningful, and imaginative, but still true. Thank you, thank you, thank you to Sarah Dessen, Megan McCafferty, Jennifer Weiner, Sophie Kinsella, and the late great Maeve Binchy.

PROLOGUE

"Do you think the Earth will always exist?"

Orion picked a small white wildflower from the grass and plucked one of its delicate petals. He examined it before surrendering it to the warm, late-summer breeze.

"Doubtful," I replied. "The universe is too random. Sooner or later some asteroid or comet will come along and—blam!" I clapped my hands too hard and the trees behind us shook, sending dozens of birds squawking overhead. "Bye-bye planet."

Orion glanced around as a couple of startled rabbits bounded by.

"Poetic," he said with a smirk. "Back in my day Eros had a reputation for subtlety."

I tore the petals off another flower and blew them toward the sun, where they swirled like a tornado before dispersing to all corners of the globe. "A lot can change in three thousand years."

Orion rolled onto his side, and I watched his arm and torso muscles flex beneath his white T-shirt. A tanned knee peeked out through a stringy hole in his distressed jeans as he crooked one leg. I smiled in a covetous way. As much justice as the leather vest and loincloth did him back in the day, this boy was born to be dressed by

2 • kieran scott

Levi's. It had taken him a couple of weeks to get used to the denim's chafing, but trust me, it was well worth it.

"What will happen to us, then?" he asked as he trailed his fingertip along the inside of my arm. "When the world ends?"

I took a deep breath, enjoying the pleasant shivers his gesture sent through me. "I wouldn't worry about it, since you probably won't live long enough to see it happen. You are, after all, mortal."

I was going for lighthearted honesty, but his deep blue eyes darkened and he flopped onto his back again, heaving a sigh.

"Don't remind me."

I felt a familiar pang and lifted my head from the ground. My long, unruly black hair tangled and caught in the unkempt grass. Talk about things changing. In the days BCE, Orion would have scoffed at my claim and declared he was going to live forever. But after thousands of years trapped in the heavens, he had new and complicated feelings about mortality. Feelings even he was still trying to sort out.

"I'm sorry," I told him, not for the first time. "I can always hang you back among the stars if you want me to. Say the word and you can loiter up there forever."

I held my breath as I awaited his response. What if he did want to go back? What if being here was too much for him, and his love for me not enough reason for him to stay? Not that I was entirely sure I *could* put him back among the stars anyway. It had been over six months since that fateful Valentine's night when I'd torn him from the heavens, and I still didn't know how I'd done it. An irksome, somewhat frightening fact that was one of very few secrets I was keeping from him, even though I'd sworn I'd always tell him everything. If there's one constant in love, it's the keeping of the little white secrets. And I should know. It's kind of my job.

"No. Absolutely not. Don't even think it." He clasped his warm hand around my waist, and I released the breath, relieved. "I'd rather spend whatever short time I have here with you than hang among the stars watching life go on without me. Watching you go on without me."

We looked into each other's eyes for a long, breathless moment. And then we cracked up laughing.

Orion sat up fully, kneading his forehead between his thumb and forefinger. "Yeah, that was a little over the top, wasn't it?" he said with a self-deprecating chuckle. "There's just so much pressure, trying to be the boyfriend of the Goddess of Love," he added, turning one palm toward the sky. He tipped his head back and laughed again, enjoying the sun on his face. "What have I gotten myself into?"

I loved watching him laugh. He'd been so pensive for the first few weeks of his new life, it had been difficult to watch. Over the past couple of months, he'd gradually started to stabilize, started to relax, but it was still a relief to see him happy.

"Technically, it's my mother who's the Goddess of Love," I reminded him. "I do her grunt work."

I was the one who spent countless hours piercing the hearts of mortals with my golden arrows. I was the one who read their souls and matched them with the very partners who would complete them and make them feel whole, safe, and eternally loved. And how did the mortals repay me? By calling me, still, by that awful name the Romans had given me—Cupid—and depicting me as a fat, half-naked male baby.

I tried to find the whole thing amusing, but it was a bit much for a goddess to take. I was Eros, the mighty creator of love on Earth. I deserved a smidgen of respect.

"Yeah, yeah. You keep telling yourself that," he teased.

"Come on. Being my boyfriend isn't *entirely* bad," I said, nudging him with my knee. "We have fun, don't we?"

As the words left my tongue I wanted to take them back, half expecting him to object. Lately Orion had been hinting that he wanted to go check out the fishing village nearby, to be among other mortals and try out the new twenty-first-century vocabulary I'd been teaching him. But even though I knew his rejoining society was inevitable, I didn't want it to happen yet. I wasn't ready to let him go.

"I suppose," he joked, looking over his shoulder at me.

"You *guess*," I chided. "No one says 'suppose' anymore. At least no one under the age of fifty."

"Yeah, but I'm, like, two *thousand* seven *hundred* and fifty," he said, squinting one eye as he did the math.

"Nice use of the pointless interjection of 'like'!" I congratulated him. "You're my prize pupil!"

"Your only pupil," he said. With the deftness of a panther he flung himself over me, bracing a hand on either side of my body and holding himself up so no part of our bodies touched. The wide neck of his T-shirt hung open so I could see every line of his perfectly toned chest, and the silver necklace I'd brought for him—a perfect arrow its pendant—tickled my collarbone. For a second I thought he was going to kiss me, but instead his expression grew sheepish. "I am your only pupil, right?"

I reached up and touched his face, the light stubble rasping my fingertips. "Never ask me that. You know you are."

He nodded and looked away, and I wondered what he was thinking. Did he really not trust me, or was it some ancient memory that was darkening his heart? Could he possibly be thinking of his first love, Merope, who had broken off their engagement just days before their wedding? I hoped he didn't think me as fickle as she.

"Hey," I said, lightly kicking the inside of his leg with the outside of mine. "Care to have some of that fun right now?"

"You know I would," he replied with a smile.

"Then catch me."

And I took off at roughly the speed of light.

Orion laughed and cursed under his breath as he scrambled to his feet and chased after me. I, of course, slowed my pace to make it fair. This was one of our favorite games, pursuing each other over the wild hillsides and meadows of our quaint North American island. I dove through the woods, nimbly avoiding brambles and fallen trees and foxholes, and grabbed my bow and quiver—filled with silver-tipped hunting arrows rather than my magical golden arrows—from the clearing where we'd left them earlier that day after a spirited hunt. Orion must have snatched his as well, because seconds later an arrow sliced so close to my ear I could hear the feathered fletching rustle. It split the bark of a birch tree dead ahead and I whirled on him, even though I knew he'd missed on purpose. Orion was the only being in existence, mortal or immortal, who was a better shot than me. Not that I would ever admit that.

"Are you trying to pierce my ears?" I demanded, shoving his chest as he arrived, heaving for breath, in front of me.

Orion dropped his weapon and pulled me to him with a grin. He tilted my head to the side, smoothing my hair back, and gently rubbed my earlobe between his finger and thumb. "And mar these perfect specimens? Never."

Then he kissed my neck and wrapped his warm, strong arms around me, enveloping my slim frame against him. I sighed simply, happily, a now-familiar sensation of peace swirling through my heart. Of all the romances I'd had, of all the people and gods and demigods I'd known, of all the realms I'd visited on Earth and in the heavens, the only place that had ever felt like home was right here. Right here in Orion's arms. I didn't understand it, would never have believed it a few months or years or millennia ago, but it was true. Orion was my soul mate. Orion, who had bedded Eos and dallied with Artemis and gotten himself killed by her and her awful brother, Apollo. Orion, the notorious egomaniac, the most reckless thrill seeker who'd ever lived, a mortal I was still getting to know. He was, in many ways, my polar opposite, but he was my one and only home.

"Don't ever leave me," I said into his shirt. "I'd rather die than live without you."

"What?"

My eyes popped open. Damn. I had said that aloud, hadn't I? My heart began to race as I struggled for an explanation. For words that could have been misheard to sound like the words I'd actually said. His fingers tangled in my hair and he tugged my head back gently, but firmly, forcing me to look at him. His eyes were alight with merriment.

"What did you just say?" he asked, amused and maybe a bit intrigued.

"I—I didn't—I mean, I said—"

A deafening crack of thunder shook the ground beneath our feet, sending us staggering together into the nearest tree trunk. Wind whipped my face and rain pelted my skin. The sky above us darkened so quickly there could be only one cause. Terror seized my gut and forced the breath from my lungs. My fingers curled like a vise around Orion's forearm, clinging to him for dear life.

He was coming. No. He was already here.

"Run!" I screamed at Orion. "Run!"

Grasping my hand, Orion turned and fled toward the center of the forest, the thickest cover, the spot that would act as shelter from any natural storm. But I knew this tempest was not natural, and after twenty paces, my fears were confirmed. Ares, the God of War, appeared before us in all his fiery glory, his face streaked with mud from the field of battle, a nasty gash oozing blood over one arm, his visage contorted with a blend of fury and hatred I'd never before seen. Orion stepped in front of me as if to shield my body, but it was no use. The god had only to extend his palm and Orion flew off his feet, hurtling forward like a boneless, weightless rag doll. I reached out for him, but managed to grab only his silver chain, which tore from his neck as he flew. He slammed against Ares's chest, his head snapping back with a crack. Ares flung Orion around to face me, crooked his elbow around my beloved's neck, and held him fast against his sweat-soaked skin.

"Daddy, no!" I shouted, clutching the tiny silver arrow pendant inside my fist.

He ignored me. He always ignored me.

"How dare you debauch my daughter?" he growled in Orion's ear. "I should tear your head from your feeble mortal body right here."

"No!" I screamed. My knees gave out and I hit the ground. Orion struggled, but it was pointless. So very, very pointless. There wasn't a stronger god on Mounts Olympus or Etna than my father. It was so hypocritical, him taking issue with my having formed a relationship with a human, while he and the other upper gods and goddesses went around bedding whomever they wanted—god, mortal, or beast—like it was their right. "Daddy, please! Please! He hasn't done anything wrong. It's my fault. I brought him here. I hid him from you. I'm the one who should be punished."

My father glanced at me, and I saw his eyes widen. For a moment I thought I glimpsed fear there, confusion, but then it was gone and I knew I had imagined it. Fear was alien to Ares. He instilled fear, but he never entertained it. He wouldn't know how to feel it if he wanted to.

"I think King Zeus will disagree about that. He doesn't take kindly to humans who try to mingle with our kind," he spat, tightening his hold on Orion until his eyes bulged. "Let's go to him and see, shall we?"

I tried to scream a protest but choked on my own desperation. Throwing Orion on Zeus's mercy was akin to tossing him to a pack of rabid, starving wolves. If I let my father take him, he was as good as dead. Without thinking, I reached for my weapon, the necklace still clasped inside my fingers. The moment I took aim, I felt a steely calm overcome my heart. With a bow in my hands I never failed. With a bow in my hands I was the purest version of myself. I pulled back and let fly. The hunting arrow zipped through the air, headed directly for its target. Headed for my father's heart.

At the last second, he lifted his free arm, deflecting the projectile with a dented bronze cuff. My trusted arrow, my last resort, ricocheted to the ground with a pointless *plink*.

My father leveled a glare that assured me I would be punished for that act of insubordination later. Not that I cared. Not that I mattered one iota in that moment. I would have given anything, my powers, my immortality, my life, to save Orion. But before I could even put those thoughts into words, the God of War disappeared in a fantastic swirl of ashen clouds and hail, taking the love of my life with him.

• • •

"Mother!" I screamed, swirling into consciousness in the center of her bedroom chamber. It was a huge space, made cozy and romantic by the presence of several goose-down mattresses; hundreds of pillows in hues of red, pink, and violet; and the swaths of luxurious silks and furs strategically draped over walls and windows. "Aphrodite! I need you!"

"Eros? What is it?" My sister, Harmonia, appeared next to me, her red hair, exactly the same butt-grazing length as mine, still floating weightlessly around her face from the breeze kicked up by my entrance.

"It's Ares. He's taken Orion to Zeus. They're going to kill him," I said, grasping her arm, trying to keep my voice steady.

"What?"

My mother, Aphrodite, the original Goddess of Love, stepped into the room from the balcony. She wore a low-cut white robe, a slit up its flowing skirt to expose her long, tanned leg. Her thick blond hair was piled atop her head in a perfectly haphazard bun, with tendrils falling to surround her gorgeous, heart-shaped face. Her blue eyes had often been described as "startling" because of their unnaturally light hue, but to me, they were simply a reflection of my own and Harmonia's eyes, about the only trait that linked us as family. My brothers Deimos and Phobos had my father's eyes— dark as the deepest pitch in the underworld.

"He found us. I don't know how, but he found us," I said, rushing to my mother and seizing both her arms. "You have to take me to Zeus's palace, Mother. Now."

My mother's perfect brow furrowed. "But I—"

"They're going to kill him!" I wailed, desperate. Zeus had never been known for his patience or fairness, and when my father was in a rage, he had a tendency to tear people apart one limb at a time, making their death as drawn-out and excruciating as possible. Orion could be suffering that fate right now. He could already be gone forever. "Please, Mother. I can't go there without you. You know this. Please."

My mother searched my eyes, and then her mouth formed a grim line. "Fine. We shall go. Bearing in mind Hera's abhorrence of unannounced visits. Especially when yours truly is involved."

"I'll find a way to pay you back," I swore to her.

"Yes," she said simply. "You will."

She took my hand, and I felt the ground begin to spin beneath me. At the last moment, I reached out and grabbed Harmonia's arm, taking her with us. I felt the telltale sucking sensation in my gut, my mind went green, then gray, and a split second later we arrived on the marble floor of Zeus's receiving hall. His throne at the top of the room was empty, the colorful favors pinned around the windows fluttering in the breeze. All seemed incongruently peaceful, until I heard Orion scream.

We whirled around and there he was, bound to the marble floor by iron chains, his chest exposed as my father thrust a spear toward his heart, the tip glinting in the sun.

"Nooooo!" I wailed.

My father, nimble as ever, stopped with the sharp point pricking Orion's skin. He and Zeus both looked up. My father's chest heaved, as if Orion had put up a struggle, but Zeus was calm. His golden beard curled above the collar of his breastplate, and his blond hair was slicked back from his head. The skin of his face was, as always, ruddy and pocked, but his green eyes were clear. He looked amused, not alarmed, to see us there, and snapped his fingers. Guards flooded the room, wearing the traditional garb of the Roman Empire, which Zeus had appropriated after the fall of the Greeks and favored even after these many years. He held up a hand to stop them from advancing on me, my mother, and my sister. For the moment.

"Aphrodite," he said, his voice like thunder. "You're a party to this?"

My mother released my hand and clasped her own. "My purview is love, Your Highness. My daughter is in love with this boy and therefore, it is in my interest to bring her here."

I gazed into Orion's eyes. Sweat poured from his brow as he fought for breath. His fists clenched, straining against the iron clamps around his wrists. He was terrified, but trying so hard not to show it. I loved him more in that moment than ever before.

"I wouldn't be so sure about that," Zeus said with a sneer. He looked at my father. "Do it."

My father lifted the spear again. Orion turned his head to the side and braced himself. Without thinking, I threw myself over Orion's chest, landing sideways so that our bodies formed an X, and waited for the spear to gut me.

Nothing happened.

"Eros! You have no idea what you're doing," my father roared.

"I know exactly what I'm doing," I spat back, rolling awkwardly onto my back but not daring to remove myself from Orion's chest. "I'm saving his life."

"You know I can remove you from here with a flick of my wrist," Zeus said, hovering over us.

"I know that, Your Highness," I said, placating. "But I'll do anything. Anything you wish. Just please, for the love of Hera, don't kill him."

"I apologize for this insubordination, Your Majesty," my father said under his breath. "I swear to you I will—"

Zeus held up a meaty hand, stopping my father cold. He looked down at me, one eyebrow cocked. "Anything?"

I slid off Orion's chest, sitting on the floor next to him. I reached for his hand and held it, warm and slick, inside my own, his necklace still clutched in my other hand. Through my back, I could feel his heart pound. Still alive. I had to keep him alive. "Anything."

Zeus studied Orion and me. "Your father tells me you claim to have rescued Orion yourself, from his place among the stars."

In the corner of my vision, my mother and sister exchanged a glance.

"Yes," I said, clearing my throat.

Zeus's eyes narrowed. It was as if I had spoken in a language he didn't quite understand, which was, of course, impossible. There wasn't a language spoken by man that we gods didn't speak fluently. After a moment, he paced away from us. While his back was turned I slowly, deliberately, moved my gaze around the room. There were two dozen windows, but four dozen guards, and my father. Even if I could somehow release Orion from his chains and get past them, which was not only unlikely, but impossible, Zeus would be able to track us anywhere. He was the king of the gods, more powerful than any being anywhere in the universe. I had been an idiot to think I could fool him.

But no. I *had* fooled him, with some help from my mother. For months now I had kept Orion safe, traveling back and forth from Olympus to Earth at will, while my mother had made sure our position was cloaked from his sight. Had he known what I'd done in February, he would have snatched us back to Mount Olympus the moment I'd done it. But here it was, the end of the summer, and here we were. Now. Why now? Why hadn't he known before today, and how had he found out?

I glanced over at my mother and Harmonia, the only two goddesses I had entrusted with my secret, as Zeus continued to pace the room and brood. I was certain neither of them had betrayed me. Harmonia was my sister, my best friend, the only being who would never turn her back on me no matter what. My mother had been known to put her own interests before those of her children in the past, but not on this. She wanted Orion's and my love to succeed. If she didn't, she would have found a way to split us up at the very beginning, rather than helping me visit him and nurse him back to health. I hadn't even told my friends Nike and Selene about my secret sojourns to Earth, since Nike sometimes placed her quest for my father's approval above everything, and Selene had a tendency to speak out of turn. So how? How had Ares and Zeus found out?

"In that case, Eros, I will strike a bargain with you," Zeus announced finally, causing an interested murmur to undulate around the lofty chamber.

"A bargain?" I asked cautiously, sitting up a bit straighter.

"Yes. I've been disappointed by your results of late. The kindling of true love is down, and the endurance numbers are sickening, to say the least. You haven't been producing, my dear," he said, stepping toward me and lifting my chin with one finger. Then his eyes flicked dismissively, disgustedly, to Orion. "And now I know why."

He hauled off and kicked Orion in the ribs so hard I heard the crack. I let out a wail as Orion coughed and sputtered, writhing away from us as best he could with his limbs bound. Harmonia buried her face in my mother's shoulder as Aphrodite's expression went stoic. I wanted to spit in Zeus's face, but I held back.

"This is my offer," Zeus continued. "You will be banished to Earth without your powers. You will be, essentially, a mortal."

My mother and sister gasped at this. Even my father shifted his weight.

"You will then prove your worth to me by forming true love between three couples with no godly tricks up your sleeve," Zeus continued. "Only then will you be allowed to return to Mount Olympus."

"And Orion?" I asked, my voice cracking.

"If you succeed in this task, I will spare his life," Zeus said with a dismissive wave of his hand. "Until then, he is to be my slave."

The king glanced at my father, who gripped his spear tightly in both hands. "What say you to this, Ares? Is my proposal fair?"

Everyone present knew it didn't matter whether my father thought it was fair. Zeus was only testing Ares's allegiance to him, assuring himself that he meant more to my father than his own daughter did.

"Fair, wise, and benevolent, Your Majesty," my father said, looking directly at me.

"Good," Zeus said with a nod. "Oh, and Aphrodite." He turned to my mother, who raised her chin.

"Yes, Your Grace," my mother said with a slight curtsy and bowed head.

"Since it's abundantly clear that you were complicit in all this, you will be banished as well."

"What?" my mother shrieked. "Zeus, no! Please! You mustn't send me to that awful place."

Harmonia and I glanced at each other, alarmed. My mother had a flair for the dramatic, but she was also the strongest goddess we knew. I'd never heard her voice reach such a frantic pitch.

"I can and I will," Zeus replied, impassive.

"I beg of you!" my mother wailed. "I will do anything you ask of me! Anything!"

"You may go now," Zeus said.

As he flicked his wrist, I turned and grasped Orion's hand with both of my own, pressing the arrow pendant into his palm. My mother sobbed, falling to her knees on the floor as Harmonia clung to her. I could already feel my cells vibrating, my mind begin to go weightless. I had only minutes. No, seconds. Desperately, I locked my eyes onto Orion's.

"I will be back for you," I told him, holding on to his fingers for dear life. "Depend upon it, Orion. I won't let you down!"

"I love you," he said through his teeth, as my fingers began to slip from his. "I believe in you."

I tried to tell him I loved him, too, but before I could respond, I was ripped away and the only sound my voice could form was a scream.

CHAPTER ONE

True

Pressure. Pain. My head was wedged inside a vise. Squeeze release, squeeze release, squeeze release. I pried my eyes open and winced as the sunlight stabbed at my retinas. My skin felt tight, dry, and cold. My scalp tingled. My toes were numb. As the room around me gradually came into focus, I realized why. I was buck naked and the room was freezing. Shivering from my very core, I grabbed the rough brocade blanket beneath me and wrapped it up and around my shoulders. Something fell to the floor with a clang.

A small, silver arrow glinted in the sun on the hardwood. Orion's necklace. I had tried to give it back to him. I had thought it would be something for him to hold on to. But I had failed. I had failed him in so many ways, and now he was trapped in Zeus's palace, alone and terrified, and I was the only one who could save him.

I bent to pick up the arrow, then double-knotted the broken chain around my own neck. The pendant felt warm against my cold skin and I touched it with my fingers, closing my eyes and trying to send a message to Orion.

I will save you. I will return for you.

As I pushed myself up off the floor, a slice of pain through my temples sent me off balance and I staggered sideways into the ice-cold iron radiator attached to the wall. The pain moved to my forehead, throbbing with each pump of my heart. I closed my eyes and breathed, pressing one hand against my skull, and waited for the ache to subside.

If anything, the throbbing intensified. I pulled my trembling fingers away to stare at them. They weren't warm. They didn't glow.

Seized by panic, I whirled toward the window, leaning against the glass as the pain gripped me all over again. Outside, the world was bright and full of motion. Cars whizzed by on the street. A couple jogged along the sidewalk in matching sweat suits, weights strapped to their hands. On the corner a woman in uniform held up a stop sign and waved a group of skipping children in front of stopped traffic. Verdant trees lined the brick walkways, a pair of tiny dogs yipped as their owner cleaned up their excrement, a mail carrier tipped his hat at the driver of a bakery truck idling near the curb. American flags adorned the porches, and the license plates read New Jersey. So at least I now knew where I was.

It was so picturesque and adorable, I felt an almost irrepressible need to scream.

"Sent me to the happiest place on Earth, didn't you, Zeus?" I muttered, casting my gaze toward the heavens. The King of the Gods had a wry sense of humor. But, I supposed, it could be worse. At least in a place like this, people would be open to love. He could have sent me to a dank cave in some oppressive, war-torn country devoid of hope. The fact that he hadn't, said something. It said that on some level, Zeus wished me to succeed. This was a very good thing.

Taking a deep breath, I braced both my hands on the desk surface, letting the blanket fall to the floor. I homed in on the mail carrier, focusing every ounce of energy on his heart. If I had my powers, his inner yearnings would reveal themselves to me. I concentrated and held my breath and prayed to the gods, but nothing happened. He simply stood there, whistling as he went through his mail. I felt no inkling of his true self, no surge of emotion; I didn't even hear his name or his age or his status. My heart sank so low I could have crushed it under my heel. This power was innate. Not having it . . . it was like not having the ability to blink or to breathe.

Any surge of defiant adrenaline I'd felt back on Olympus withered and died inside my chest. I didn't know how to do this without my powers. How was I to begin? I'd never been to Earth for more than a day or two at a time, aside from my weeks spent alone with Orion. And other than Orion, I'd never interacted with a human in my existence, not for more than a few minutes.

Something crashed inside the house. I turned, and the mail carrier froze in his tracks at the foot of our front walk, his jaw hanging toward the ground. Oh, right. Naked. I shrugged at him and snapped the blinds closed.

"Mother!" I shouted, going to the closet on the far side of the bed. The inside revealed a paltry selection of clothing. I grabbed a baggy white sweatshirt and pulled it on. On a normal day, I simply closed my eyes and imagined a gown or a dress or hunting apparel and it would appear on my body, perfectly fitted and flattering. Another power I was sure I would miss. "Mother! Where are you?"

I heard a groan. The wooden hallway floor creaked beneath my feet as I staggered toward the noise. I passed another bedroom, a bathroom, and the top of the stairs before coming to the largest bedroom yet. It was situated at the back of the house with windows facing north, south, and west, but every single one of the blinds had been closed and the drapes flung down, so that hardly a sliver of light shone through. In the center of the four-poster bed, a mound of blankets writhed.

"Mother?"

Her slim white hand emerged from beneath the covers. "Here."

I walked to her bedside. She sat up with a bottle of wine, her blond hair stuck to her forehead with sweat, and flung the bottle at the floor, where it clinked and rolled toward the dresser. It was already empty. She pulled another from under her covers and popped the cork.

"Where did you get that?" I asked.

My mother gulped down half the contents and dragged the back of her hand across her mouth before answering. "Wine cellar. Well stocked. Zeus has shown some mercy."

"Mom, you have to get up. We have to figure out what we're going to do," I pleaded as she hunkered back against the huge, downy pillows.

"That is where you are wrong, Eros," she said, taking a sip and smacking her lips. "You must devise a plan. You have a mission to complete." She gestured at me with the bottle. "I was sent here out of spite and therefore, I drink." She lifted the bottle in a toast to no one and brought it to her lips.

"But mother, I have no powers!" I shouted, throwing my hands out. "I've never done this without them. How am I supposed to match people when I have no idea of their inner needs? When I can't read their thoughts? When I—"

"Enough of your incessant whining!" my mother spat, throwing the now-empty bottle at the wall so hard it shattered, exploding shards of glass across the antique armoire and ancient, worn throw rug. My heart stopped, but she didn't even pause. "Let us make one fact perfectly clear, Eros," she seethed, shoving herself out of bed, wearing nothing but a long black T-shirt. "It was your carelessness that exiled us. I have never been banished to Earth before. Never! Do you know how many gods can make that claim? I was a legend, and now I am nothing." She looked down at herself, her fingers, her toes, and clutched the shirt with both hands as if she might rend it from her body. "Nothing but a *mortal*. And it is all down to you."

She teetered slightly, then turned and crawled back into bed. "I should never have helped you go to him that first day. I should never have let you stay. I should have known this would happen. I should have seen it in the stars. But did I? No. Why? Because you were so blissfully happy that I, for some unknown reason, felt the need to indulge you in your ongoing, unrealistic daydream."

Her words stung. It had been some source of pride to me that my mother had aided and abetted my relationship with Orion, that she'd done so willingly, even merrily. I had felt, for the first time in a long while, like I truly meant something to her.

"Could it have been motherly love?" I asked hopefully.

My mother scoffed and pulled the covers over her head. "Sentimentality is for the weak, Eros. Now get to work."

My throat was dry, my stomach tight with disappointment and fear. But I knew when not to argue with my mother. She was wallowing. And when she was wallowing, there was no reasoning with her. I was alone here. On Earth. Mortal and friendless and alone.

I turned toward the door but paused, my hand on the molding. "I just have one question," I said. "How? How did Ares find out about us?"

"I know not," she replied without lifting her head. "I told no one and my cloak was never breached."

"Why didn't he come to me?" I asked. "Why didn't he talk to me about Orion instead of kidnapping him off to Zeus?"

"You've now asked three questions," my mother pointed out impatiently. "Now go!"

The floor creaked beneath my feet and she sat up, heaving a sigh. "Your father did what he did because he cares about only two things: himself, and the favor of Zeus. He knew that if Zeus found out and realized Ares hadn't told him, or worse, that Ares hadn't even *known* what his daughter was doing, that it would lower him in Zeus's eyes. Your father is an egotistical megalomaniac, Eros. He always has been, and he always will be. As much as I once tried to convince myself otherwise, he loves no one more than himself."

She dropped back onto the bed. "Now please," she said wearily. "Do your job."

Silently I turned and left the room, closing the door behind me. As the catch clicked, I suddenly longed for my sister. She always knew the right thing to say, the right thing to do. But even as I wished for her wisdom, I knew we were better off with her on Mount Olympus. She would keep an eye on Orion. She would do what she could to make sure Zeus didn't get out of hand, didn't go back on his bargain. I needed her right where she was.

Taking a deep breath, I closed my eyes and tried to hear Harmonia's voice. In my heart I knew what she would say. I was a goddess. I was powerful. I'd brought Orion down from the stars. I'd traveled back and forth from Mount Olympus to Earth for months with no one suspecting. I had nursed him back to health. I was a scholar, a hunter, a daydreamer, a soul searcher. I could do this. I had to do this. I had to save Orion.

The question was, where to start.

Slowly I wandered back to my room, my skull still radiating pain. There were billions of people in the world. How was I supposed to know who was single and who wasn't, which people had found their soul mates and which hadn't, without being able to read their hearts? Not every soul on Earth was desperate to be in a relationship, not everyone was open to it. Where was I going to find hundreds of souls willing to be paired up? Ready for and open to true love?

Inside my room, I heard a horn bleat a staccato rhythm. Something big and yellow and loud stopped outside my window and hovered there, rumbling. A school bus. I took a step forward and my breath caught as a couple of gangly teenage boys climbed the steps. They both paused to gawk when a pack of girls strolled by, giggling and whispering and glancing over their shoulders. Then the door squealed shut, the brakes released, and the monstrosity rumbled on.

Every inch of my skin tingled. High school. Of course. Who longed for love more than a community of hormonal, attention-starved, drama-addicted teenagers? I needed to go to school.

For the first time, I noticed a manila folder sitting in the center of the desk. Next to it was a large hourglass hewn of ash and filled with dark red sand. It was already running, gravity releasing the sand at the top of the timer through the minuscule hole at the center, spraying the tiny red particles across the bottom of the glass. My heart thumped.

Undoubtedly, it was a gift from Zeus. But did I have this much time to complete my first pairing, or to complete all three? For the moment, I decided not to dwell on that awful question.

I opened the folder and found a smiling photograph of my own face. It was attached to a transcript from a high school in Maine called James Monroe. The transcript boasted straight As in everything but psychology, where I'd received a C. A school in Maine, where Orion and I had hidden. Only average at psychology, the study of the soul. Very funny, Zeus. But at least he'd seen fit to provide this for me. The meaning of the gesture was not lost. It was important to him, to each and every one of the gods, that love continue to thrive here on Earth. Without it, the balance of good and evil, of right and wrong, would be forever altered. Without love, all would be lost.

Of course that didn't mean that he wouldn't enjoy torturing Orion while I was stuck here, carrying out his little mission. Zeus was a complex god.

At the very top of the page in front of me was a space for my name and my birth date, which had been left blank. At least the king had given me that, the chance to choose my own name.

I stared out the window and considered, then picked up a pen and wrote it in. True Olympia. It would be a daily reminder of my mission—to save my true love and return myself and my mother to Mount Olympus. My birth date was, of course, February 14, and I quickly did the math, writing down a year that would make me sixteen today.

Another horn honked outside, and my head exploded along with it. I closed my eyes and brought my fingertips to my temples again. Still nothing. It wasn't bad enough that I was stuck on the mortal plane without my powers and with a seemingly impossible mission, but I had to be in debilitating pain as well? Talk about adding injury to insult. But it was nothing. Nothing compared to what Orion was going through. It was time for this goddess to suck it up.

I took a deep breath, walked back into the closet, and readied myself for my first day as a mortal.

CHAPTER TWO

Katrina

It's going to be fine. It's going to be great. But you're going to have to actually get out of the car.

"What did you just say?" Ty asked as he put his vintage Firebird in park at the curb in front of Lake Carmody High.

I blushed. One strand on the fringe at the end of my gauzy scarf was wrapped so tightly around my finger, the tip was turning white. I quickly unwound it. "Oh, sorry. I didn't realize I said anything out—"

"Ugh. Did you forget the sugar?"

My mouth snapped shut. Ty Donahue, my very own tall, dark, handsome—not to mention older, employed, license-having—boyfriend was digging through the brown paper bag from 7-Eleven like a bear pawing at a picnic basket. The large coffee I'd bought him at our morning pit stop was wedged between his legs on the driver's seat, his pride-and-joy roadster having been built in a time before cup holders.

"No. It's in there somewhere," I said.

"No, Katrina, it's not."

I swallowed hard. There was nothing I hated more than when

he used my name like that. Like I was some stupid kid, when he was only three years older than me. And if I'd forgotten to grab sugar on the way out the door of the convenience store, it was only because I was so nervous this morning, not because I was callously trying to deprive him of sweetener or something. I opened the glove compartment and dug through it until I found four crumpled, but full, sugar packets from Dunkin' Donuts and slapped them into his hand.

"Thanks," he grumbled, shaking the packets before ripping them open.

"Why are you in such a bad mood?" I asked quietly, letting the dark waves of my hair fall forward as I picked at a dried stain on my vinyl backpack. "It's my first day of school."

"So what? It's school." He dumped the sugar into the steaming coffee. "Hang out with your friends, torture a few teachers, and I'll be here to pick you up before you know it. You going home tonight or are we hanging at my place?"

"Your place. My mom worked the night shift, so she'll be sleeping."

My mom *had* left a note on Friday asking me—no, ordering me—to go to the grocery store to get the basics, but I hadn't done it yet, having spent the whole weekend at Ty's. But what did it matter if she was going to be sleeping and I wouldn't be there?

I looked out at Lake Carmody High, the red brick walls and multipaned windows glaring judgingly back at me. Sophomore year had sucked, plain and simple. After breezing through freshman year with my head buried in my books and a string of straight-A report cards, I'd been bumped from three honors courses to five as a sophomore and had suffered through the summer as the only person I knew who was looking forward to going back to school.

Not that I knew that many people. My best friend Raine Santos was pretty much my only friend and had been since we'd bonded in kindergarten over our similar last names and the fact that we were both obsessed with Minnie Mouse. But unlike her, I liked learning. I liked figuring things out. And I lived for the huge grin that would break out on my father's face whenever I brought home an A test or paper.

But then, one icy day in January, my dad had gone to work with a wave and a smile as always and had never returned. One slip of his tires and he was gone. Forever. The rest of the year was a blur, and my grades? Let's just say if my father had seen them, he never would have believed they were mine. After my epic fail, I'd been demoted to the regular college-prep-level classes this year, which for me was weird. It made me feel like a loser, and like I'd disappointed my father. Not that I'd ever tell anyone that.

At least I had a few classes with Raine now. I was doing my best to look on the bright side.

"I don't know," I said quietly, my eyes finding the window of the school shrink's office—the room I hated more than any other room in the school. That was where they'd brought me the day my father had died—where they'd carefully delivered the news. That was where I'd seen my mom break down into convulsions on the floor. My tough, impassive mother. Broken. And she'd been broken ever since.

Before my father died, my mom had always been strict. She had always held me to the highest standards. But she had also shown me she loved me in a million different ways, like hiding encouraging notes in my lunch box, attending my academic decathlon meets in middle school—even if it meant finding someone to take her shift at the hospital—or taking me out for a special breakfast once a month, just the girls. Since my dad died? Nothing. It was like she couldn't even look me in the eye anymore, and I hadn't once seen her smile. Not once. Obviously I had let her down with my grades last year. Obviously I'd become a huge disappointment. Just when she'd suffered the most crushing loss she'd ever faced. That either of us had ever faced.

"I'm kind of hoping things'll be different this year." Major understatement.

Ty tilted his head. He reached out and cupped the back of my neck with his rough hand, giving me a quick, comforting rub. "You're gonna be okay," he said. "If anyone messes with you, send 'em to me."

I smiled. He'd completely missed the point, but at least he was trying. I picked up the wax bag of doughnuts from the floor, and Ty reached in to grab one. He was bringing it to his mouth when I realized it was the only sugar-coated jelly.

"Don't eat that! That's for—"

Too late. He'd already pushed half of it past his lips.

"I got that for Raine!" I complained as I opened the door.

"Sucks to be her," he said with a laugh.

Great. Earlier this morning Raine had reminded me that the only thing that was going to get her through the first day of school was a jelly doughnut, and now she was going to think I'd spaced when I hadn't. As I climbed out of the car, Ty revved the engine, making it growl, and a few girls in cardigans and preppy little skirts turned to look. One of them, Cara Tritthart, used to be a semi-friend—at least a during-the-school-day friend—back in middle school and freshman year when we were in the accelerated classes together. She'd even come to my dad's funeral and offered to study with me when I'd started getting Ds and Fs. Not that

I'd taken her up on it. Back then, studying had felt so pointless, and after a while, we'd stopped talking between classes like we used to. Now I saw her eyes flick judgmentally over me, the car, and Ty. I slammed the door, walked around the front, and leaned toward the window for a good-bye kiss, my face so hot it could have melted rubber.

"Have a good day, baby," Ty said, sucking a dot of jelly off his finger.

"Thanks for the ride," I replied.

When we kissed it was like the last five minutes hadn't even happened. He tasted like sugar, and being so close to him reminded me of how lucky I was to have him, to have someone who loved me. When I leaned back again I was smiling, Cara and the prepsters forgotten.

"You look hot," Ty said, his eyes traveling possessively over my skinny jeans and black high-heeled boots. "These high school losers best behave."

I reached out and ran my fingers over his dark buzz cut. "I'll see you later."

He ground the engine one more time, then peeled out, making sure every kid in a five-mile radius was watching. That was Ty. He loved to be the center of attention—something I'd never be able to figure out. I tucked my chin as I walked up the concrete stairs toward the school, trying to ignore Cara's friends, who were obviously whispering about me, and suddenly I felt icky and hot on the inside. Why? I didn't care what they thought about me or about Ty, because what they thought was wrong. I wasn't just some poor half-orphaned Latina girl, and he wasn't just some dropout mechanic. They didn't know anything about us that wasn't superficial. So why did I *feel* like I cared?

As I was about to stride through the front door, I noticed some kid staring at me. His shaggy blond hair was pushed forward over his forehead, his bright blue eyes peeking out from under it. White wires dangled from his ears, connected to an iPod in his front pocket. His posture was slightly hunched, and a pair of worn-looking drumsticks stuck out of his red backpack. He had on a blue-and-white-striped polo shirt that was too pressed to go with the rest of him, which made me think his mother might have picked it and laid it out for him this morning.

Dork, I heard Ty say in my mind.

But still. There was something about the way he was looking at me that made my palms sweat all over the wax doughnut bag. I ducked inside and paused for a breath in the Pine-Sol-scented hallway, trying not to glance back through the glass doors. I took in the fall-colored bulletin boards, the club sign-up sheets, the huge WELCOME BACK! banner. I could smell fresh coffee brewing in the Café—the seniors-only area off the cafeteria—and the scent calmed me.

It was a new year. I was going to be new me.

I promise you, Dad, this year is gonna be different.

My throat tightened like it annoyingly did every single time I even thought the word "Dad," and then I did glance back, but the guy was gone. Staring at the gleaming floor, I turned and walked straight down the middle of the deserted hallway, to the arts wing at the back of the school. I was still twenty feet away from the girls' room when I heard Lana Auriello's cackling laugh. I opened the door and a cloud of acrid smoke hit me in the face.

"Ramos!" my friends sang out. The three of them were sitting on the floor, ashing into a plastic cup. Lana held open a compact with one hand while applying mascara with the other, her glossy dark hair pulled over one shoulder. Raine and Gen Moore made gimme gestures at the doughnut bag.

"Hi, guys," I said, walking over to the window to crack it. I tried to breathe in some fresh air, but still got two lungs full of smoke. "How long have you been here?"

"Fifteen minutes, tops," Raine said, rifling through the bag with her cigarette clamped in the corner of her mouth. "Where's my jelly?"

I pressed my lips together. "Sorry."

"And you call yourself my best friend," Raine joked, finishing up her smoke before biting into a cinnamon doughnut. She'd highlighted her curly hair over the summer, and it had looked sun-kissed for a few days before turning its current shade of Florida orange. Last week Gen had called her "Garfield," and the slap fight that followed would have gotten us a million hits on YouTube if me or Lana had been quick enough to record it. No one had brought up Raine's hair since.

"Do you have an eyeliner I can borrow?" Lana asked, pushing herself up off the floor. Her mother didn't let her wear eye makeup, so the rest of us had become her own personal Rite Aid.

"I think so." I slid my backpack off my shoulder and opened the zipper.

It was hard to believe that at this time last year I'd barely spoken two words to Lana or Gen. Back then they were Raine's "other friends"—the girls she hung out with when I was too busy studying or hanging out with my dad. But after the accident, the four of us had spent most of our time together, cutting classes, hitting the mall, and borrowing Lana's brother's car to go down the shore when it was nice out.

"Where's my makeup bag?" I muttered. Lana stood on her toes

to peer inside my backpack, and her eyes widened. By the time I realized what she'd seen, it was too late. She'd snatched the typed report out of my bag. I closed the zipper before she could spot my black notebook, too.

"*What* is *this?*" Lana asked, holding it up between elaborately manicured fingers. Each pink nail had two white stripes painted diagonally across it, and there were clear rhinestones on the thumbnails. Lana worked at Burger King and spent her french-frying money on her nails. And on eye-makeup remover.

"Give it," I said through my teeth. But she was already bending over to show Raine and Gen.

"You did the summer homework?" Raine asked, gaping up at me. "Are you trying to reclaim your nerd status?"

I snatched the pages back from Lana and shoved them into my bag, wincing as they wrinkled. "What? I thought it was mandatory."

The three of them exchanged a look and then doubled over laughing. I turned toward the window, smoothing the pages flat across the front of one of my brand-new notebooks. I cleared my throat and zipped the bag closed.

"Don't any of you, like, want to go to college?" I asked. "Get the hell out of here?"

"Please. No one ever actually gets out of here," Gen said, flicking an ash into the cup. "That's a line they sell you so they can pad their graduation percentages and get more money from the state."

Gen's dad had graduated from our school twenty years ago and was now one of its janitors. We always joked about how his bitterness had rubbed off on Gen, who was so cute and petite and blond she could have been a cheerleader if she had one ounce of school spirit. But I had to believe that if I did well enough in school these next two years, I could still get into a good college. I had to believe it because I couldn't imagine any other way to get out of my house permanently, and with my dad gone and my mother basically hating me, getting out was my only option.

"When did you even have time to read a book?" Raine asked, getting up. "Every time I called you this summer you were either pushing groceries at the Stop and Shop or hanging out with Tiiiiy." She sang out his name and clutched her hands under her chin.

"I don't know," I said, hoisting my bag onto my shoulder. "I guess I . . . figured it out."

The truth was, I'd been fired from my job at the Stop & Shop in July after Ty had forgotten I needed a ride—again—and I was more than half an hour late for the third time in a row. The next day my mom was home from work, which meant I needed to be somewhere else, so I'd walked the two miles into town. It was so hot, I'd slipped into the library to cool off, and that was when everything had changed. I'd been wandering the aisles, feeling aimless and conspicuous, when Mrs. Pauley, one of the librarians—a skinny middle-aged lady with a nice smile—had told me they had my school's summer reading list, if I was interested. She'd helped me pick out a book, *A Separate Peace*, and I'd spent three hours in a cushy chair, lost in the reading. For those three hours I hadn't been obsessing about my pissed-off mom or my dad who I was never going to see again or how I was going to sock away cash for college without a job. I'd escaped to this whole other place. By the time Mrs. Pauley had come over to tell me they were closing down, I felt like she was waking me up from a really good dream.

I went back there every day for three days and read two more books. On the fourth day, she offered me a job. Almost every day since, I'd worked mornings shelving books and spent my afternoons reading. I'd read my way through the entire summer reading list, actually. Not that I'd ever tell my friends that.

The first warning bell rang.

"Yay. First day of school," Lana said flatly.

"Is there enough room in here to do a cartwheel?" Raine joked.

"Come on. My dad'll kill me if we don't clean this up." Gen got up, tugged down on her denim miniskirt, and dumped the plastic cup full of ash into the garbage. Then the four of us spent a couple of minutes pointlessly fanning the smoky air toward the window.

"Hey, Kat, did you see the new guy?" Raine asked as we shuffled toward the door.

My heart slammed against my ribs, remembering the way he'd looked at me. "You mean the one with the drumsticks? Yeah. Why?"

"What a complete loser," Raine said.

She and Lana laughed as Gen yanked open the door. "We finally get some new blood around here and he has to be Justin Bieber?"

"You are *so* lucky to have Ty," Lana said, giving her eyes one last check in the mirror.

"*So* lucky," Raine added, slinging an arm around my neck.

Bet she wouldn't say that if she knew what had actually happened to her jelly doughnut. I remembered how he'd snapped at me about the sugar; how he'd acted like today was no big deal, even though he knew how much it meant to me to get my grades up. But I wasn't about to tell them any of that. They didn't understand what I was trying to do here, so I knew they'd take Ty's side. Everyone always took Ty's side. He was that guy.

So I bit my tongue and smiled as the hall filled with students, telling myself I was not keeping an eye out for a pressed blue-and-white polo shirt.

"Yeah," I said, leaning into Raine's side. "Lucky me."

CHAPTER THREE

Charlie

I counted fifteen judging stares before I even got to the office and one sneering glare at my drumsticks. I had thought that maybe moving to the Northeast things would be different, but no matter where I went in the great USA, people were tools. They didn't like change. They didn't want to meet anyone new. They didn't want to be friends. Not really. I wondered why I hadn't gotten used to it yet.

Like that girl outside, for instance. She was so bogglingly beautiful. So clearly clueless to it. So obviously sweet and shy and vulnerable. I mean, she couldn't even hold eye contact without practically breaking into hives. So of course she had a boyfriend. Some douche in a predictable car who probably didn't appreciate her and totally exploited her weaknesses. She could do better. Way better. But would she? No. Why? Because this place was no different.

I found the door marked OFFICE. Grasped the cold silver handle. Tugged my earbuds from my ears and silenced my iPod. Another year, another school. Time to get it over with. I yanked the door open, and Mrs. Leifer looked up with a smile. At least, that was what her desk placard said. MRS. TANYA LEIFER, ADMINISTRATIVE

ASSISTANT. She was a large woman with gray curls that formed a perfect helmet around her head.

"Well, good morning!" she said brightly. "Are you one of our new students?"

Near the wall, a trio of big jocks in school colors—blue and white, like the shirt my dad had made me wear this morning—took interest. They looked me up and down slowly, and I felt conspicuous. These were exactly the kind of guys who loved to mock me. One was tall with brown spiky hair and a tan, the second had dark skin and a fade, and the third had red curls cut close and pale skin. They made me think of my brothers, who were basically good guys, but obsessed with sports and born with the annoying ability to be total dicks when they felt like it, and usually out of nowhere. So of course, I instantly wanted these guys to like me . . . which made me hate myself. Nothing like a heady dose of self-loathing on the first day of school.

"Yes, ma'am," I said, trying to ignore my audience. "My name's Charlie Cox."

"Cool! You're mine!"

One of the school spirit dudes shoved away from the wall. The tall, tan one. He had a backpack on one shoulder and held out a small book to me. The title read *Lake Carmody High School Handbook*.

"Yours?" I asked warily.

"Charlie Cox," Mrs. Leifer said, standing up from her desk and handing over a schedule. "This is—"

"Josh Moskowitz," he said. His chin was perfectly square and hovered about a foot above mine. "Your peer guide."

"Oh." I took the book and stared at it. I'd been to one school with peer guides before. George W. Bush Middle School outside

Dallas when I was in fifth grade. By the end of the first day I'd been stuffed inside a garbage can in the girls' locker room with a rotting banana peel shoved down my pants.

"And one of the stars of the junior class," Mrs. Leifer said, looking Josh over like he was some kind of god. "Every year we recruit the school's best to show our new students around," she added with a nod to the other dudes.

"So is your dad David Cox? The new coach over at St. Joe's Prep?" Josh asked. There was an LB on his sleeve. Linebacker. Perfect.

I stared at the charging ram on the cover of the handbook. The local paper had covered my dad a couple weeks earlier when we'd gotten to town and he'd started up football practices at the Catholic school. They'd made him sound like he'd descended from heaven to fix the formerly great team. They'd even done a sidebar on my superstar brothers, Chris and Corey, the Quarterback Twins. Honestly. That's what they were. Every town we moved to they got enrolled in different schools—one private, one public—so they could both play starting quarterback. The clipping was now framed on the mantel of our fireplace, even though 75 percent of our boxes were still packed.

"You've heard of him?" I said, flipping the pages of the handbook.

"Are you kidding? I wish we'd've gotten him! Your dad is like a miracle worker," Josh told me.

Like I didn't know this. This was why I'd been at a new school every two years for my entire life. Some school with a crappy football team hired Dad, he swooped in, fixed things in one season, stayed around for one or two more to win a championship, and then we were out. Next project. It was all about Dad and where he was going to play the hero next. Never mind whether anyone else in the family wanted to stay in one town, make a friend, maybe even get a girlfriend.

"We're playing St. Joe's in our opening game. What's he think of his QB over there, Keegan Traylor?" Josh asked. "Does he really believe he's better than Peter Marrott?"

I'd heard my dad mention this Keegan guy on the phone and stuff, but I hadn't known he was the quarterback. My dad doesn't exactly talk business with me. But now that I knew, I used my awesome powers of deduction to figure out that Peter Marrott was Lake Carmody's quarterback. I considered my response before answering.

"Let's put it this way: my Dad doesn't take on a new team unless he thinks he can win with them," I told him. And it was the truth.

Josh nodded slowly with narrowed eyes, as if I'd said something seriously deep.

"You play?" he asked doubtfully, obviously noting my scrawniness.

"Uh, no," I said with a scoff.

"What about track?" Josh asked without hesitation, tilting his head. "You got the build for it. Cross-country tryouts are this afternoon. You should show. Right, Bri?"

"Totally," answered Brian, the lanky black dude. His voice was deep. Like, baritone deep. "We need fresh meat."

"Running's not really my thing," I answered.

In fact, I hated running. Ever since I was eight my dad had forced me to go out on morning runs every weekend with him and my brothers. Mercifully, this ritual had stopped once Chris and Corey went to college—different schools, but within driving distance of each other, of course. Now it was just me, Mom, and Dad, and there was no point.

I glanced over my schedule. Band was ninth period. It was going to be a long day.

"Too bad," Brian said. "If you change your mind, we meet behind the gym after last bell."

I narrowed my eyes, trying to figure their angle. Did they want me to show up behind the gym after last bell so they could kick the crap out of me? But no. They looked . . . sincere. There wasn't a single mocking smile. Which was weird. Because guys like this normally couldn't hide their excitement if they thought they were pulling one over on you. I'd been victimized by enough popular kids to know.

"Yeah, that's not gonna happen," I said.

"We'll convince you by the end of the day," Josh said confidently.

"Come on over and get your picture taken for your ID," Mrs. Leifer said, beckoning me toward a square of blue construction paper taped to the wall.

"Then we'll go check out breakfast in the caf," Josh told me. "There's always pancakes on the first day."

I stood in front of the blue square, confused. Something was not right here. Had these guys not seen the drumsticks in my bag? Did they not notice my shirt was from Old Navy and not Hollister? That I didn't have a jock bone in my body?

"Say Lake Carmody!" Mrs. Leifer called out from behind camera.

I blinked as the camera flashed. Then the door swung open, slamming back against the wall. A framed certificate crashed to the floor. Mrs. Leifer gasped.

"Is this where I'm supposed to sign up?"

We all stared. The girl was crazy tall, with the longest hair I'd ever seen, tangled in a million knots. Her eyes were this startling blue, and her face was perfect. One hundred percent perfect. She was wearing a white sweatshirt about ten sizes too big and pink shorts that showed almost every inch of leg. But craziest were the brand-new, shiny, red-and-purple cowboy boots. Which I think she was wearing with no socks. I'd worn cowboy boots before. Those things hurt. *With* socks.

Totally weird. I instantly liked her.

"And you are?" Mrs. Leifer asked, picking up her phone. There was a beep, and she spoke into the receiver. "Mr. Moore to the office, please! We have broken glass!" her voice rang out over the speakers in the hall.

"Er—True," the girl said. "True Olympia." She slapped a folder down on the counter. "I'm a new student." She turned and looked at me, then Josh, then Brian, then their third jocky friend. Her eyes flicked over us appraisingly, like we were horses up for auction.

"Are any of you single?" she asked.

Josh's jaw fell open. Brian laughed. The red-haired guy sauntered over to her.

"I'm Trevor," he said, leaning against the counter and blatantly checking out her chest.

"Hello, Trevor." She looked him in the eye. "Do you have a girlfriend?"

"Are you applying for the job?" he asked, making Josh and Brian cackle.

She laughed like that was the funniest thing anyone had ever said. Ever.

"No. I'm taken," she replied, tugging a necklace out of her collar and holding it up. Like it was an engagement ring or something. "So what do you look for in a girl, Trevor? Humor? Intelligence? Loyalty?"

"He's a boob man," Brian supplied, making the others laugh.

"Lovely," True said with a grimace.

"Watch it, Mr. Lawrence!" Mrs. Leifer scolded, but was holding back a smile. She leafed through a stack of papers on her desk. "Ah. Here it is. Your schedule, Miss Olympia."

"Really?" True seemed shocked. She snatched the paper from Mrs. Leifer. "Well. Look at that."

"Veronica?" Mrs. Leifer glanced over her shoulder toward the back of the office. "Your new student is here."

A curvy blond girl in a tight skirt and even tighter sweater stepped out from behind a cubicle divider. When she smiled, I saw nothing but teeth. Big, white teeth. She was like a walking Victoria's Secret/Colgate commercial. A sparkly V dangled around her neck, landing right at the top of her cleavage.

"Hey, babe," Josh said, his whole face lighting up. She stepped into his arms and they kissed, sharing gallons of spit.

"So I guess *you* have a girlfriend." True seemed disappointed.

Veronica was not amused. "Yes. He does," she said, locking her arm around Josh.

"Veronica Vine, this is True Olympia," Mrs. Leifer said. "Veronica is one of the student volunteers here in the office. She's going to be your peer guide."

"Great," Veronica said sarcastically, sucking her teeth.

"I don't need a peer guide," True said. "I'm fine."

"Perfect!" Veronica took Josh's hand and tugged him toward the door. "Come on, Joshy. Let's go."

"Not so fast," Mrs. Leifer said. "Every new student gets a peer guide. It's Principal Peterson's most prized program."

I clenched my teeth to keep from laughing at the tongue twister.

"Really. I don't need any help," True insisted. "I can manage to navigate one measly little school that's less than a hundred thousand square feet." She chuckled and glanced down at her schedule. "Are honors classes the most challenging you have on offer? I bore easily."

Everyone gaped at her. She didn't seem to notice. Instead she looked at me. "What about you? What's your name? Do you have a girlfriend?"

At that exact moment, the girl from the Firebird walked by the door. She clutched a few books to her chest, her eyes trained on the floor. My heart did this awful dance. There I went again, always wanting the girl I couldn't have.

"Charlie," I told her. "And no. I don't."

True smiled.

CHAPTER FOUR

True

By the time I trailed Veronica and her followers into the cafeteria that afternoon, I understood why my mother had refused to get out of bed this morning. This place was a nightmare. It was far too closed in, every hallway tighter than the last, the ceilings impossibly low, the classrooms like cages. At moments it felt as if I had to gasp for air. There were people—everywhere. Chewing gum, singing along to songs played directly into their ears, sniffing and sneezing and coughing and cackling and breathing. But more than anything, it was loud. Too loud. Did every girl on Earth have to greet every other girl on Earth with a scream and a hug and an uncomfortable knee-knocking, bouncing-up-and-down ritual? Plus, the boys seemed to have the lung capacity of elephants, bellowing down the halls in what turned out to be the one language I didn't understand.

"Fa-LEECE! Whad-UP? Where you been at, PLAYAH? WTF is on in the beat-down lose-ah?"

Honestly, what did that *mean*?

To make matters worse, the teachers were adamantly opposed to talking in class, which meant I hadn't met anyone aside from the boys in the office that morning and Veronica and her horde. It was torture, taking orders from these figures of authority, each of them younger than my newest set of arrows back home. I knew better than to talk back and get thrown out of school, but my pride was not happy. These adults, as it were, were getting in the way of my mission—a mission that was far bigger than them and their pedantic lessons. If I couldn't talk to these kids, there was no way I was going to be able to set anyone up.

When we entered the cafeteria, however, my spirits perked considerably. This lunch hour seemed like a free-for-all—students moving about at will, hopping from table to table, talking to whomever they wished. WELCOME BACK banners and cheerful posters hung from the walls, and there was not a teacher in sight. Perhaps I could get some work done here.

As we walked along the side of the cafeteria, my feet cried out in pain with every step and my hair itched my face. I pushed it away, but it kept falling back again. Honestly. How did humans deal with this sort of constant insubordination from their own bodies? Back home, and even in Maine with Orion, my hair was always clean and fell perfectly in place, and every item of clothing I conjured for myself fit perfectly. But these shoes were torture devices, and my hair had a mind of its own. We passed by an open bag on a chair and I saw a pretty plaid scarf peeking out from inside. I grabbed it and tied my hair back from my cheeks. There. Much better.

Now if only I could find a spare pair of sandals lying around.

"Darla!" Veronica suddenly screeched at a deafening pitch. "OMG! There you are!"

I winced as the two girls screamed and pawed at each other, closing my eyes and touching my forehead, willing the headache to heal already, willing my fingertips to warm and make it go away.

But my power refused to return, and my headache was getting worse and worse as this interminable day dragged on.

"Hi," Darla said, looking me over curiously. She glanced at Veronica, and I noticed they were wearing almost the exact same outfit, except that Darla's skirt and sweater were blue, and her D pendant was slightly smaller than Veronica's V. "New girl?"

"Hello," I said. "I'm—"

"New girl," Veronica confirmed, interrupting me. "Leifer says I have to let her follow me around, but only for today."

The four girls looked me over with disdain. I might not have been able to read their souls, but after shadowing Veronica this morning, I was certain of one thing: The girl was a two-faced bitch. She gossiped about everyone, even her friends, going off about one girl's fake tan the *second* said girl walked away from her. She'd slammed some poor freshman's locker closed to get to her own, told an adorable guy his girlfriend was cheating on him with absolutely no sympathy, and even crushed a ladybug under the toe of her pointy boot—on purpose. If I *could* read her soul, I was fairly certain it would have that murky, purple-black quality usually reserved for dictators and torturers. Normally, I would have been bent on finding a girl like her a good match, knowing that love's healing powers would tame her a bit, make her more sympathetic and kind. But she already had a beautiful boyfriend, and she was still a raving bitch. That type couldn't be saved. Not even by true love.

Oh, how I wished Harmonia, Nike, and Selene were here with me. Our combined beauty would have intimidated Veronica into submission in a blink.

"Well, I'm Darla," Darla said finally.

"I'm True," I replied.

"Don't *talk* to her," Veronica hissed, rolling her eyes.

She'd rolled her eyes so many times today I was surprised her skull could still hold them.

I lifted my chin and pushed past her, trying not to limp. "I'm hungry."

There was a line of people waiting in front of steaming silver vats of food, but none of it looked appealing, so I went right to the produce section and grabbed an apple and a banana. There was a tray on a shelf, so I put my things on there and looked around for something to drink.

"Hey! That's my tray!" a boy with many, many pimples whined.

My brain felt like it was slamming against my temples. It was the first time a mortal had ever dared protest something I'd done, and in my current mood, I could have lifted a finger and reduced him to ash for it. One more power I would miss. Instead I pointed at a stack of similar trays near the door.

"There are others," I told him. Then I reached past a tiny girl with blond curls and took a carton of milk and a brown roll.

"You're cutting the line," she said.

"Get over it," I snapped.

I gave the woman the meal card Mrs. Leifer had issued me that morning and took my food outside, wincing with every step. Other students had claimed tables and were starting to eat. I concentrated on a sad-looking girl sitting alone and tried to read her feelings. *Come on. Give me your name. Your heart's desire. Something. True love is just the thing to turn that frown upside down.* I gritted my teeth, held my breath, and focused. The only sound was that of my blood thumping in my temples. And now the pain radiated down my neck and into my shoulders. Perfection.

"Hey, True." Charlie Cox walked up next to me with a tray full of food. "Lunch at a new school. Sucks, doesn't it?" he said quietly.

"Does it?" I asked, distracted by the throbbing.

"Always," he replied with a tentative smile. "So . . . wanna sit together?"

Kindness. Interesting. That was new.

"Sure," I said.

Then the three virile boys from the office that morning—Trevor, Josh, and Brian—walked up behind him.

"Where're you going? You're sitting with us," Josh said, hooking his arm around Charlie's neck in a friendly way.

"Oh." Charlie looked perplexed. Maybe even alarmed. "I guess we're sitting with them."

We walked over to a table under a lovely elm tree and settled in on the benches. My feet pulsated, so I took the opportunity to tug the boots off. The cool air rushed over my bare toes like a soothing balm. A pair of girls shot me a disgusted look, so I stared them down until they went away. The sun pierced my eyes, and I held one hand over them for shade.

The Virile Trio took out their cell phones and started texting. I bit down on my tongue. All day it had been like this. People texting their friends across the classroom, in the halls, at their lockers, standing *right in front of each other*. Why not talk to the people around you? Look them in the eye? Connect on a human level? No wonder the true love connection was faltering. Texting "I love you" was simply not the same as saying it out loud while staring deeply into your beloved's eyes. . . .

My heart ached, and I touched Orion's arrow. Three couples. That was it. I would see him again once I matched three couples.

"So. What do you think of Lake Carmody High?" Charlie asked.

I bit into the apple and eyed him carefully beneath the cover of my fingers. I already knew he was single, and he'd been in a couple of my honors classes that morning, where I'd seen a few different girls appraising him. Clearly they liked this scruffy, twenty-first-century-artist look he had going. Plus, he was the only human human I'd met today, the only one who'd offered me even an ounce of consideration.

I could work with Charlie Cox. If only I could read his soul and find out exactly what he wanted in a girl. If only I had my gold-tipped arrows. Ever since I'd left the house that morning, I'd been missing the heft of my quiver and bow on my back. Now I squirmed, my spine actually tingling with longing.

"Not much," I answered. "What about you?"

Charlie's eyes trailed along the table toward the VT. "It's . . . weird. These guys? At any other school I've been to? Would have kicked my ass by now. Or at least tried to shove me into a locker."

I nodded knowingly, thinking of Orion. "The alpha males. They're born with the primal need to assert themselves. To show everyone around them who's in charge."

Charlie laughed and took a bite of sandwich. "I've never thought of it that way, but okay."

"They seem to genuinely like you, though," I mused.

"I know! That's the weirdest part. No one has ever asked me to sit with them on the first day before. Four schools in ten years and not once," he said.

I smiled, touched. "Is that why you asked me to sit with you?"

Charlie shrugged. "I know how it feels. And it doesn't feel good."

"Thank you," I said earnestly.

He grinned. "Anytime."

I decided I liked Charlie. That kind of empathy is rare in the teenage population. It illustrated a depth that I, as someone who had been around for countless millennia, appreciated. I sat back and gazed around the courtyard, munching on the apple and trying to discern if any of these girls were worthy enough to deserve him.

"Where'd you move from?" he asked, popping open a bottle of iced tea.

"Maine," I said flatly.

That iced tea looked good. Refreshing. I picked up the bottle and gulped down half of it. Charlie stared. I placed it down and sighed. My head throbbed a bit more dully.

"Um, that was mine," Charlie said.

"What is with everyone and this *mine* thing?" I asked. "'That's my desk, you took my pencil, mine, mine mine.' Doesn't anyone on Earth share?"

He narrowed his eyes at me, and I realized with a start that I might have said too much. Normally, I was not one to complain, but this day—and this headache—were frustrating me to no end. It was so difficult, getting used to these new rules. Normally I simply visualized what I wanted and it would appear before me. My brothers and sister, my friends back home . . . we'd never wanted for anything, and we'd never had a problem with anyone taking something from us, because we could always conjure another.

Except for our loves, of course. We always took issue when someone tried to steal our loves.

Suddenly a plain girl with gorgeous auburn hair paused at the end of our table. "Did you take my scarf?"

I sighed as I reached back to untie it. "See what I mean?" I handed the scarf to the girl, who stared. "What? I don't have fleas."

She ran to her friends to whisper. A tall, handsome boy with shaggy brown hair and the letters *QB* on the arm of his jacket shot

me a disturbed look before ushering her through a door marked
THE CAFÉ, her friends trailing behind. A stiff breeze blew my hair
into my face. Mental note: *Tomorrow, braids.*

"Ooookay," Charlie said. "Can I have your milk, then?"

"Sure," I said, taking another bite of apple. Why did he even feel
the need to ask? "I can always get another."

A car motor gunned and we both looked up. Idling at the bottom of the stairs leading from the courtyard to the parking lot was
a sleek black car. A pretty girl in tight jeans jogged down the steps
and over to the driver, who got out and laid a serious kiss on her.
He wore an oil-stained baseball cap, and even from here I could tell
his fingernails were black with grime. He picked up his girlfriend
and sat her down on the hood of the car, where they went at it like
dogs in heat.

I grimaced. Those two, I had not matched up. I would have
remembered.

"Ever wonder what people are thinking?" Charlie sounded
mildly disgusted.

My eyes narrowed. I used to always *know* what people were
thinking. But now I would have given anything for the smallest
inkling.

"All the time," I said.

Charlie shook his head and picked up the sandwich again as
Veronica, Darla, and their hangers-on arrived with trays piled high
with greens. Darla shot me the smallest of smiles, then sat down
next to Charlie, angling away from us. Veronica slid into a chair
next to Josh, wrapping her arms around his neck and leaning in for
a kiss. Then she glanced over at the couple on the car.

"God. Do we really have to watch that?" she asked, scrunching
her nose.

"I know," Darla put in, pushing her salad around with her fork. "And she used to be so normal."

"Katrina Ramos? Please," Veronica said dismissively.

Darla's cheeks turned pink. "Well, she was *semi*-normal. We used to have a lot of classes together. She was nice."

Veronica scoffed and widened her eyes. "And look at her now," she said derisively.

"Come on, V. You gotta cut the girl some slack after what happened," Josh said. For a long moment, everyone at the table was silent.

"Why?" Charlie piped up. "What happened?"

Darla leaned toward him. "Her dad died last year. In a car crash," she whispered. "This huge pileup on 78. It was on every news channel for days. After that, she just kind of . . ."

"Turned slut?" Veronica suggested.

The guys laughed. Darla shifted in her seat. Charlie watched Katrina and her boyfriend for another few seconds, and I could tell he felt for her. The boy definitely had heart.

"Charlie, I'm going to find you a girlfriend," I announced, pressing the tip of Orion's arrow into the pad of my finger.

"What?" Trevor said with a laugh.

Charlie paled.

"Yeah . . . what?" he squeaked.

"I'm going to find you a girlfriend," I repeated, taking another swig of iced tea. "I'm really good at matching up couples. It's a special talent of mine."

Veronica rolled her eyes. "Who *is* this freak?" she whispered to Josh.

"You think I need a girlfriend?" Charlie asked, fiddling with the ripped top of the milk carton.

"Everyone needs love," I told him. "It's a universal truth."

Charlie chuckled.

"She's right about that," Josh announced, kissing Veronica's cheek.

"Don't you want a girlfriend?" I asked, perplexed. "Or is it that you want a boyfriend? Because either way, I can help."

Trevor almost choked. Brian eyed Charlie curiously. Loud music blasted through the windows of the black car. I winced, touching my fingertips to my temples. Almost everyone in the courtyard stared. Charlie's ears turned pink.

"Girlfriend. I'm a girlfriend kind of guy," Charlie specified. "And, um, sure. I guess."

"Then I'm going to get you one."

Charlie shifted in his seat, and his shoulders hunched. It was like he was trying to grow smaller. "Why do I feel like I don't have a choice here?"

I tilted my head. "Because you don't."

He glanced along the table. Veronica and Josh were now feeding each other cucumber slices. Down in the parking lot, the dirty guy was nuzzling his girlfriend's neck while that awful guitar music assaulted everyone's eardrums.

"Okay, fine," Charlie said. "Why the hell not?"

"This should be interesting," Veronica said under her breath.

I ignored her. "Good," I said to Charlie. I smiled and took a cookie off the plate in front of him. Charlie watched me bite into it, crestfallen. I rolled my eyes, broke off half, and handed it back to him.

"Now tell me everything there is to know about you."

CHAPTER FIVE

Katrina

I had Ms. Day for English again. This was a good sign. Ms. Day was one of the only teachers who had been nice to me after my dad died last year. Most of the others could barely figure out what to say to me. But Ms. Day, she'd offered to help me with makeup work a few times—an offer I'd always turned down—and had even given me a Christmas present—a gift card to Barnes & Noble. "Escapism is good for the soul," she'd said. Until this summer I'd had no idea what that meant. But even knowing the teacher was a non-nightmare wasn't stopping my nerves about handing in my paper. In five minutes everyone was going to know I'd done the summer homework. In my old honors classes, this wouldn't have been a big deal. Everyone else would have done the homework too. But in these classes, people laughed at you for doing the work. They stared. They whispered.

I hated that.

It doesn't matter, I told myself. *This is not about them. Fresh start, fresh start, fresh start.*

As I came around the corner into the literary arts wing, I tripped, and my stack of new, uncovered textbooks slipped out of my arms.

Of course everyone in the hall applauded. Originality was not big at my school. My face burned as I bent to check on the poor freshman I'd collided with. She was still crouched at my feet, the laces of her shoe in each hand.

"I'm so sorry!" I said. "I didn't even see you!"

"It's all right," she replied, tying her shoelace. She stood and shoved her big glasses up on her nose. She had dark skin, brown eyes, and black hair pulled back in a perfect ponytail. "I get that a lot."

Then her eyes shifted past me. When I turned around, I stopped breathing. Not-Justin-Bieber was standing there, holding my books out to me in a neat stack. Except up close he looked nothing like Justin Bieber. His cheeks were more square and his eyes very, very blue. He was hotter than Justin Bieber. By a lot.

"That looked painful," he said with a smile. His voice made my heart feel fuzzy and warm, like hot chocolate on a cold day.

"We're okay," I replied, glancing over my shoulder at the frosh, mostly to force myself to tear my eyes off him. "Right . . . ?"

"Zadie," she replied, lifting a hand. She had on about twenty Hello Kitty bracelets, some beaded, some silver, some string. "I'm Zadie."

"Nice to meet you, Zadie," Not-Bieber said. "I'm Charlie."

They both looked at me. "Oh, Katrina. That's my me. I mean name. I'm Katrina."

Charlie's smile widened. "I think these are yours."

"Oh. Right." I realized with a start that my black poetry notebook was still on the floor and had fallen open, exposing my latest attempts at haiku to the world. I grabbed it and took my books from him, feeling like an idiot for making him stand there holding them for so long. And also for not being able to speak. My face was hot as I clutched the books, and my poetry, to my chest. "Thanks."

"Um. Okay. Bye," Zadie said, turning around.

"Bye! And sorry! Again!" I called after her.

She waved and smiled and was gone, leaving Charlie and me standing there alone.

"So," he said.

I opened my mouth to say something to him, when I was suddenly dragged off by the arm.

"Raine!" I protested.

"You're welcome!" she sang, looking down at her phone.

She practically flung me into Ms. Day's room. I glanced over my shoulder at Charlie, who had pushed his hands into his pockets and was loping away, and realized maybe I *should* thank her. If I'd kept talking to him, I probably would have said something else as brilliant as "That's my me." Ugh.

"Katrina! Hello!" Ms. Day greeted me as I shuffled through the door.

Every kid in the room stopped talking and turned to look at me. It was like I had the words "Teacher's Pet" stamped across my forehead. I bowed my head as Raine slipped by and took a seat toward the back of the room.

"Hey, Ms. Day."

My heels clicked loudly as I rushed after Raine and plopped into the seat next to hers, my cheeks pulsating. Raine's thumbs flew over the screen on her phone.

"Lana says hey," she told me. "She says Mr. P got hot this summer."

I snorted a laugh. Mr. P was an ancient, shriveled history teacher. He wore polka-dotted bow ties with plaid shirts and stopped every five feet in the hallway to lean against the wall and catch his breath.

Suddenly my own phone vibrated. My heart leaped when I saw that it was a text from Ty. But why was he texting when he'd left me in the courtyard exactly one class period ago? Maybe he'd remembered that I had English seventh period and wanted to wish me luck! I clicked the text.

CANT GET THERE TILL 4. SRY.

Damn.

His place was too far to walk to from school. I could walk home, but I didn't want to go home. My mom was always crankier than usual after the overnight shift, and I hadn't even seen her in two days. I also realized suddenly that I hadn't dusted or vacuumed the house, and if I went home, that meant I'd have to go grocery shopping first. With no ride from Ty.

Sometimes I hated my life.

I slumped in my chair until my whole butt hung off the edge. The guy next to me, a senior whose name I didn't know, hunched so fully he looked like a turtle, his leather jacket covering everything but the tips of his frosted blond hair as he rested his cheek on the desk.

"Welcome back, everyone!" Ms. Day said brightly, standing at the front of the room in her bright-green dress and brown flats, her black, gray-streaked hair pulled back in a bun. "I hope you all had a fun, productive summer."

A couple of people sighed. Someone outright laughed.

"How many of you did the summer reading assignment?" she asked, lifting her chin as she surveyed the room.

Raine looked at me and smirked. "Katrina did it, Ms. Day!" she announced.

Ms. Day's eyebrows shot up.

"Raine," I said through my teeth, clutching my bag in my lap.

"What?" she said, lifting the hand that wasn't holding the phone. "Like you weren't going to hand it in?"

Chrissa Jones and Elana Rosen laughed.

"Which book did you choose, Katrina?" Ms. Day asked, walking toward my row.

"Um . . . *The Perks of Being a Wallflower*?" I said, tugging the paper out. My makeup bag, a pen, and three quarters flew out with it, tumbling to the floor. More laughter. Ms. Day picked up the makeup bag. Raine got the pen. The guy next to me snagged one of the quarters.

"Finders keepers," he said, clutching it in his fist. Then he turtled up again.

"Good choice." Ms. Day traded my makeup bag for the paper, which shook as I handed it over. "I look forward to reading this."

"Um. Okay."

Suddenly I was sweating like I was in gym class, doing the dreaded squat thrusts. But then Ms. Day gave me this proud smile, like she was impressed. By me. And something inside me unclenched. I sat up straight and put my things back in my bag.

"Anyone else?" Ms. Day asked.

Two other kids had written papers. Josh Harper's was handwritten and on *The Catcher in the Rye*, and Casey Catalfo had read *The Secret Life of Bees*. It made me feel much less conspicuous, and I realized one of the windows was open, pouring sweetly scented late-summer air over our desks.

"Thank you, Katrina, Josh, and Casey, for taking your teachers seriously when they told you this was a mandatory assignment," Ms. Day said, walking back to the front of the room with our papers. "As for the rest of you, congratulations. You now have until

Monday the sixteenth to read one of the books on the list and write a five-page book report."

A groan went up around the room. Turtle boy snored.

"If you need a copy of the list, see me after class, or you can check the school's website or visit the Lake Carmody library, as you could have done throughout the summer. As for the three of you who did the assignment, congratulations are due to you as well. You will have no homework from me for the first two weeks of school."

"Yes!" Josh Harper cheered, pumping his meaty fists.

I bit back a grin.

"Goody-goody," Raine muttered mockingly. Then she shot me a smile.

"These will be your textbooks for the year," Ms. Day announced, circulating the room with a pile of books. "They contain the knowledge you'll need to ace the English portion of your SAT."

More groans. But as the book slid onto my desk, I felt a sizzle of excitement and anticipation. I cracked the book's spine and inhaled the plasticky, new-book scent. Ms. Day caught me smiling and winked, which made Raine roll her eyes, but I didn't even care. I'd handed in the paper and hadn't died of humiliation. Maybe this year really would be better than last.

CHAPTER SIX

True

The honors English teacher looked like a Hun and had the personality to match. You'd think she'd be happier, considering she was sporting a gold wedding band and had a picture of herself and her handsome husband framed on her desk. People around here obviously took true love for granted. I would have liked to have seen how she would behave if she'd had that big hunk of masculinity ripped away from her for the gods knew how long. Maybe it would soften her a touch.

I blew out a sigh. I really missed Orion.

But we'd been sitting in class for thirty minutes already, and the teacher had done nothing but quiz us on the authors and themes of the titles they'd read last year. So far, I'd learned exactly nothing. Other than the fact that the chairs these humans forced their young people to sit in day after day were excruciatingly hard.

"Does anyone recall who wrote *Of Mice and Men*?" the teacher asked.

A girl in the front row raised her hand like a shot. She had, in fact, raised her hand to answer every question the teacher had posed. Her strawberry-blond hair was pulled back tightly from her head and tied into a French braid like Harmonia liked to weave into my hair when she was bored, adding a daisy or a sprig of lavender here and there. She had a smattering of freckles across her cute, upturned nose, and very pretty pink lips. And from what I could tell, she was the smartest girl in the room, not to mention the most eager.

"Would anyone other than Miss Halliburn care to answer?" the teacher asked, looking over the class with an imperious raise of her chin. Her shoulders were almost perfectly square, and she had pointy sideburns that did not flatter her round face.

Miss Halliburn was practically falling out of her chair in an attempt to raise her arm even higher. I knew the answer but didn't care to share it. My head still hurt, and I didn't exactly feel challenged. Plus, ever since lunch the skin on my face had felt tight and hot and stung whenever I touched it. I closed my eyes and carefully pressed my fingertips to my temple. My skull warmed and the pounding ceased.

I stopped breathing and my eyes flew open. Could it be? Was my power back?

But then, with a slam of pain, the throbbing returned full force, so bad I had to concentrate to keep from mewling like a tortured kitten. Wishful thinking.

"Anyone?" the teacher repeated.

Next to me, Charlie carefully raised his hand.

"Yes, Mr. Cox?" the teacher said.

"John Steinbeck?" he asked.

Miss Halliburn turned around in her seat. "You're right!" she said, as if surprised.

"It happens occasionally," Charlie replied.

Everyone laughed. Charlie's ears turned pink and Miss Halliburn smiled. Then she turned around in her seat, awaiting the next question with an excited air about her. I looked at Charlie. He was smiling to himself. I glanced at Miss Halliburn. Leaning up against the legs of her chair was a long black box with a handle. A flute case. Charlie's drumsticks lay across the pile of books under his desk.

They were both musicians. Check.

At lunch, Charlie had told me he loved to read, which this Miss Halliburn person clearly did as well. Check.

But he had also told me that his favorite subject was math. I slid down in my seat for a better look at Miss Halliburn's books. A fat trigonometry text anchored the pile. Check.

Charlie had also told me that he came from a football family, whatever that meant, but that he didn't play himself. I couldn't imagine that Miss Halliburn was a football fan or a player, with her tiny wrists and ankles and the copious amounts of pink she was wearing. Check.

I smiled to myself, staring down at my fingertips, which I could have sworn were still tingling. Could it be? Did I have my first match?

As soon as the bell rang I zipped right over to Miss Halliburn's desk. A gold plate around her neck told me in dainty script that her first name was Stacey. Charlie Cox and Stacey Halliburn. It had a ring.

"Hi, Stacey," I said brightly, gritting my teeth against my headache.

She stood up and looked around, like she was worried I was about to pounce. "Uh . . . hi?" she said like a question.

"My name's True," I told her with the friendliest smile I had in me. "And I have a proposition for you."

CHAPTER SEVEN

Charlie

The band room was worth waiting for. I'd never seen anything like it. Six risers for the musicians, a state-of-the-art recording system, a sheet music collection like no other. But it was the drums that really got me. They couldn't have been more than five years old, and they gleamed like they had been polished that morning. Three schools ago the snare drums had been drawn on with permanent marker, and when I'd asked if they had kettles, they'd laughed. In my face.

I was in heaven. And when Mr. Roon, the band director, handed me the mallet for the bass drum, then the sheet music to the Harry Potter score, I almost cried. I didn't even care that the other guys in the drum corps were shooting me annoyed looks throughout class. The orchestra was awesome. And I kept the beat perfectly the whole time, if I do say so myself.

Maybe living here wouldn't suck so bad. It seemed like only five minutes had passed when the bell rang.

"Thank you, everyone!" Mr. Roon called out as chairs scraped and music sheets fluttered. "Remember, if you haven't signed up for marching band yet, and you're interested, see me in my office!"

I couldn't stop grinning. Then I bent to grab my backpack off the floor, and someone bumped into me from behind. My forehead hit the cinder-block wall and then my knees hit the floor.

"What the hell?" I said.

The beefy guy in the *Phineas and Ferb* T-shirt who had been on the snare barely glanced at me. "Sorry. Didn't see you."

Yeah, right.

I shoved myself up but didn't have time to think up a comeback. Mr. Roon was suddenly right in front of me. He had shaggy reddish-brown hair that stuck out at a million angles like a scarecrow, tiny glasses, and a wispy goatee.

"Charlie, if you don't mind, would you play something for me on the drum set?" He raised his arm out elegantly toward the smokin' black kit in the far corner. "I like to know what I'm working with."

"Sure," I said eagerly.

I'd been eyeing that drum set ever since the first bell of the period. It was beautiful—nothing like the crappy old kit in my garage. Not that I didn't love my drums. My mother had saved up and then scoured the garage sales for me last spring when we were still in Austin. Aside from practicing on them whenever I could, I had pounded on them after every argument I'd ever had with my father. Very helpful in that way. My drum kit was my favorite thing in the world. But it was still crappy and old.

I shoved my music into my backpack and shouldered it. As I crossed the bustling room, I noticed Phineas and Ferb and two of his friends had slowed to a crawl. I drew my sticks out of my pocket, adjusted the stool, and started to play the jazz solo I'd been working on for the past few weeks. A few musicians who had been chatting and straggling stopped to watch. Self-consciousness seeped in and I closed my eyes, blocking them out. This was the one part about playing that I didn't love—the audience. I'd never loved being the center of attention. With two superheroic older brothers, it had never been my natural state of being. But as long as I closed my eyes and felt the music, it didn't matter. And now, I was in the zone. When I was done, I reached out to steady the cymbal and sighed. That felt good.

A few people applauded. Mostly girls, I couldn't help noticing. Instantly I thought of Katrina, and those offhanded comments the girls had made at lunch. I couldn't believe she'd lost her dad. It had sounded, in fact, like she'd lost a lot more than that. I wished I'd said something to her in the hallway before, but what?

Oh, hey. You don't know me, but sorry your dad died? Not likely.

"Fantastic, Charlie. Absolutely fantastic," Mr. Roon said.

"Thank you, sir," I replied, trying to focus.

The guys from the corps snorted, like they'd never heard anyone use the word "sir" before. Mr. Roon glanced at them. "Looks like you gents have lucked into a talented new member."

"Great." Phineas and Ferb sneered at me. The other two said nothing.

I got my stuff together and headed for the door. The three corps members stood close enough together that I couldn't get through. I stared each of them in the eye.

"Excuse me," I said.

"Excuse us, *sir*," the short one said pointedly, backing off with his hands in the air.

I shook my head as I blew by them. So much for making friends in orchestra. At least they were good. That was something. Not that I'd ever tell them that if this was the way they were going to be.

"Hey, sir! Wait up, sir!"

They were following me. The little hairs on the back of my neck stood up.

"Hey you, new guy. We're talking to you, *sir*!"

I gritted my teeth and kept walking.

"Is there a problem?" I said quietly.

"Our problem is we've been playing together for three years. We're finally seniors. And we don't need some punk-ass hick coming in here and screwing up our corps," Phineas and Ferb said, getting in front of me.

I backed up into the wall. This kid had, like, a hundred pounds on me and I could see up his nostrils. He was pissed.

"I just want to play drums," I said, hoping to appeal to him on common ground. "I don't care which ones or on what songs. I just want to play."

"Well, we don't want you here, sir," he said, shoving my chest so hard my head knocked back against the wall. "So tomorrow you're gonna go in there and tell Mr. Roon you want to switch to the glockenspiel or the harp or something. Whatever you want. But you're not gonna be a part of our corps."

He shoved me again, and this time my head cracked so hard I saw stars. I was trying to figure a way out of this when a hand came down on Phineas's shoulder.

"Lay off him, Fred."

Fred. So his name was Fred. Well, Fred paled at the sound of Josh's voice. Then he paled some more when he saw Brian and Trevor were with him.

"I wasn't doing anything," Fred said, raising his meaty palms.

The other two drummers were already halfway down the hall. Looked like they weren't the type who had their friend's back.

"It's fine," I said to Josh. "Really."

Josh didn't look convinced. He gave Fred a menacing stare. "Why are you still here? Go!"

Fred flinched and took off after his buddies. I cleared my throat, standing up straight. The back of my head radiated crackles of pain. "Thanks, man."

"No problem. That kid's been a bully since we were in kindergarten and he was the big bad first grader," he said. "Luckily, I'm bigger than him now," he added with a grin.

I laughed and rubbed at the bump forming on my head.

"I woulda pounded on him some for ya, but his band's playing my party next Friday, so I don't wanna, like, create bad blood or whatever," Josh added.

"Or break his arms," Brian put in.

They both laughed. "Or break his arms," Josh agreed.

"He's in a band?" I asked, jealous against my will.

"They're called Universal Truth," Trevor said with an eye roll. "But they're good."

"Annoyingly. They're so good I actually have to pay them for the gig," Josh put in. "Anyway, I gotta get to football practice, but Brian's on his way to help Coach Ziegler with cross-country tryouts. You in?"

"Come on, man," Brian said, raising his palms. "You only gotta run a three-mile course. It's no big."

I had that put-on-the-spot feeling that I didn't love. "I don't know, you guys. . . ."

"You make it, you get a varsity jacket," Trevor told me, opening the lapel of his own like he was modeling it. "The ladies love the varsity jacket."

I laughed.

"And hey! You get to *come* to Moskowitz's party next weekend," Brian said, slapping my chest with the back of my hand. "It's varsity athletes only. Well, and girls. Lots of girls."

"And Universal Truth." Trevor rolled his eyes again.

A party? I hadn't been invited to a party since the fourth grade. And this was a real party. A popular crowd party. With a live band. For a second I stood there, trying to wrap my head around this. All day I'd been waiting for these guys to suddenly pants me in the cafeteria, or lure me into a bathroom for a swirly, or worse. But now the day was over and they were still not torturing me. It was getting harder to believe that they didn't actually want to be friends.

But did I want to be friends with them? I mean, they weren't exactly my type of guys with their thick necks, school spirit, and sports-obsessive attitudes. They were more the Quarterback Twins' type of guys. But then, wouldn't rejecting their friendship on superficial criteria be as bad as the kids at the other schools rejecting me for what *I* looked like? For the things I was into?

My brain was starting to hurt. And Brian, Josh, and Trevor were waiting. The adrenaline from the near miss with Fred was still coursing through my veins. Maybe I could work it out with a run. Just this once. It wasn't like I was going to actually make the team.

"What the hell," I said with a shrug. "I'm in."

"Yes!" Brian cheered, throwing his arm around my shoulders. "You will *not* regret this."

"Aw, yeah," Josh said, slapping hands with Trevor behind my head. "I knew we'd get him!"

I tugged out my cell phone as we loped toward the locker rooms. For kicks, I texted my dad.

HOME LATE. TRYING OUT FOR XCOUNTRY.

He was probably running drills on the football field over at St. Joe's right now. I imagined the whistle falling out of his mouth as he stared at the phone in shock. That simple image would make a three-mile run totally worth it.

CHAPTER EIGHT

True

"I can't believe I'm doing this. Why am I doing this? I'm not even supposed to date. My mother would freak out if she knew I was here. I mean, she would *freak*. *Out*."

Stacey rubbed her knees together as we waited near the back door of the gym, her ribbed stockings making a *shush, shush, shush*-ing sound. There were a few other packs of kids hanging around, some in blue-and-white soccer uniforms, others in football pads, others in plain clothes. Half of them were texting instead of talking to their friends. Ugh.

At least I'd lost the awful red boots. When I'd taken them off in the locker room for last-period gym, the gym teacher had spotted the open sores on my feet and sent me right to the nurse. Now I sported several bandages, a clean pair of white socks, and a pair of blue-and-white cheerleading sneakers someone had fished out of a supply closet. They were heavenly. I was going to wear them every day for the rest of my exile.

"Do you really think he'll like me?" Stacey asked. "What if he doesn't like me?"

I looked her up and down through the silver-framed sunglasses

I'd taken from an open locker, thereby fixing the glaring sun problem, and smiled in an encouraging way. My heart went out to her.
Somehow, even with her big brown eyes, her appealing smile, and
her obvious intelligence, the girl had serious self-esteem issues.
Being with a good, stable, sweet guy like Charlie would work wonders on her. That was one of the many incredible things about love,
its power to change a person's life.

"Why wouldn't he?" I said.

Stacey's eyebrows shot up, and she smiled. "You're so sweet!"
She looped her arm through mine and clutched me to her side. "I'm
so glad you moved here. I think we're going to be best friends."

I smiled, moved and relieved by the contact. No one aside from
the nurse had touched me today. Not once. At least I now knew
that people did still want to connect around here. Perhaps all was
not lost.

"There he is!" she breathed, rising up onto her toes.

Charlie had just crested the hill with one of the VT—Brian, he
of the dark skin and ridiculously winning smile. Charlie's face was
ruddy, and his hair was wet around the ears. His gray T-shirt was
stained with sweat, and he was grinning from ear to ear. He looked
strong. Vibrant. Manly. He was oozing testosterone. I could see the
attraction written across Stacey's face, and why not? Men gave off
abundant amounts of pheromones when filled with the adrenaline
of battle.

"Charlie!" I shouted, waving.

He said his good-byes to his VT friend and jogged over. This
was it. Their first impression of each other. I felt a flutter of nervousness inside my chest.

"True! What're you doing here?" Charlie asked pleasantly.

"We followed you after school and asked the coach what you

were doing," I said. "He told me the cross-country tryouts would take about forty-five minutes, so we waited."

His brow knit, and he eyed me curiously. "Okay."

"So did you make the team?" Stacey asked, biting her bottom lip.

"I did, yeah," he replied.

"That's amazing!" Stacey cheered, gripping me even harder.

"Um . . . thanks?" He shot me a question with his eyes.

"This is Stacey," I told him, smiling my encouragement. "She loves to read, excels at math, and plays the flute in the school orchestra. Oh, and she detests football."

They both seemed nonplussed by my introduction, but Stacey recovered first.

"I saw your audition after class today," she told him, touching his forearm with her fingertips. "You were . . . amazing."

Charlie blushed. "Wow. Thanks. You play the flute?"

"Second chair," she replied, looking at her feet. "It's not as cool as drums."

"No, no. Flute's cool," Charlie said.

They both laughed. They grinned and shifted their feet and turned all sorts of colors. I might not have had my powers of intuition, but even I could see that these two were hitting it off.

"Why don't you guys go out and celebrate?" I suggested, detaching myself from Stacey's side. "You made the team!" I cheered, tilting my head toward Stacey and hoping Charlie would get the message.

"Yeah?" Charlie said, eyebrows raised.

"Totally!" Stacey enthused. "You're new here, right? Have you been to Goddess yet? It's amazing!"

"Um . . . no. I—"

"Good! Let's walk into town. I'll show you around," Stacey suggested, gathering up her things. Charlie bent to pick up her flute case and Stacey preened. Perfect. They were perfect. Or, perhaps, *amazing*.

"Okay. But I have to hit the locker room and get my stuff."

As the two of them moseyed off together, Charlie turned around and gave me a double thumbs-up, the flute case hooked around two of his fingers. I grinned and waved, watching them until they'd disappeared inside, Charlie holding the door open for his lovely girl.

With a breath of relief, I reached up and laid my hand over Orion's arrow. My heart swelled and tears stung my eyes, remembering the first time we'd met. It was almost three thousand years ago, and a love connection was not in the cards—at least not for us—but still, it was a memory I now cherished. I walked to a nearby bench and sat with my eyes closed, my face tipped to the sun, letting the remembrance embrace me.

"Come one, come all! Come god, come mortal! None of you can best me when there's bow and arrow in my grasp!"

Orion threw his sinewy arms wide, turning in a slow circle at the center of the wide, sun-dappled hills of the poppy field, a favorite meeting place for the lower gods and goddesses near the apex of Mount Olympus. I had heard tales of his bravado, but this was the first time I'd ever seen it for myself. I understood why so many women in the heavens and on Earth had fallen for the guy. He was a perfect specimen. Obnoxious, to be sure, but otherwise perfect.

I approached, my bow at my side, my quiver fastened, as it always was, to my back.

"We have a taker!" he crowed to the clumps of gods and goddesses lounging in the flowers along the knoll. I saw my nemeses—the twins Artemis, Goddess of the Hunt, and Apollo, God of Light—draped

over each other, along with Artemis's Titaness friend Hecate, who was even more awful than they were. Her black eyes were trained on me as she leaned toward Artemis's ear to whisper. "And you are?" Orion said to me.

"She is Eros, the Goddess of Love!" Artemis shouted. "She fancies herself the greatest archer on Mount Olympus."

A few of the other gods laughed, and I smiled. "It is not a fancy," I called back, "but a proven fact."

"You have not tested me," Artemis replied, a shadow passing through her eyes.

"Then come forth," I shouted back. "Orion has the test laid out for us!"

I gestured to the target Orion had fastened to the tallest tree at the edge of Gaia's Wood, a dark and magical forest, home to all sorts of exotic and unnatural beasts. Artemis squinted at the bull's-eye, her hand held up to guard against the sun.

"She will not take the bait," Orion said, leaning toward my ear. The masculine scent of him was very appealing, the odors of sweat and blood and wine. "Of all the goddesses, I find Artemis to be the most vile. She has the bark, but not the bite."

"And you?" I said, looking him up and down. "What do you look for in a mate?"

He smiled wickedly, and I opened my inner ear to his heart of hearts. "Submission," he replied, even as I read his real desire. He longed for someone who could be his equal. Someone who would challenge him. A great beauty with whom he could forge new adventures. Someone who would fight by his side and love him forever.

A mischievous plan formed in the back of my mind. I turned to the hill.

"Come, Artemis!" I shouted jovially. "Let us play!"

The other gods and goddesses cheered, goading her on. I saw my sister Harmonia and her friend Hephaestus, the divine craftsman, stand up and applaud on the opposite hill. They made an intriguing pair. While Harmonia was as pristine, regal, and sweetly smiling as ever, Hephaestus was covered in the soot of his forge, which made his already dark skin appear black as pitch, and he wore his ever-present stoic and suspicious expression. Nike and Selene and several of the other lower gods and goddesses were there as well, obviously excited by the prospect of a contest. It was perfection. Artemis might have backed down from the challenge with some flimsy excuse if we were alone, but with an audience, I knew she'd never yield. After another whisper from Hecate, she rose to her full, willowy height and strolled down to us, her bow and quiver clutched in her hands.

"Fine," she said as she stood next to me, her brown curls bouncing around her shoulders. "Who shoots first?"

"I do," I told her. "For it was I who issued the challenge."

"Actually, I believe it was I who issued the challenge," Orion said.

"Oh, well," I replied innocently, lifting a shoulder.

Then, before either of them could react, I pulled out two of my golden arrows and shot them each through the heart. Artemis stumbled back a few feet, clutching her chest. Orion did the same. The crowd gasped. Then the pair of them looked up into each other's eyes and melted.

"Orion!" Artemis cried.

"My love!" he replied.

"No!" Apollo wailed from the knoll.

But he was too late. The cockiest man on Earth fell into the waiting arms of the most awful goddess on Mount Olympus. Victory was mine.

"What have you done?" Apollo demanded, appearing at my side in a blink. Hecate remained on the hill, seething, her fists clenched at her sides.

"*I believe they are well matched,*" I replied, laughing as Artemis pushed Orion to the ground and climbed on top of him.

"*You have defiled my sister,*" Apollo seethed, his dark eyes aflame. "*You will pay for this!*" He let out a mighty screech and whirled off as Harmonia and Hephaestus appeared at my side.

"*Ugh. No one needs to see that,*" Hephaestus said, staring at the couple nonetheless.

"*I think it's sweet,*" I replied giddily.

"*You're too capricious, Eros,*" Harmonia scolded me.

"*Please! They deserve each other!*" I cried. "*There are no two more obnoxious beings on Earth or in the heavens.*"

Harmonia sighed. "*This is the type of thing that can come back to haunt you.*"

"*I'm not afraid,*" I told her, lifting my chin. "*I'm never afraid.*"

A door slammed and I blinked myself back to the now, back to Earth. My headache suddenly felt less severe, with Orion so vivid in my memory. I could do this. I *was* still good at my job. In fact, I pretty much *kicked ass* at my job. Less than eight hours and already I'd matched the perfect couple. It would be no time before I saw Orion again for real. Before I held him in my arms. Sensing that Zeus was watching, I looked up at the sky with a cocky sort of scowl.

I hoped he knew what I was thinking right then.

One down, two to go.

CHAPTER NINE

Katrina

"Katrina! I've been meaning to come find you."

Dr. Krantz, the school psychologist, gave me his biggest, friendliest smile as he walked toward me in the main hall. The school was mostly deserted, and there was nowhere for me to run. I should have known this was coming, but I still felt a spark of anger at the sight of him. I knew what he wanted—to sit me down and pick my brain and ask me how I was feeling—and there was nothing I wanted to do less.

"So," he said, cradling a book in his arm as he paused in front of me. "How was your summer? How *are* you?"

I always knew when people were really asking me whether or not I was still crushed about my dad by the way they pronounced the "are."

"I'm fine," I told him. "I was just going to the library to get some studying done, so . . ."

His bushy eyebrows shot up. "Studying after school on the first day? Well. We've come a long way."

I pressed my teeth together. What was I supposed to say to that?

"How's everything at home?" he asked. "How's your mom?"

"Fine. Busy," I said curtly. Did he really think I wanted to talk about this stuff with him? Every time he'd stalked me down during classes last year, I'd sat in his office, silent, until he'd finally given up. Maybe he thought that since I was clearly ready to do schoolwork, I would also be ready to spill my guts to a relative stranger. Not likely. "Can I go now?" I said finally.

His face fell. "Sure. But come by my office soon to chat. I want to help you, Katrina. That's all."

Stifling a groan, I slipped inside the air-conditioned library. I still vividly remembered his face when I'd stepped into his office last year, clueless that my life was about to be turned upside down. He'd said the right sympathetic things, but when my mother had buckled to the floor, I swear there was this gleam in his eye. Like on some level he was glad. Like he relished having a potential real patient with a real problem, instead of the girls who went to him every day sobbing over a breakup.

I would never forgive him for that.

The school library was silent and still. I walked past the larger study tables, their chairs tightly tucked in, and headed for the windows where the smaller, two-person tables were set up. I almost tripped when I saw Zadie in the corner. She had a laptop open in front of her, the logo for the school's literary magazine— the *Muse*—plain across the top of the page she was typing into. I sat down at the table farthest from her, and she gave me a quick, uncertain wave.

Hi, I mouthed.

She smiled, pushed her glasses up, and went back to her typing.

"Can I help you with anything?"

I nearly jumped out of my chair, startled by the full-voice question. Mr. Carlson, one of the school librarians, hovered behind me.

He wore his hair in about a million braids that he tied back with a standard tan rubber band, and his blue cotton tie was loosened around his neck. There were a bunch of earring holes in his ears, but no earrings, which had led to the rumor that he'd once been in a hard rock/reggae band but burned out young, landing himself a high school job instead.

"No. I'm fine," I said.

He didn't move, but kept his dark eyes fixed on me. My palms started to sweat.

"Is it—I mean—am I not supposed to be here?" I asked.

"Depends on what you were planning on doing," he said.

I tugged my history text out of my backpack. "Um, studying?"

Mr. Carlson blanched slightly. "Oh, I'm sorry. We've . . . last year we had a lot of issues with students using the library for other . . . inappropriate—"

My face burned, and I wasn't sure if it was for him or for me. What did he think I was going to do? Smoke a joint? Meet a guy to hook up? What?

"Dad! God!" Zadie hissed.

We both stared at her. She widened her eyes, and Mr. Carlson backed away.

"I apologize," he said formally. "Go about your business."

He shot Zadie a look and quickly walked back to the front desk. It took a good two minutes for me to feel comfortable again. I eyed Zadie as I reached for my poetry notebook. So she was Mr. Carlson's daughter? Interesting.

"Katrina! There you are!"

Ms. Day had appeared as if from nowhere. Was everyone at this school trying to give me a heart attack?

"Dr. Krantz said she saw you come in here. I'm so relieved."

She was out of breath, her hand over her heart. "Would you mind coming with me?"

"Um . . . sure."

I was already shaking as I shoved my stuff back into my bag. I caught Zadie watching me and pretending she wasn't. I knew what she was thinking. *What did that girl do?* I was thinking the same thing. Was I in trouble? For what? It was only the first day of school. I couldn't possibly have done anything wrong yet, could I?

Keeping my head down as I passed Mr. Carlson's judging eyes, I followed Ms. Day along the dark-gray carpet and out into the hall. She led me past students straggling at their lockers and teachers chatting over schedules, into the English department's office. It was a cramped space with two cluttered, badly lit square rooms. Sitting in the second room behind a huge desk was Mrs. Roberge. She was in charge of the English department and taught honors classes, and she was totally intimidating. Her shoulders were wide and square, and she wore her brown hair clipped close to her head like a helmet, with two points coming forward over her ears. Two streaks of dark-pink blush marked her cheekbones, and she had on enough eyeliner to keep Lana happy for a year. I stood in front of her and waited for her to speak, wrapping the fringe on my scarf around my index finger. Then she shifted, and I noticed that on her desk was my paper.

"Katrina Ramos . . . ," Mrs. Roberge said, eyeing me suspiciously. She lifted my paper, pinching opposite corners with her fingers so I could see it. "You wrote this?"

My heart jolted. Was that what this was about? Did they think I'd plagiarized my paper or something? My throat closed over and I nodded. "Um . . . yes?"

Great. That sounded confident.

Mrs. Roberge's face lit up. When she smiled, she looked pretty and about ten years younger. I hadn't known that before because I'd never seen her smile.

"It. Is. *Excellent*," she said, enunciating each syllable.

A *whoosh* of air filled my lungs. "Really?"

"Really," Ms. Day said behind me.

"It's so excellent that we'd like to move you into my honors English class," Mrs. Roberge continued, laying the paper down again and folding her fingers on top of it. "Ms. Day has always taken issue with your being demoted to standard levels this year, and now that I've read this, I have to agree."

I beamed at Ms. Day.

"It involves switching your econ section," Mrs. Roberge continued, "but we've already spoken to your guidance counselor and he raised no objections."

"That would be great," I said. "I . . . thank you."

"Good. Then tomorrow you will be with me sixth period and have economics directly afterward," Mrs. Roberge said. "Come ready to challenge yourself."

"I will. Okay," I said, glancing over at Ms. Day, then at the door. "Should I—?"

"I'll walk out with you," Ms. Day offered.

"Bye," I said to Mrs. Roberge. She lifted a hand but had already moved on to reading something else.

Out in the hallway, I felt like I didn't know where I was. I looked left and right, wanting to scream. I was going to be back in honors English. I was on my way. My dad would be so—

Suddenly tears sprang to my eyes and my whole chest felt heavy. My dad. My dad my dad my dad. I wished I could tell my dad.

"Congratulations, Katrina," Ms. Day said, squeezing my arm.

"I'll miss having you, but you definitely deserve to be bumped up."

I cleared my throat. "Thanks, Ms. Day. I'll, um . . . I'll miss you, too."

She laughed, tucking a few strands of hair behind her ear. "You don't have to say that."

"No. I really will," I said, trying to cling to the excitement and not let the heaviness take over. "Thanks for everything."

Ms. Day nodded. "You don't have to thank me. You did the work," she said, checking her watch. "I should be going. I'll see you around the halls!"

She walked off toward her classroom, but I felt frozen. I didn't want to go back to the library now, but I couldn't go home, and Ty wouldn't be here for another half hour. I looked out the window through the open door of the main office. It was beautiful outside, sunny and blue and bright. Maybe I'd celebrate by writing under a tree somewhere.

Taking a deep breath, I watched my feet as I walked down the hall, through the lobby, and out the front door. I would have killed to be able to call my father, but instead I imagined what he would say if he were here right now.

I knew you had it in you, mija. *You're your daddy's girl.*

I smiled sadly, longing to hear his voice, and tears stung my eyes. I fished out my phone to call someone, anyone, to keep from crying. The word HOME stared up at me.

Bad idea, Katrina. She won't care and then you'll be disappointed. But she would have to care, right? We'd had so many fights last year about my failing grades. This was a big deal. Maybe she'd be excited. Maybe we could even have a celebratory dinner together. It could happen.

I hit HOME, then instantly regretted it. But it was already ringing. I couldn't back out now, because if the phone did wake her, and I hung up, she'd freak even worse. Shaking, hoping, holding my breath, I brought the phone to my ear. It rang twice. Three times. I felt sick to my stomach. The line connected. There was a scrabbling sound—her bringing the phone to her ear across the bed—then a yawn. I almost hung up.

"Katrina?" Her voice was thick with sleep.

Bad idea. This was a really bad idea.

"Hey, Mom," I said, hating the hopeful sound of my voice.

"What is it?" she snapped. "I was sleeping."

My fingers hurt from gripping the phone. "I know, I . . . there's something I wanted to tell you."

She sighed. "Well? What?"

Why was I doing this? Why? Why had I hit HOME? "I—I found out I'm going to be moved back into honors English."

Dead silence. "That's . . . really? That's great."

My heart was about to burst. "Yeah? I mean, yeah. I know. I was just sitting in the library and Ms. Day came in and I—"

"Was that it? That's the only reason you're calling?" she interjected.

I swallowed hard. "Um, yeah. I—"

"Okay then. Let me go before I'm too awake to fall back to sleep."

"Oh. Okay."

"Katrina," she sighed. "Please don't give me that tone. I just worked a twenty-hour shift. We can talk about this when you get home." She paused, and when she spoke again, her words were clipped. "Or is this your way of telling me you're not coming home? Again."

"I—I didn't—"

"I'm going back to sleep."

The line went dead. Stupid. Stupid, stupid, stupid. Trembling, I gritted my teeth and hit Ty's name on the contact screen. He picked up on the first ring.

"Hey, baby," he said. There was laughter in the background. And clanging. And the sound of hip-hop on the stereo. "Look, it doesn't look like I'm gonna get there at four. The garage is slammed. You might hafta walk home."

"Oh," I said, my bottom lip trembling. Didn't he remember I didn't want to go home? But then, he was busy. And I didn't want him to think I was some crazy, needy girl. "Um . . . okay."

"You okay?" he asked, as the sound of a buzz saw squealed through the speaker.

"Yeah," I said, trying to sound bright. "I'm fine. I'll talk to you later."

There was a huge crash. "Asshole!" he shouted. "What the f—"

I hung up. I thought about calling Raine, but she had a job too—at her father's pizza place—and had a shift right after school. I felt suddenly and completely alone.

Someone breezed by me down the stairs, so close my hair whipped up. I looked around at the trees, their green leaves rustling in the wind. The JV football team was loading onto a big yellow school bus. A mom herded a girl and her friends, toting matching duffels from the local ballet school into her minivan. A pack of skater kids hung out on the concrete steps to the staff parking lot, sucking on Blow Pops and flipping tricks. Everyone was doing something fun. Everybody seemed happy. So what the hell was wrong with me? Why did I have to feel like this?

That was when I spotted Charlie, loping down the hill next to the gym. He was wearing shorts and a T-shirt, his blond hair matted with sweat, his cheeks red from exertion. He was yards away, but we locked eyes, and for a second, everything went away. The sorrow, the self-deprecation, the dread of going home. Everything. There was this inquisitive look in his eye, as if he knew something was wrong, even though that was fully impossible. I felt this sudden, irrational urge to talk to him, to tell him everything. I even started to raise my hand to wave, with no clue what I'd say if he waved back.

Then someone shouted and he stopped. A girl stepped out from behind the gym. Stacey Halliburn. One of Cara's friends, who I also used to have classes with. She jogged up to Charlie in her flippy plaid skirt and her adorable flat shoes. They grinned and kept walking. Together. Not holding hands, but together.

My heart sank. Clearly I was imagining things. He probably hadn't even been looking at me, and now they were getting closer. I could even hear Stacey giggling.

I ducked my head before they could catch me staring and turned around to walk, as slowly as I possibly could, toward home.

CHAPTER TEN

Charlie

"So then *last* year they told us that we were going to get to go play at Disney World on Thanksgiving, but then when the school year started they said it wasn't in the budget and instead we were going to Hershey in the spring," Stacey babbled. "And we were all like, 'Boo!' You can't tell people they're going to Florida and then bus them to Pennsylvania. Is that not so wrong?"

I didn't answer. My mouth was full of Oreo cupcake. "Goddess" had turned out to be Goddess Cupcakes, where apparently, every kid my age in a forty-mile radius went to hang out after school. Yeah, I was at the cool hangout. A place I'd never even found at my last school. And not only had I not gotten my butt kicked today, I was now a varsity athlete. Which meant I had the potential to have actual friends. To not sit alone at lunch every day. To maybe even be looked up to like my brothers always were. And to top it off, I was hanging out with a girl. A pretty, smart, musically inclined girl who seemed to like me.

There was this odd feeling inside my chest, and I kept smiling. If my brothers could see me now, they would die. Or fall on the floor laughing. Probably both.

Stacey and I were crammed into a tiny table in the corner. Four guys in green-and-yellow baseball jackets from St. Joe's hovered nearby. They were waiting to take our table and clearly talking about me. Being my dad's kid sometimes meant being a quasi celebrity.

"Anyway, Mr. Roon is a total jerk." Stacey sipped her water. She hadn't touched her hummingbird cupcake. Which made no sense. This Oreo cake was the best thing I'd ever tasted.

"I don't know. He seemed nice," I said, wiping my mouth with a napkin.

The edges of Stacey's cheeks turned pink. "Oh, yeah. I mean, yeah, he's nice sometimes. But he can be a jerk."

"Like how?" I asked, reaching for my water.

"How?"

"Yeah. I mean, how is he a jerk? Give me an example," I prompted.

"Sorry. I didn't know I was gonna get the third degree."

Stacey flipped her braid behind her shoulder and took out her cell phone, which had a pink polka-dot case. She started texting and I squirmed. Behind her, the door opened with a jangle of bells, and Veronica and Darla walked in. I lifted a hand and Darla smiled, but Veronica shot Stacey this look. This kind of appalled look. She grabbed Darla and steered her toward the counter.

That was weird. What did Veronica have against Stacey?

"So. When're you gonna get your varsity jacket?" Stacey asked, the smile suddenly reappearing. "You have to get the one with the leather sleeves. The wool one is so last millennium."

"Um . . . I hadn't thought about it," I said.

Me. In a varsity jacket. I had to call Corey and Chris.

"When's your first meet?" Stacey asked, her green eyes bright.

She opened the calendar on her phone. "I'm totally coming. I'll bring water and snacks. What're good after-race snacks?"

I opened my mouth to respond but didn't get a chance.

"Oh! I know! I make this homemade granola? It's amazing!"

She typed a note into her phone.

"You should probably get new sneakers," she said, eyeing my feet under the table. "I'm sending you a link to this coupon for Fleet Feet. They have the most amazing selection in town."

My phone buzzed. I looked at the screen. It was from Stacey.

"How did you—"

"Get your number?" she asked. "I checked your phone while you were in the bathroom before. If we're gonna hang out, I have to have your number."

Suddenly my underarms started to sweat. She'd checked my phone? That meant she went into my backpack. That was kind of invasive. Maybe even stalker-level invasive. I found Darla and Veronica at a table in the far corner, splitting a pink cupcake. Veronica leaned in to whisper something to Darla. They were both watching us, and was it me, or did they look concerned?

Who the hell had True set me up with?

"So when's your birthday?" Stacey asked, her thumbs hovering over her keyboard. "I make the coolest birthday cards from scratch. They're amazing!"

"It's, uh . . ."

Right then, the door to the shop opened and my dad walked in. I'd never been so happy to see those massive shoulders in my life. He wore a green polo shirt with the letters SJP embroidered on the chest, and his black SJP FOOTBALL cap covered his blond hair. He scanned the room, all wide chin and narrowed eyes.

"Dad!" I called, standing up and grabbing my stuff.

He nodded when he saw me. The crowd parted for him as he walked to our table. His whistle was tucked into the pocket of his chinos, the red cord dangling down the side of his leg.

"Thanks for coming to get me, sir," I told him.

"Hang on a sec, son." His breath smelled, as always, like peppermint. "Introduce me to your friend."

"Sorry. Dad, this is Stacey. Stacey, this is my dad, David Cox."

"So nice to meet you!" Stacey beamed, standing and offering her hand.

My dad flicked a smile, impressed. "Nice to meet you, too," he said. "Now tell me, is it true that Charlie here tried out for the cross-country team?"

"And he made it!" Stacey eyed me proudly like we were a couple. "He ran a 5K in twenty-six minutes, fifty-eight seconds."

I shook my head. "How did you—"

She turned her phone's screen toward me. "I texted Brian and asked for your time. Our families are old friends."

The Oreo cupcake turned in my stomach. Stalker. One hundred percent stalker.

"That's an impressive time, son," my dad said.

"Yeah. Can we go now, please?" I felt the sudden need to get away from Stacey as fast as humanly possible. Darla and Veronica were still watching, and I didn't want them to get the idea that I was *with* Stacey. At least not until I figured out if she was crazy. It was still my first day, and I knew better than anyone that first impressions can make or break you. It's not pretty, but it's the truth.

"Sure. We need to go home and call your brothers," my dad said. He turned to Stacey again. "It was a pleasure to meet you, Stacey. I hope to see you again."

"Oh, you will," Stacey said, giving me a knowing smile.

No. You won't, I added silently.

"Bye," I said, practically pushing my dad toward the door.

Outside, I took a deep breath. The streets of downtown Lake Carmody were busy with shoppers, popping in and out of the artsy shops and restaurants. The sun shone and birds twittered in the trees that lined the sidewalk. Confronted with the normalcy, I started to think that maybe I had overreacted. Maybe Stacey really liked me, and shouldn't I be glad that a smart, pretty girl like her liked me? Then my phone buzzed. I checked the screen. It was a text from Stacey.

MISS YOU ALREADY!

Ugh.

"Well, you've had quite a day, haven't you?" my dad asked, looking me up and down with this sort of awed expression.

"I guess," I replied.

"Are you kidding?" my dad bellowed, slapping me on the back "I almost peed my pants right in front of the team when I got your text!"

"Dad!" I said through my teeth. Two little old ladies shot him disapproving looks as they strolled by.

"I said, 'Cross-country? My Charlie? No way.'"

"It's not that big of a deal," I said, embarrassed.

"No. Let's give credit where credit is due," he said, giving me a half squeeze, half shake as he turned us up the sidewalk. I saw his red pickup parked near the curb. "You not only survived your first day at a new school, but came out of it with a spot on a varsity team and a very pretty girl. She in the band too? I saw she had one of those instrument cases."

"Yeah. And the band was awesome," I told him, slipping my backpack onto my shoulder. "Plus, the director loved my solo." I chose not to tell him about the assholes in the drum corps. I felt hot and humiliated around the collar just thinking about it.

"That's great, son. I'm glad things are finally working out for you," my dad said, his eyes shining. "I'm really proud of you."

I stared at him as he rounded the car, fishing his keys out of his pocket. My chest radiated warmth.

"What?" my dad asked, popping open the driver's-side door.

"Nothing," I replied.

But as I got in beside him, I had to bite down on my lip to keep from laughing. He was proud of me. My dad was proud of me.

CHAPTER ELEVEN

Katrina

I stood on the sidewalk outside our small split-level house and stared at the numbers next to the door, 777. My father had hand-screwed those numbers to the siding, smiling down at me from the top of the stepladder.

"It's lucky, *mija*," he'd told me, concentrating to make sure the screws went in straight. "Seven, seven, seven. As long as we live here, we'll have good luck."

A rock formed between my throat and my heart, threatening to suffocate me. I missed him until it hurt. I missed everything about him—the scratch of his five o'clock shadow atop my head when he hugged me, the musky-dusty scent of his clothes after a long day in the reporter's room at the paper, the way his face lit up whenever he saw me.

Lenny Crisco, the guy who lived next door, zipped up to the gate in front of his house, dropped his bike against the fence, and bounded inside, letting the door slam behind him like it was nothing. And that was it. Right there. That was what I missed more than anything—being able to walk into my house without even thinking about it. Without knowing I would have to tiptoe around. Without being scared a screaming fight waited around every corner.

My mother and I had never fought before my dad died. Not once. She had always been kind of a tense person, but my dad always knew how to chill her out, how to make her smile—talents I was not blessed with. Now it was like I never knew when she might explode.

I could always go over to Ty's and wait for him to get out of work, but the thought made me tired. Now that I was here, I realized that I wanted to be in my own room, in my own space. I wanted to sleep in my own bed and not listen to Ty and his friends playing World of Warcraft for hours on end. I wanted to be home. And besides, I was out of clean clothes.

I trudged up the brick steps, avoiding the one crumbling corner, and gathered up the pile of newspapers that had been collecting atop the worn welcome mat. As always, the door was unlocked. I pushed it open as quietly as possible, but it stuck when I closed it and I had to give it a shove. I flinched at the resounding bang. The air inside was stifling and stale. I heard my mother's shuffling foot-steps at the top of the stairs.

"You're home."

I turned around slowly. She was wearing her gray sweatpants and my dad's Seton Hall sweatshirt, her dark hair pulled into a messy ponytail. A sleep crease zigzagged across one cheek.

"Hey," I said, trying for a smile. "How was work?"

"Fine. Busy," she said. "Two new babies in the NICU. I'm starving. What do we have to eat?"

She plodded down the steps to the kitchen. There was a time when my mother would kiss me on my forehead whenever I came home. When she'd hug me. When she'd ask to see my homework and ooh and aah over my poems.

I could hardly remember it anymore, but I knew it had happened. I dropped my backpack at the top of the stairs leading to the basement and followed her. She slammed the refrigerator and crossed her arms over her chest.

"I thought you were going to the supermarket," she snapped.

My throat was tight. Should have seen that coming. "I'm sorry. I didn't have time."

"Why? Because you were too busy sleeping around?" she demanded, walking to the cabinet and taking out a box of Ritz crackers. She banged the door shut and went rummaging in the pantry.

"Mom! I'm not sleeping around!" I protested. This was what she was like now. I did one thing wrong and suddenly she was on me like a pit bull about everything. "I have one boyfriend. One."

"Who lives with a houseful of hoodlums," she said, emerging with a half-empty jar of peanut butter.

"They're not hoodlums," I said with a sigh, leaning back against the counter.

"Don't you sigh at me!" she shouted, opening and slamming a drawer. "How am I supposed to know what they are or what they're not? You're never here! You never introduce your friends to me. I've barely said two words to this boy, and now he has you forgetting to go grocery shopping. You have responsibilities around here, Katrina. I can't do everything myself." Her body seemed to shake as she spread peanut butter on a cracker. It splintered between her fingers and she flung it into the sink, then reached for another. "Do you even realize that I've spent twenty long hours at the hospital? Is it so much to ask that there be milk for my coffee and something to eat other than this crap?"

Tears stung my eyes as she shoved a cracker into her mouth. "I'm sorry. I—"

"Forget it," she said with her mouth full, gathering everything up in her arms and storming past me. "I'm taking this up to my room."

"Mom, wait," I said, my voice cracking. "We can go to the supermarket now. We can still make something. We can get burgers. Or I can make that fried chicken you like?"

She paused at the bottom of the steps, and her head fell forward. For a split second I felt hope. She was going to say yes. We were going to have a normal night. We could buy those biscuits that come in the blue sleeve and maybe even make a salad. Then I would tell her about my first day of school and how shocked I was to be asked back into honors English. Maybe I'd even tell her about Charlie. And Zadie, too, of course. The idea of me, having potential new friends might make her feel better about Ty.

"It's too late," she said. "I'm tired." She looked over her shoulder at me, and I could see the red veins shot through her eyes. "Go make it for your boyfriend."

Then she stomped up the stairs and slammed her door. I gripped the countertop, a hole where my heart used to be. Two tears slipped down my cheeks, and I let them fall to the linoleum floor.

I didn't need this. I hadn't done anything wrong. Well, I'd done one thing wrong, but I'd offered to fix it, and she hadn't even considered it. Slowly I walked to the bottom of the stairs and glared up at her closed door. Clearly she didn't want to be around me. Well, that was fine. I would text Ty, then go hang out at the library with Mrs. Pauley until he could pick me up. At least Mrs. Pauley would be happy about my honors English placement. In fact, I didn't know why I hadn't thought to go there sooner.

I stomped up to my room, grabbed two pairs of jeans, two T-shirts, and my sneakers, and shoved them into an old Gap bag. On my way back downstairs I grabbed my backpack and then stormed out of the house, making sure to slam the door as hard as I could behind me.

CHAPTER TWELVE

Charlie

"Well, Elaina, you're never going to believe it," my father said, dropping his work stuff near the door. We walked past piles of unpacked boxes and bare walls toward the kitchen at the back of the house. The scent of my mother's favorite beef stew made my stomach grumble.

"What's that?" my mother asked, smiling as she looked up from the vegetables she was chopping. Her blond hair was pulled back in a messy ponytail, and she wore her favorite red sweater and no makeup. I could tell she'd been unpacking most of the day by the amount of stuff laid out on the counter—pots and pans and ceramic plates, our cow-shaped cookie jar, and about a dozen wooden spoons. "Charlie!" she said, seeing me. "How was your first day?"

I opened my mouth to reply, but my dad cut me off.

"Charlie here made the cross-country team!" my dad crowed, already reaching for the phone on the kitchen counter.

My mom stopped chopping. "You tried out for cross-country? You hate running."

I lifted my shoulders and slid onto one of the stools at the kitchen island. "It's just something to do after school."

"Well, that's great, but are you sure it's something you want to spend your time on?" she asked, handing over a few carrot sticks. "Won't you be busy enough with your schoolwork and band and—"

"Don't try to talk him out of it, Lanie," my dad barked as he held the phone to his ear. "Look at him! He's beaming!"

My mom and I exchanged a knowing smile. Really it was more my dad who was beaming. She reached over and ran her thumb down my cheek, then gave it a pat.

"Well, if you want to run, then I'm proud of you," she said. "Wait till your brothers find out!"

"Christopher!" my dad said into the phone. "Glad I caught you! You're never going to believe this. Charlie made the cross-country team!"

My dad chuckled and put the phone on speaker, placing it down on the counter. The sound of Chris's laughter filled the bare kitchen. My cheeks turned red. Then my phone beeped. It was a text from Stacey.

DO U LIKE MOVIES? WE SHOULD GO TO THE MOVIES.

I sighed and blanked the screen.

"I'm sorry," Chris finally said. "But that's funny."

"What's so funny about it?" I asked.

"Oh. You're there? Wait . . . he was serious? You really joined the cross-country team?" he asked.

"Yes. And if you laugh again, I'm gonna drive out there and dead leg you," I replied, crunching into a carrot stick.

My phone beeped again. A list of movie times for the local theater this weekend. My mother glanced at it and her brow wrinkled.

"Like you could," Chris scoffed. "But seriously, that's awesome, man. Good job. We can finally call you a Cox."

My last bite of carrot felt like a rock going down my throat. I reached for the glass of water my mother was drinking from. "Thanks a lot."

My father took him off speaker and they chatted for two minutes. Then he hung up and called Corey. This time, he left it on speaker from the moment it started ringing.

"Hello?" Corey said.

"Hey, Corey," I said, jumping off my chair to get closer to the phone. "Dad's about to tell you that you're not gonna believe it, but I joined the cross-country team."

"Damn right!" my father said, clapping me on the back.

There was a pause. "Wait. What?"

"I joined the cross-country team," I said. "You can laugh now."

"Well, you're right, I don't believe it," Corey said flatly.

I glanced at my father. His happy grin faltered.

"You, Charlie? Come on," Corey said. "That's not possible."

My face burning, I grabbed the phone and hit the talk button, then brought the receiver to my ear. I saw my mother and father exchange an alarmed look.

"What do you mean, that's not possible?" I said, gripping the phone so hard my knuckles turned white. "Is it that hard to believe I could somehow be a jock? That I could be like you guys?"

"That's not what I said," Corey replied.

"Screw you," I blurted.

"Language!" my mother admonished as I handed the phone back to my dad.

"I'll be in the garage."

I grabbed my drumsticks from my backpack as I stormed across the foyer and out the side door into the cool, brightly lit garage, the dry scent of cardboard boxes permeating the air. My drum kit was set up in the corner. I sat down behind it and started to play as hard and as fast as I could.

But it didn't make a difference. I kept hearing their words over and over in my head.

You're never going to believe it.

That's not possible.

We can finally call you a Cox.

And Chris's laughter, like a bass line beneath the chorus.

I closed my eyes and kept drumming, trying as hard as I could to pound it out of my head, until my mother finally called me in to dinner.

CHAPTER THIRTEEN

True

I clomped up the creaky stairs to the second floor of my new home that afternoon, wincing with pain as each step seemed to radiate inside my head. There were a few doors off the west-side hallway that I hadn't noticed this morning. At some point I was going to have to actually explore this house. If my head didn't explode first.

From the direction of my mother's room came a clatter, then a crash. I rushed down the hall and found her in a heap on the floor with a lamp next to her. The room was still dark. There were ten bottles of wine strewn about the rugs. Crumbs covered the bedspread, and a half-mauled hunk of bread lay on one pillow.

"Mother," I muttered, bending to grab her under her arms. "Have you been in bed all day?"

"Lmee 'lone," she muttered. Her breath smelled like rotten grapes. I maneuvered her back onto the mattress and flung the covers over her legs. Her hair was matted in places, and puddles of drool marred one pillow.

"I would leave you alone, but I have something to tell you," I said, leaning my hands into the foot of her bed. "I matched up my first couple today!"

"Fabentastical," she said, then hiccuped. "Now kindly leave me."

She flung one arm over her eyes, the other hanging loosely down the side of the bed. The bread chunk slid down the pillow and rested against her elbow. I glared at her prone form. This morning she'd basically ordered me to get my mission over with as quickly as possible, and now she didn't even care that I was a third of the way there?

"Fine. I'll go. But can you please tell me one thing?" I asked, pressing the heels of my hands into my temples as hard as I could.

She rolled one limp hand around, prompting my question.

"What do humans do to get rid of headaches?" I asked.

Aphrodite flung her arm off her eyes and reached under the heavy covers. She drew out a full bottle of red wine and thrust it toward me. "Drink this."

"Wine?" I took the bottle from her, and her arm dropped onto the bed with a *thwump*. "Really?"

"It will cure you," she said, rolling onto her side. Her nose pressed against the crusty bread, and she didn't even flinch. "I pwahmise."

Her tongue fell out of her mouth and she hiccuped, then started to breathe heavily. Passed out. I turned toward the door, popping open the bottle. When I brought it to my nose and sniffed, my stomach grumbled in anticipation.

I'd always had a taste for red wine, but I'd never used it for a headache. I'd never had to try it. I tipped the bottle toward my mouth and chugged half of it down, then drew my arm across my lips. It was appropriate, really. This was a celebration. Right now, Stacey and Charlie were out there somewhere, falling in love, all thanks to me. Their lives were going to change for the better, all thanks to me. And most importantly, Orion was now one step closer to freedom and a nice, long life. With me.

I walked down to my room and stood at its center, staring at the timer on my desk. It still ran, the red sand slipping at a frantic speed from top to bottom. I felt sick at the sight of it. Part of me had hoped that the sand would have reset, indicating I'd done my job. But that was illogical. They weren't in love yet. In a few days' time, I was sure the timer would turn and I'd get a new deadline for couple number two. At least, I hoped that was true.

Deadline. What a horribly appropriate term. I wished I could simply point my fingers at it and turn it myself. I took a swig of wine and tried.

Turn!

Nothing happened.

Turn!

The sand kept right on slipping.

Frustrated, I flung my hand at the timer. "Turn!" I shouted.

A pencil on the desk surface shifted half a millimeter. I held my breath, my heart slamming against my chest like a charging rhino. I tried again, this time focusing my energy on the pencil. I raised my hand and whispered.

"Turn!"

The pencil shuddered.

I took a startled step back. Outside the window, the back gate of a truck crashed closed. My powers. Were my powers starting to work here? Could I get them back?

Suddenly the constant throbbing inside my skull didn't seem so bad. If I could get my powers back, I could be done with this so-called mission in a snap. If I could get my powers back, I'd unite a hundred couples and return to Mount Olympus a conquering hero. No one would ever dare doubt me again. Not Zeus, not my father. No one.

Zeus. Zeus had specifically said I had to match three couples without my powers. He'd taken them from me. So why did they seem to be returning? Had he allowed this to happen? If he hadn't, then how could I have possibly done what I'd just done?

I knew one thing for sure. If Zeus hadn't decided to return my powers, he would *not* be pleased to know that they were working again. That I had somehow regained them without his help, without his permission. Any indication that his power was not absolute would send him into a mighty rage.

Slowly I let my eyes trail toward the timer. I was dying to try the pencil again, but if Zeus was watching right now, I could be in deep trouble. As could Orion. I wanted to run to my mom, to ask her what this meant, but she was dead to the world. Besides, I wasn't sure I could trust her. I wouldn't put it past her to tattle on me to Zeus, make it like this was my fault, like I was purposely circumventing him. She would do anything to get home to Mount Olympus. Even betray her daughter.

Telling her would put Orion's life on the line. I'd seen him die once before, when I didn't know what he would one day mean to me, and I couldn't do it again. . . .

"Eros? Have you heard?"

My brother Deimos burst into my chambers as I was about to pierce the heart of a young handmaiden who had caught the eye of a handsome goatherd. I miss-shot and hit one of the goats instead. That would make an interesting pair.

"*Deimos!*" *I shouted, whirling on him.* "*I've told you countless times never to surprise me like that!*"

Deimos shrank back in fear as if he believed I was about to beat him with my bow. I took a deep breath and raised a calming hand. Sometimes I forgot how skittish he could be.

"*I'm not going to hurt you, brother,*" *I said.* "*What news do you bring?*"

He stood up straight, his eyes wild. But then, they were always wild. My poor brother was born the God of Fear and spent his days either instilling irrational dread in the people of Earth or developing new phobias himself. He was terrified of thunder, of spiders, of our father. I'd once seen him run and hide at the sight of his own shadow. Before long he would divine a white-walled fortress for himself and never come out again.

"*It's Artemis! She's killed her love!*" *Deimos cried.*

My heart dropped. "*Orion? Orion is dead?*"

He nodded eagerly, as if my reaction buoyed his spirits. "*Killed by her own arrow. Come! They all gather in the moor.*"

I grasped my brother's hand and together we whirled into Nyx's Moor, a bleak, rocky plain north of Gaia's Wood, which bordered the Bay of Circe, our access to the Mediterranean Sea. Lightning flashed and a driving rain flattened the brown grass. The sky was a heavy, mottled gray, but I could make out a group of gods and goddesses huddled near shore. Deimos clung to my hand, bent almost in submission as thunder growled around us. Even over the howling wind and raging weather, I could hear Artemis's anguished wails.

"*Eros!*"

I saw Harmonia rise to her feet, her red hair matted and dark with rain. My sister's role, as always, was to be there for everyone, no matter what, as she was now there for Artemis, even though we couldn't stand the goddess on a normal day.

*I trudged toward the huddled mass, dragging my brother with me.
On mud-slicked rocks near the water's edge lay Orion, an awful wound
torn open in his temple, oozing blood and brains into the sludge. Orion,
who had been so virile in life, so cocky and sure and full of swagger,
was now reduced to a carcass, and an unpleasantly scented one at that.
Artemis was bent over him, her handsome bow and leather quiver tossed
aside, her slim frame racked with awful sobs. Her twin brother Apollo
knelt nearby, catatonic, his face an utter blank. Hephaestus was there
too, his skin as black as the night, glowering at Apollo, his hand on the
intricate hilt of his sword.*

"What's happened?" I demanded.

*"It was him!" Artemis sobbed. She pointed across the body at her
brother, who was both her best friend and worst tormentor. "He tricked
me! He challenged me to hit a moving target on the lake, but it was
Orion! I didn't know!"*

*She bent her face into her hands and wept awful tears. I gaped at
Apollo. He was known for his cruelty. For his games. But even though
he and Artemis fought almost constantly, I couldn't imagine why he
would do this to her. Why steal her one true love? It had been months
since I had matched the two of them, and I thought that Apollo had
finally accepted Orion's role in his sister's life. Clearly something had
changed.*

*Artemis tipped her head back and raged at the heavens. Suddenly
the storm quieted and the clouds parted, revealing a star-blanketed sky.*

"What are you doing?" Harmonia asked her.

*I was surprised too. Artemis was so self-involved it wouldn't have
shocked me if she'd kept the rain going for months on end while she
mourned, making the rest of us miserable right along with her.*

"I can't take it. I can't look at him anymore," Artemis cried, tears

streaming from the corners of her eyes, across her temples and into her soaked brown hair. She touched her fingertips to Orion's pale cheeks and shook like a spiderweb in a windstorm as she leaned in to touch her lips to his. Then, with a shuddering wail that trembled the very ground beneath our feet, she flung her arm toward the sky. Orion vanished into a swirl of sparkling dust. The cloud that was once human flesh floated to the heavens, where it exploded into seven pinpricks of light. Seven stars forming shoulders, legs, and a bright, shining belt—a memorial to Artemis's beloved.

It was quite touching, actually. And very out of character.

"Let him hang there for eternity," Artemis said, "so that I might be reminded of my folly in listening to you," she spat at Apollo, rising to her feet. "So that you might be reminded of the cruelty you visited on your own sister."

Apollo never shifted, never blinked. He hardly seemed to breathe. Artemis turned on her heel and, whipping her leather cape around her, disappeared, leaving her prized bow and quiver behind. Hephaestus stood. He took two steps toward Apollo, his fingers tightening around the hilt of his sword. There was something awful brewing inside his eyes. Hatred, anger, jealousy, fear. I wasn't sure. Harmonia reached out and touched his arm. He stared into her eyes for a long moment, and there was the slightest softening in his features. Something passed between them, a communication I couldn't begin to decipher, and in a blink he, too, was gone.

I dropped to my knees in front of Apollo. He and I had once been friends, he the god of poetry, of music, of light—elements that were so closely linked to love. But we'd grown apart as he had begun to enjoy toying with mortals, with other gods, even with his own sister.

"What were you thinking, Apollo?" I whispered, trying to look into *his blank eyes. "I know I matched them as a bit of a lark myself, but they were truly in love. Your sister was truly happy. Why take that from her? What did she do to deserve this punishment?"*

His eyes sparked to life, and the force of his ire as he glared at me chilled me to the core. I rose, flicking one of my iron arrows—the ones I only rarely used—from my quiver and taking aim at his heart. The iron ones bred hatred instead of love, not that Apollo needed any more reason to hate anyone. But while it wouldn't kill him, it would slow him down and cause him a lot of pain.

Apollo blinked at the arrow and laughed. He laughed so hard he keeled over, bracing one strong hand on the rocks beneath him. He laughed like a madman, like a god unhinged. He laughed as if he would never stop. And then, suddenly, he whirled into nothing.

I lowered my bow and stepped closer to Harmonia, shivering from head to toe. Only when everyone else was gone did Deimos finally rise to his full height, though he reached out to cling to Harmonia's gown like a nervous child. Together, the three of us stared up at the stars. Three shining points in a row marked Orion's belt. She had tossed him up next to the Scorpion, I noticed. The beast she had slain a few days prior, as it traveled the lands in search of her love.

"Why would she do that?" I whispered. "Why set him up there to be chased by that monster forever?"

"Because she wanted to punish him too," Deimos said. "As much as she wished she could save him."

"But why?" I asked, agape.

Harmonia looked at me, her blue eyes full. "She punishes him," she said, "for leaving her."

Outside the window, headlights flashed. Slowly I walked over to my bed, carefully removed my new sneakers, and slid under the covers, trying to shake that memory of Orion—the sight of him drained, pale, lifeless. Curling the bottle of wine toward my chest, I settled in for the night.

"I'm coming for you, Orion," I said, touching the arrow pendant against my chest. I stared at the pencil, imagined him alive, well, and happy, and smiled. "I'll be there soon."

CHAPTER FOURTEEN

True

I couldn't open my eyes. They were welded shut. I tried to move my arms, but they didn't budge. It was as if they had the weight of the gods on them. I brought my hands to my face, but of course, that did nothing, so I took a breath and tasted bile and wine. It was so potent it stung the back of my nose.

What new torture was this?

Concentrating, I rolled onto my side. My hands hit a cool, dry pillow. Still in bed. That was something. At least I hadn't been transported to the underworld in my sleep. I focused and forced my eyes to open. They were as dry as the sands of the Sahara and the bright sun sliced through my retinas, sending a bolt of pain sizzling through my skull. Tears squeezed out, dripping down my face.

I groaned. "Bad idea. Opening eyes, bad idea."

But the sun continued its assault, turning the insides of my eyelids a bright, blinding pink. I shoved myself out of bed. My head weighed five million pounds. No. Five trillion. I pried one eyelid open, staggered toward the window, and somehow found the string for the blinds. With a yank, they mercifully fell shut. I turned, tripped, and went sprawling onto the cold, hard floor.

My stomach clenched, sending an awful, heaving feeling up my airway. A sour, burning sensation filled my throat. My head still ached. So much for my mother's suggestion that wine would solve that problem.

Wine. The very thought made me heave all over again.

On the street a horn honked, and I heard the school bus's air brakes release. My eyes darted open, and I blearily found the clock on my nightstand. It was eight fifteen, Tuesday morning. My second day as a mortal. And I had fifteen minutes to get to school.

Another groan escaped as I sat back against the side of my bed. My foot hit one of the wine bottles and it rolled toward the window, clinking against the second, which I'd removed from the basement around midnight and finished at about two a.m. More than anything I wanted to crawl back into bed and sleep. Sleep was the only escape from this headache, not to mention these new and disgusting symptoms. Did humans feel this way all the time? How did any of them function? Perhaps I had underestimated their fortitude.

I pushed myself up, and the whole room tilted, including the evil sand timer, which continued to run. Apparently, Charlie and Stacey had yet to find love, but was there really anything I could do about that today? No. Not in this state. Bed. I was going back to bed. I flopped onto my stomach, and Orion's arrow pierced my skin.

My heart all but stopped, and I sat up again.

Orion.

I had a job to do. I had to save him. Maybe I couldn't make Stacey and Charlie move any faster, but I could start trying to find a second couple to match.

I slipped to the floor and tried to stand, but the room and its many colors and lights and shapes spun around me. The floor seemed the safer route. I crawled into the closet and closed the door. The mirror on the back of the door startled me. I sat there and stared.

This could not be my reflection. The hair in tangles, the gray swipes of color under the eyes, the red nose with its skin peeling along its bridge. I leaned forward, horrified. Was that a pimple on my chin?

"No!" I cried, the tears flowing freely now. "This was not part of our deal! No one said I was going to deteriorate!"

Back home, my skin had never been marred by anything—not a blemish, not a wrinkle, not a scar, and certainly not this awful burning sensation. And I didn't have to do anything to keep it that way. I was simply beautiful, every moment of every day and night. As were my mother and my sister and every other female on Mount Olympus. It was who we were. Goddesses. Unless an upper god chose to take my beauty, that was the way I was to be. Always. But here on Earth . . . here on Earth I was turning into a Harpy.

I lay down on the floor and cried, clutching Orion's necklace. If he saw me right now, I was sure he'd turn away in disgust. Imagining his face at the sight of my own made the sobs turn to convulsions. I couldn't do this. I couldn't go out there like this. I was going to fail him. I was going to fail us.

Eros, stop this now. This is not about you.

I took in a broken breath. Harmonia's voice surrounded me.

"Sister?" I said, my voice cracking.

This is not about your vanity, she said. *This is about saving your love. It's about proving yourself. It's about being the goddess I know you to be.*

"But how?" I whimpered, pulling my knees up under my chin as another awful wave of discomfort hit me. "I can hardly lift my head."

Find your strength, Eros. Pick yourself up. Focus on your mission. You only have a short time to complete it.

I opened the door a crack and peeked out at the sand timer. Still running. Taking a deep, broken breath, I dried my eyes with the backs of my hands. I wasn't sure whether Harmonia had found a way to communicate with me, or whether I was deluding myself, but either way the voice in my head was right. This was no time for self-pity. I pulled on a pair of baggy jeans, shoved my aching feet into white socks and the blue-and-white sneakers, and tugged on a flowing white top. When I touched my hair, I winced. It even smelled awful. If only Harmonia were really here to brush and braid it. Instead I wrapped it into a bun as best I could and found a red baseball cap, which I jammed down over the mess.

On my way down the hall, I passed the bathroom. The bathroom. Of course. A bath. That was what I needed. I had always enjoyed baths in hot springs and cool lakes as a matter of pleasure, but here they were a clear necessity. I eyed the faucet longingly, but there was no time.

Bathing would have to wait. Right now, I had to find my next lucky couple. I teetered to the top of the stairs, clung to the railing, and somehow found my way out the door.

CHAPTER FIFTEEN

Charlie

My phone beeped as I locked my bike to the bike rack on Tuesday morning. It had been beeping for hours. Since before I woke up. Stacey telling me what she was having for breakfast. What she was wearing. Who was being interviewed on *Today* while she ate her Special K. Stacey texting me her address, her home number, her favorite color. Every time the phone beeped, my shoulders tightened a bit more. There was also one text from Corey telling me to call him—like that was gonna happen—but most of them were from Stacey.

I mean: What. The. Hell? I didn't have a whole lot of experience with girls, but this couldn't be normal. I knew for a fact that Chris and Corey had never had to deal with this kind of thing from the girls they'd gone out with. Of if they had, they'd never told me about it.

I let the lock clang against the bike as the next text came in. The sun beat down on the back of my neck. I scanned the crowd hanging out in front of the school doors. True. I had to find True. So I could strangle her.

A car door slammed behind me. "There you are! Charlie!"

I stopped and closed my eyes. The sound of my name had never made me so tense. I reached for my drumsticks and gripped them both in one hand, wishing there was a kit nearby. These flashes of irrational anger were the one thing I had in common with my dad and brothers, and I hated them. Of course, my brothers used to take out their angst on me or each other with surprise wrestling matches, but I had no one to pound on like they used to. Instead I had my drums. So I took a deep breath, started playing my jazz solo in my mind, and gripped those sticks. There. Slightly better.

Slowly I turned to face Stacey, who was jogging up the steps after me. She wore a purple T-shirt with flowers embroidered around the collar, and her hair was in one long braid. She really was pretty. Or she would have been. If she wasn't psycho.

"Where were you? Didn't you get my texts?" she asked, her brow wrinkling.

"I . . . I turned my phone off last night, and I guess I never turned it back on this morning," I lied, twirling one stick between my fingers.

"Oh. That sucks." She pouted slightly. Behind her, a school bus pulled up and a bunch of kids poured out. No True. "I thought you were gonna pick me up."

"Pick you up?" Not one of her texts had said anything about picking her up.

"I texted you my address," she said, like that made sense.

"I didn't get it," I lied again. Twirl, twirl, twirl. Faster, faster, faster. "And I don't have a car."

"You don't?" She seemed disappointed. Good. Maybe now she'd break up with me. Not that we were together, but it was pretty clear she thought we were.

"Nope. My dad dropped me off yesterday and I rode my bike

today," I told her, nodding my chin toward the half-full bike rack.

"Oh." She looked slowly over her shoulder, and for a moment I was staring at her braid and a tiny brown mole on the back of her neck.

Please let this be a deal breaker. Please let this be a deal breaker.

"That's okay," she said finally. "Walking together is much more romantic anyway."

She reached for my hand, but the drumstick stopped her. Caught between giving her what she wanted and having no desire to hold her hand, I shrugged. So she wrapped her arm around mine instead. Right. So Stacey was smart, but not so good at the hint taking.

Ugh. Why couldn't I be a man and tell her I wasn't interested? Honestly. There was something wrong with me. It was like I'd been born with my default setting on "polite" and that's where it would always stay. Even if it meant I had to go out with someone I didn't even like.

"Come on," she said, pulling me close to her side. "I want to introduce you to my friends! They're dying to meet you!"

I didn't know how she'd had time to tell them about me, considering how many texts and e-mails she'd fired at me last night. Obviously the girl was an overachiever. I saw the pack of them notice us as we approached, nothing but bright colors and big smiles and lots of giggling. One of them looked me up and down like she was sizing me up for herself, and my fight-or-flight reflex kicked in. If I got in with Stacey's friends, it would be that much harder to get out. At least, that's what my instincts were telling me.

"Actually, I gotta go," I told Stacey, slipping from her grasp. "I told Roon I'd stop by before class."

"Why?" she asked.

"Because I . . ."

Have to lay into the drums before I explode?

"Told him I would," I mumbled instead.

"Oh. Okay. Well, I'll see you—"

The rest of her sentence was drowned out by the guilty, embarrassed pounding in my ears as I sprinted toward the front entrance. First I was going to hammer out some aggression on the drums, and then I was going to very calmly, very rationally, kill True Olympia.

CHAPTER SIXTEEN

Katrina

"Honors English? Seriously? Isn't that, like, a lot of work?"

Lana leaned back against the windowsill next to me and blew a stream of smoke at the ceiling. She'd finished applying false eyelashes seconds before, and now she couldn't stop blinking.

"I did it last year," I said, scrolling through the calendar on my phone to check my mother's schedule.

I saw that my mom was working this afternoon and evening and breathed a sigh of relief. I could go home, do some laundry, and be out of there before she got back.

"Yeah, and you flunked out of it," Raine pointed out.

"Thanks a lot," I said.

"What?" She raised her hands, then ashed into the cup she and Gen were sitting around. "Do I not speak the truth?"

"Well, now I got back in," I told them, bumping the toe of my boot against the floor. I dropped my phone back into my bag and zipped it up. "And I don't mind doing the work."

"Really?" Gen asked.

"C'mon, KitKat. I was psyched we were in that class together,"

Raine said, pushing her legs out and crossing them at the ankle. "Who'm I gonna cheat off of when we have a quiz?"

I laughed. She didn't. Neither did Lana or Gen. They really did think I should stay in CP English for Raine. So she could cheat. Suddenly I was reminded of the fact that Lana and Gen had been Raine's friends first. And clearly, still were.

"Raine, you're going to be fine. Ms. Day is a great—"

At that moment, the door flew open and we froze. A tall, scrawny girl in a red baseball cap lurched into the room. Her nose was clearly sunburned, but the rest of her face was so pale she was practically see-through. Before any of us could react, she opened her mouth, let out this awful, choking burp, and spewed all over the floor.

"Holy shit!" Gen shouted, jumping up. A dark brown chunk slid down to the hem of her skirt and dropped off, splatting into the puddle that was oozing over the tiles. My nostrils filled with a horrible, sour stench.

"Omigod, I'm gonna barf. I'm gonna barf," Lana rambled, waving at her face with her free hand while she held her cigarette at arm's length with the other. She was blinking like crazy, and I was sure she couldn't see where she was going.

"You're supposed to puke *in* the toilet!" Raine shouted, flattened back against the wall. I didn't even know how she'd gotten there. Two seconds ago she was sitting on the floor, where the vomit lake was slowly expanding. Now she strong-armed Lana, almost slamming her head into the paper towel dispenser to keep her from stepping in barf.

The puker didn't hear a word anyone said. She was bent over in the doorway with one hand clinging to the handle as she heaved for breath. Her long dark hair hung forward over her face, a whole clump of it tangled and dripping.

"Are you okay?" I asked, not breathing.

"What *was* that?" she demanded, looking up with her eyes without moving her head. Even in the chaos, the gorgeous shade of blue stunned me. But she looked totally terrified. Like she thought she might be dying or something. "What did I just do?"

"Uh, you upchucked everywhere, you freak," Raine said, skirting the lake of barf and dragging Lana with her.

The girl moaned and leaned against the doorway.

"I have to get out of here." Lana tossed her cigarette into the nearest sink and blindly shoved past the puker into the hall. Gen and then Raine followed.

"Are you coming?" Raine demanded.

"Shouldn't we, like, help her?" I asked.

Raine's eyes widened and her lip curled. "Girl, *that* is gross." And then she was gone.

The puker turned her head and groaned. A tiny drip of brown goo clung to her chin. I grabbed a paper towel, wet it, and tiptoed around the ooze, pulling her out into the deserted hallway. Once the door closed behind us, I sucked in a huge breath.

"Here." I dabbed at her chin with the towel, and her face fell forward. She let out a rancid sigh and I almost heaved. Alcohol. I could smell alcohol behind the stench of puke.

"Are you . . . hungover?" I asked, scrunching up my face.

The girl's eyes popped open and she stared at the floor, unfocused. "Oh my . . . maybe!" she said, her forehead wrinkling. "But that's not possible. I had only two bottles of wine!"

"Two bottles? Yourself?" She was definitely tall, but even skinnier than Gen. A lightweight like her could never handle that much wine.

"What? It's never affected me before," she semi-whined, leaning her shoulder into the wall. She slid forward and went down on her knees. I somehow managed to catch her before her face hit the floor.

"Okay. This is not good," I said, hooking my arms under hers and dragging her to her feet. She weighed practically nothing, but she was limp. As I tried to get her to stand up, we both slammed against the wall.

"Hey, Katrina! What're you—"

Zadie stopped in her tracks as she came around the corner, her thumbs crooked around the straps of her pink Hello Kitty backpack. She looked at the puker and grimaced.

"Is she okay?"

"Not exactly," I said, pushing the girl against the wall. Her eyes were at half-mast. "You've gotta go home," I told her. "If any of the teachers see you like this, you're screwed."

"No!" the girl wailed loudly, her voice bouncing off the walls. She threw her arms around my neck and let herself go, hanging her full weight on me. "I can't go home now! I have work to do! One down, two to go!"

Somewhere nearby a door slammed. A hushed conversation echoed down the hall.

"That's my dad!" Zadie hissed, her eyes wide.

"Crap," I said under my breath. "We have to get her out of the hall."

"What about the bathroom?" Zadie asked.

I shook my head emphatically. "Not an option. Trust me."

The girl hiccuped and burped. It was totally foul.

"Okay. I have an idea. Zadie, can you take one side?" I asked.

Zadie nodded and ducked under the girl's arm. "Got it."

I slung her other arm around my back. "Band room, on three," I directed. "One, two, three."

Together, Zadie and I struggled down the hall and around the corner, somehow managing the girl's dead weight between us. At the door of the band room, I stood on my toes to peek through the high square window. Empty. I yanked open the door, and Zadie and the girl tripped inside.

"Here."

I opened the heavy door to the first soundproof rehearsal room and flicked the light switch. The old fluorescent fixture blinked to life with a hum. Pushed up against one wall was an ancient leather couch stacked with boxes of weathered sheet music, one broken snare drum, and a teetering pile of programs from last year's graduation. I leaned the puker against the door.

"Can you clear the couch?" I asked Zadie.

She jumped right to work and shoved everything into the far corner, next to the broken-down piano with the random missing keys.

"You can sleep it off here," I told the puker. "My friends do it all the time."

"Thank you."

She took two blind steps forward, fell face-first onto the couch, and passed out, her hair trailing over her shoulder and down to the floor. For the first time I really looked over her outfit—a long white summer dress that was practically see-through over a pair of baggy jeans, and brand-new cheerleading sneakers with fuzzy white socks. Plus the red baseball cap. Where the hell had this girl come from? Mars? The Amazon? Victoria's Secret? Although, if she'd come from there she'd probably be wearing a bra.

"I'll come back to check on you later," I promised. Not that she could hear me. There was a band jacket on a hook near the door, and I tore it down and tossed it over her, then snuck quietly out. Zadie waited for me in the open area of the band room.

"Thank you," I told her.

"No problem," she said, bouncing on her toes, jittery. "Is she gonna be okay?"

I lifted my shoulders. "I hope so. I don't even know her name."

"Well, I guess I should get to homeroom," Zadie said. She took a step, then hesitated. "Are you going to the library again today?"

"I don't know."

"Well, if you do, I'll be there. I'm there pretty much every day," she said. "We can sit together. If you want."

I smiled. "Thanks."

Zadie grinned and traipsed out into the hallway. Someone grabbed the door before it could close and came inside. It was Charlie. He was wearing a white T-shirt with black sleeves and the logo of a band I'd never heard of on the front. His drumsticks were gripped in one hand. My pulse started pounding at the very sight of him.

"Hey!" he said. "What're you doing here?"

He adjusted the one backpack strap he had slung over his shoulder. I didn't want to tattle on the puker, but maybe he'd know what to do.

"I'll tell you if you swear you won't tell anyone."

"Ooh. Intrigue." Charlie rolled the drumsticks between his palms. I smirked.

"C'mere."

Opening the door to the rehearsal room a crack, I let him peek inside. The puker let out a huge snore and rolled over, her arm flung over the side of the couch.

"True?" he whispered. "What the hell?"

"You know her?" I asked, closing the door.

"Yeah, I . . . well . . . I guess she's a friend."

His phone beeped. He tugged it out of his back pocket, looked at the screen, and groaned.

"Or was," he added.

"She threw up in the bathroom."

"Ugh, really?" Charlie said. "Should we get the nurse?"

"I don't know. I think she's hungover." We heard a groan from inside. "Actually, I think she may still be drunk."

Charlie's eyebrows shot up so far I couldn't see them under his thick bangs. "Seriously? Whoa. Okay. That might explain a lot."

His phone beeped again. This time he didn't look at it. Instead he clenched his teeth and rolled his eyes to the sky.

"A *lot*."

"What do you mean?"

"Nothing," he said. "Forget it. I'll figure it out." There was a long pause, with him staring at me and me trying not to blush.

"What?" I asked finally.

"Nothing, it's just . . . it was really nice of you to take care of her like that."

My heart panged. He had this adorable dimple right next to the right side of his mouth and I suddenly, irrationally, wanted to lean in and kiss it. I actually imagined myself doing it. Imagined how his skin would feel beneath my lips. Warm and soft and sweet. I blushed, severely, and looked away.

"Please. I couldn't leave her in a pile of her own puke," I said. "Anyone would have done the same."

He shook his head at me, dubious. "Not really."

He was right, of course. Raine, Lana, and Gen hadn't stayed

around to help. Only Zadie had. My blush deepened. "Thanks."

Then the bell rang. Neither one of us moved. I could see the logo on his T-shirt moving up and down with the rhythm of his breath.

"We'd better go," Charlie said finally.

"Yeah," I replied. "We'd better."

He held the door open for me, and I strode off toward my first class. It wasn't until I got there that I realized I hadn't looked at my feet once the whole way.

CHAPTER SEVENTEEN

Charlie

There were three stacks of books on Mrs. Roberge's desk. Twenty-one worn copies of *Great Expectations*. Guess we were about to get our first assignment. Great. Not that I minded reading, but I hated overanalyzing it. Overanalyzing it meant not enjoying it.

I sighed as I sat down at the same desk I'd taken yesterday, glancing over at the couple of other kids who were already there. Stacey was in this class, and I was dreading seeing her. I'd managed to avoid her during lunch by going to the band room to practice. True had still been in there, snoring so loudly I swear I could hear her over the drums. I hadn't woken her, but I was surprised Mr. Roon hadn't heard her.

The door opened and I flinched, but it wasn't Stacey. It was Katrina. The room instantly got ten degrees hotter. She'd changed her hair since that morning, tying it back on the sides, and she looked beautiful. She glanced around uncertainly, twisting some fringe on her scarf around her finger as she edged into the room. I couldn't tear my eyes off her. She was obviously nervous, and it made me want to go over to her and take her hand. But I couldn't. Because she had a boyfriend. And I had . . . Stacey.

Finally Katrina saw me. And she smiled. And I thought I was going to die.

"You're in this class now?" I asked.

"Yeah. You too?"

I nodded and glanced at the next desk. "Wanna sit?"

Her expression was priceless. Like I'd just offered her the last slice of pizza on earth. "Sure."

She walked over, ducking her head in that perfect way of hers, and slid into the chair next to mine. The whole left side of my body felt warm.

"Do you have econ next?" she asked as she hung her bag on the back of her chair.

"Yeah. You too?"

She nodded and bit her bottom lip. "Yep."

God. Someone was watching over me right now. Then the door opened and slammed.

"Charlie! Come sit by me!"

Stacey. She walked right over and stood between me and Katrina with a huge smile. Pretty much murdered the warmth. Her friend, a tall, solid-looking girl with short blond hair, did a double take when she saw Katrina, then smiled and waved. Katrina smiled back shyly.

"I'm good here," I told Stacey.

"Please. People who sit in the front row do ninety percent better in class. It's a proven fact." She grabbed my wrist and pulled. "Come on."

"Really. I'm good," I told her, trying to sound like my dad. Like I was serious and wasn't going to budge. Instead I sounded mean. Stacey's face fell. A few people around us stared. I felt like such an asshole I actually almost moved where she wanted me to, but pride or Katrina or something kept me frozen in place.

Stacey glanced over her shoulder at Katrina, who had somehow reduced herself to half her size, hunching her shoulders and sliding down in her seat.

"Fine." Stacey was grinning when she looked at me again. "You're so funny!" Then she ruffled my hair—reached out like it was nothing, sank her fingers in there, and tousled it. No one had ever ruffled my hair before. Not even my mom. As she turned and flounced toward her 90-percent-success-rate seat, I faced forward and glowered, running both hands forward over my head. I was too humiliated to look at Katrina, who now probably thought Stacey and I were soul mates or something.

I glanced over at the chair True had taken yesterday. It was empty. Still sleeping it off, apparently.

"Good afternoon, everyone!" Mrs. Roberge walked in, wearing a blue dress with white swirls. She divided the books into five separate piles and dumped the piles on the front desk of each row. "Take one and pass them back. This is *Great Expectations*, one of the finest novels ever written in the English language, and it will be our first book of the year. I'm throwing you into the lion's den straight out of the gate, if you'll forgive my mixed metaphor."

The kid in front of me handed me two books, and I passed the last one back. Mine was dog-eared, the pages browning around the edges. Someone had written notes in the margins. Good. That could be helpful. If the kid before me had been smart.

"Each one of you will be assigned a chapter and will lead the class in the discussion of that chapter," Mrs. Roberge announced.

The class groaned. Next to me, Katrina froze. Like, froze solid. For a second I thought she was going to faint, and I imagined what I would do if she fell in my direction.

"Tonight you'll read the first three chapters, and tomorrow I will assign those chapters to three lucky members of this class," Mrs. Roberge continued, her eyes sliding over the classroom mischievously, like she knew exactly how sick she was making us feel and she was loving it. "So be ready! For now, let's talk about the author, Mr. Charles Dickens."

She turned to the board, and I leaned into the aisle to whisper to Katrina. I wanted to see if she was okay. If there was anything she needed. But the second I moved, Stacey turned around and waved at me.

I had to figure out a way to break up with this girl. But how the hell do you break up with someone you've never even asked out?

The guy at the back of the room got up to bring an extra book to the front of the class. Mrs. Roberge frowned at True's empty desk.

"Anyone know where Miss Olympia is today?" she asked.

Katrina and I exchanged a look. Neither of us said a thing. But I suddenly realized who was going to help me figure out what to do about Stacey. True. The person who'd forced Stacey into my life. I could only hope she'd be sober enough to make sense.

CHAPTER EIGHTEEN

True

I lounged in my stark-white, high-ceilinged parlor room with Harmonia and our friends Selene and Nike, eating grapes alongside my Earthen window. The window was a huge round opening in the floor of my chambers, through which I could see any point on Earth in the blink of an eye. At the moment I was focused on the Grecian court, and had just matched a jilted lover with a mourning widow when Artemis appeared near the fire.

"Artemis!" Selene cried, jumping up to hug our unexpected visitor. "You're back!"

Selene, the moon goddess, was sweet and kind, but could also be a bit of a dimwit. She always saw the best in everyone and never seemed to notice when danger was at hand, as it clearly was now. It had been months since we'd seen Artemis, but rumor had it that she'd spent her time on Mount Etna, an awful place where the Cyclopes roamed, volcanoes and earthquakes erupted without warning, and forests burned. I myself had never visited, but occasionally gods and goddesses took refuge in its dank caves and underground villages to avoid the wrath of Zeus. He didn't like to acknowledge Etna. Considered it beneath his notice. But he would pursue his enemies there from time to time, if his anger was great.

As she appeared before us now, Artemis was dressed for battle in a freshly forged breastplate, leather skins, and a fur cape. Her once peachy complexion had gone ruddy and brown, and her face and arms were streaked with black soot. She didn't move to return my friend's embrace. She simply stared at me over Selene's creamy-white shoulder. Nike, quick as a whip, rose to her feet and squared her shoulders.

"What is it?" I asked, clutching my bow as I stood. "What's wrong?"

"You," she growled. "You did this to me!"

Artemis advanced on me so swiftly I didn't have time to draw my bow. She reached out and latched her fingers around my throat, squeezing her thumbs into my airway.

"Artemis, no!" Harmonia cried. She lifted her hands to repel Artemis, but Artemis threw Harmonia against the wall with a mere blink. This was a power I'd only seen upper gods and goddesses use. The younger generation had to use our hands when battling other deities.

Nike froze in place and gaped. "How did you—"

"I learned a few things on Etna," Artemis said with a sneer, looking directly into my eyes with a strength of purpose I'd never seen on anyone, god or mortal. She was going to extinguish me, right here, right now. "Like how to crush another goddess's windpipe."

I couldn't breathe. Panic seized my gut, like nothing I'd ever felt before. I was supposed to be immortal. This was not supposed to happen to me.

"It wasn't Eros who tricked you into killing Orion!" Harmonia protested, scrambling to her feet. "It was Apollo."

"But she tricked me into falling in love with him!" Artemis shot back. My vision began to prickle around the edges. Nike's smooth dark skin went gray and hazy over Artemis's shoulder. "With a mortal!"

"But love him you did!" Selene said, gripping Artemis by the shoulder. "And you were happy. If not for Eros, you never would have been so happy!"

"*And I never would have been this miserable!*" Artemis replied through her teeth. *They had gone brown in her absence. Or was that a trick of my mind as it slowly shut down?*

Suddenly every door to every one of my many terraces slammed. The fire was extinguished. The candles were snuffed. The room went dark. And my mother, Aphrodite, appeared behind Artemis. She shoved her forearm into Artemis's back, grabbed her heart in her fist, and twisted. Artemis's jaw hung slack. Her hands went limp and she released me. I fell to the ground in a heap at her feet as my mother lifted Artemis over my head by her heart.

"*Mother, please!*" *Harmonia cried.* "*Don't do this! Artemis is suffering. It was not her fault.*"

Aphrodite pulled her hand out, leaving the heart in the body cavity where it belonged, and let Artemis drop. Her body hit the marble floor with a sickening crack. I pushed myself up to my knees, coughing and sputtering and heaving for breath. Slowly the world around me curled into focus. Artemis rolled over to her back with a groan.

"*You think you can threaten my daughter?*" *Aphrodite raged, advancing on her prone body.* "*You think I won't tear you into a hundred tiny pieces and scatter your putrid remains to the far reaches of the underworld?*"

Artemis gasped for breath. "*I don't care what happens to me. I no longer wish to exist.*"

Aphrodite narrowed her eyes at Artemis, then looked around at the rest of us.

"*Your generation baffles me,*" *she said.* "*He was one love. One measly, sniveling mortal. They are born and wither like grapes on a vine.*" *She gestured at the heaping bowls of fruit around my Earthen window, then crouched down next to Artemis.* "*You will go on existing and you will love again,*" *she said.* "*But if you touch my daughters or my sons or anyone else I care for, I will turn you over to Hades and your soul will burn for all eternity in the most blistering fires of the underworld. Do we understand each other?"*

Artemis's eyes were wide with terror. "We do."

"Then go."

Aphrodite stood, and before she had even turned around, Artemis had whirled from the room. My mother reached out an arm to me. I clasped it, and she pulled me to my feet.

"It's a dangerous occupation, this," she said, glancing at my golden arrows.

"To be sure," I rasped.

It was a ritual of ours. Something we recited to each other whenever the business of love grew difficult, worrisome, violent. She enveloped me into a lilac-scented hug, and before I could even properly thank her, she was gone.

I woke up with a gasp, a crazy beat pounding inside my brain, but this time it wasn't my own head making the noise. It was coming from somewhere outside. As the last wisps of my memory faded away, I cautiously opened my eyes. I lay in a darkened room filled with discarded musical instruments and haphazardly arranged furniture. An itchy, but warm blue jacket covered my torso, and set on the floor next to me was a full bottle of water with a handwritten sign propped next to it.

DRINK ME

I sat up and clucked my tongue. It felt like a freshly skinned animal pelt. I grabbed the bottle and chugged most of it down. Nothing had ever been so refreshing. I turned toward the door.

There was a package of small doughnuts a couple of feet away with another sign.

EAT ME

My stomach grumbled, then turned. I ripped open the package and bit into the first powered doughnuts. Then I sipped the water. It seemed to help my stomach. After I'd downed three more dough-nuts, I felt able to stand. I slid my arms into the slippery vinyl-lined sleeves of the jacket and cautiously stepped out into the light.

In the corner of a large room, Charlie was beating on a set of drums with maniacal precision. His eyes were closed and he kept the beat with his chin, occasionally shaking his head as he really felt the rhythm. He was unbelievable. He was handsome. He was even sexy. The boy was in his element.

"Hello!" I shouted.

He stopped drumming and blinked, as if shaken out of a trance. His face lit up with a smile. "Hey! You're up!"

"Yes," I said. "What time is it?"

He glanced behind me and paled. "It's after three? Crap."

"After three?" I blurted, whirling to look at the clock he'd checked. "I missed a whole day?"

"Looks that way," Charlie said. He stood up, tucked his drum-sticks under his arm, and went over to his backpack, which was resting on a chair.

I shook my head. What the hell had happened to me this morn-ing? Suddenly I had a vague recollection of a girl with dark hair and kind eyes, helping me off the floor. Wine. She'd said something about the wine. I winced at the very thought of it, that sour taste rising up in the back of my throat.

So it hadn't helped my headache one iota, and it had apparently taken an entire day from me. Mental note: *No more wine. Also, kill Aphrodite.*

"Did you leave the water and food?" I asked weakly.

"Yep." He grabbed something from a small pocket on his bag and zipped it up again. "I'm not really a drinker, but my dad gets hungover sometimes and my mom always gives him water, carbs, and this." He held out a small white packet with red lettering. "I got it from the nurse for you."

"Tylenol?" I read, scrunching my face.

"What? You've never had Tylenol before?" he asked.

My heart thumped. Clearly this was something I should have known about, were I a human. "Of course."

"Take it. It'll help the headache," he said, shouldering his backpack. He grasped his drumsticks in one hand. "You do have a headache, right?"

"Always, it seems," I replied. I ripped open the packet, and two small capsules fell out. I shrugged, tossed them into my mouth, and swallowed. They were hard and traveled very, very slowly down my throat. I coughed and Charlie took the water bottle from my hand, opened it, and handed it back. I chugged the last of it, and the capsules slid down to my stomach.

"Thank you." I sighed and recapped the bottle. "You're very sweet, Charlie Cox."

He blushed. "Listen. I need your advice." He turned around and headed for the door. "Got any ideas on how to let Stacey down easy?"

My eyes nearly popped out of my skull. Ow. "What? I thought you two were perfect for each other!"

"Uh, no," he said, shaking his head with a laugh.

I tripped over the leg of a music stand as I tried to follow, and it went crashing into another, both of them making a cacophony as they collided with the floor. My heart pounded with panic as I caught up with him at the double doors. This wasn't happening. I was supposed to be a third of the way there. Only two more couplings stood between me and my reunion with Orion. Charlie couldn't take that away from me. He couldn't.

"But why?" I asked, breathless. "She seemed so nice!"

He pushed one door open, and the noise of a hundred chatting voices, screamed laughter, and slamming lockers assaulted me. I leaned against the edge of the opposite door.

"Yeah, I thought so too. Before she went stalker on me." He pulled out his phone, hit a few buttons, and showed me the screen. "She's texted me two hundred and seventeen times since yesterday afternoon."

My brow knit. "Is that a lot?"

He barked a laugh. "Yeah, that's a lot!"

"Sorry. It's just you people are on those things *all* the time. . . ." He gave me an odd sort of look, and I cleared my throat. "I guess I'm not big on cell phones."

"Well, whatever," he said, pushing the phone back into his pocket. "What do I do? How do I let her down easy?"

I took a breath. My heart felt sick, like someone had shot me with a poisoned arrow. I couldn't believe I had to do this. That I had to advise him on how to break Stacey's heart. But he was obviously not interested, and keeping a couple together for the wrong reasons wasn't going to help my cause.

"You have to tell her the truth," I said reluctantly. "Go to her and tell her that you don't think the two of you are compatible. She'll understand."

Charlie's blue eyes were wide. "That's it? That's your advice? Tell her the truth?"

"Tell who the truth?" Josh Moskowitz walked up behind Charlie and stood there, eyeing us curiously. Veronica and Darla sauntered up next to him, and Veronica looked me up and down like I was a gremlin. I remembered what I'd looked like in the mirror that morning and could hardly blame her.

"Stacey Halliburn," I said. "He wants to break up with her."

"Who, flute girl? You two are going out?" Josh asked.

"Not exactly," Charlie replied.

"Thank God. She is *such* a loser," Veronica said, flipping her hair behind her shoulder. A pair of diamond *V*s glittered against her earlobes. Darla flipped her hair as well, and I caught a glimpse of the similar diamond *D*s decorating her ears.

"Why?" I asked. "What's wrong with her?"

Veronica snorted. "Well, first off, she's in band."

"I'm in band," Charlie said. As he held his drumsticks. In front of the band room. Veronica, it seemed, was not the most observant person. Nor the smartest. For the first time since I met her, she actually looked lost for words. Darla blushed and, at least, seemed embarrassed on her friend's behalf. But she didn't contradict her.

"Whatever. Just text the girl," Josh said. "Tell her you're not into her."

Charlie frowned, considering.

"You can't text her!" I protested. "She obviously likes you. You need to talk to her. Tell her how you really feel. She deserves to know."

"It's been one day," Veronica said condescendingly, recovering nicely from her slip of the tongue. She slipped her cell phone out of her bag and held it at arm's length, pointing it at me.

"So? She still has real emotions!" I protested. "Her feelings still matter."

"You are *so* weird," Veronica said. Then her phone clicked and she slid it into her back pocket.

"What was that?" I asked.

"Nothing," she said, wide-eyed. "I *really* like your outfit."

Then she and Darla laughed and walked away, tossing their hair and whispering. Josh and Charlie slowly followed.

"I'll see you later, True," Charlie said. "Go home and get some real food. You'll feel better soon."

As they melded into the thinning crowd, I leaned back against the cool cinder-block wall and swallowed hard. Somewhere up there, Orion was suffering. Someone up there, Zeus was making him do unspeakable things. I was the only being in the heavens and on Earth who could help him, and so far, I'd only let him down.

Zero down. Three to go.

CHAPTER NINETEEN

True

As I walked to school on Wednesday morning, I was in a foul mood. The sands of the hourglass continued to run, and my mother was no help. We had been here on Earth for two days now and she had not yet left her bed—didn't care to hear what had transpired yesterday. I had even tried to tell her about my memory/dream of the day Artemis had returned and remind her of how she used to want to assist me, but she waved me off. To make matters worse, last night I had suffered a fitful sleep, pleasant dreams of lounging in the grass with Orion turning to nightmares of his torture over and over and over again. It was killing me, not knowing what Zeus was doing to him, being unable to rescue him. I had felt so desperate this morning that I had even crawled into my closet again and called out to Harmonia, but either she wasn't listening or yesterday's conversation with her had, in fact, been the imaginings of a very drunk girl. Either way, it was clear I was on my own.

Even so, as I stepped up onto the brick walkway leading uphill to the school, I tried as hard as I could to be positive.

So Stacey hadn't worked out for Charlie. There was another girl for him somewhere in this crowd. There had to be. He was a good guy. Handsome, talented, caring, creative, thoughtful. Look what he had done for me yesterday, bringing me water and snacks. And Tylenol. Tylenol was a revelation. It was my new best friend. For the first time since I'd arrived on Earth, I was headache free. Plus, I had bathed and woven my hair into two thick braids down my back and discovered a tube of sunscreen in the bathroom cabinet. No wayward hair for me today. No itchy face. And miracle of miracles, no headache or nausea.

Life was good. And it was only going to improve when I found Charlie's true soul mate. The one person who would make him as happy as Orion made me.

I stepped across the driveway and up to the steps leading to the school's front door. Stacey and a few of her friends were huddled together next to the NO PARKING sign, shooting me nasty, pinched looks.

"Stacey, I'm so sorry it didn't work out with Charlie," I said, pausing in front of them.

"Whatever," Stacey said, turning her back on me.

A few of her friends snickered. To my surprise, my cheeks began to burn. Was I actually feeling embarrassed by these mere mortals? I scowled, trying to stop the heat from growing hotter.

"Keep on moseying, farmer girl," one of Stacey's friends said. I wasn't sure what she meant by that, but it was clearly an insult. I chose to ignore her.

"If you want, I can try to find you someone else," I offered. "Someone more compatible. Someone who can—"

"Leave me alone," Stacey snapped. "I wish you'd never moved here."

One of her friends slipped her arm around Stacey's shoulders.

I blinked. "What happened to us being best friends?"

That really got them laughing. "Oh my God! You're so pathetic," Stacey shot back. "I'm not friends with losers who can't even dress themselves."

My eyes narrowed as they turned their backs on me and walked up the stairs. Where had that come from? Suddenly she reminded me of Artemis. Sweet as a pomegranate one second and biting like an onion the next. No wonder Charlie had decided against her. The next time I saw him I'd have to apologize and then congratulate him on his good instincts.

"Charlie was right to break up with you!" I shouted after them, letting my anger get the best of me. "You don't deserve him!"

A few people trailed by me, and they each seemed to be looking me up and down. I glanced down at my outfit—a pair of light blue overalls and a black tank top with my favorite sneakers—and glowered back. It wasn't like I'd come to school naked.

I took a deep breath and mounted the stairs, eyeing the crowd, looking for a girl Charlie might like. And now I was searching for Stacey's polar opposite. The faces gave me nothing. Not one inkling. Were they kind, cruel, smart, stupid, loving, aloof?

I would have killed for my powers. Killed and maimed.

Veronica, Darla, and the VT were clumped together under the shade of a huge maple tree. They snickered as I walked by, and my neck muscles constricted. What were they laughing about? I turned to glare at them, and some jerk with long black hair snapped my picture with his phone.

"Who the hell do you think you are?" I shouted.

I grabbed the tiny device from his hand and hurled it as hard as I could toward the street. Unfortunately, with my weakened human muscles, that wasn't very far. Still, it did crack in a satisfying way against the concrete and shatter into a half-dozen pieces.

"What the hell? This bitch is crazy!" the guy shouted at me, trying to look menacing as his friends gathered around him. My fingertips itched. What I wouldn't give to zap him with my power. Not smite him necessarily, but at least cause a severe and lasting limp.

Instead I snorted a laugh, turned around, and walked into the school, feeling as if I'd done a good deed—one less human toting around a soul-sucking cell phone. The air inside the school was cool and scented with sugar. I turned my steps toward the cafeteria. Dotted around the room were various groups of friends, munching on doughy sticks and bacon. My stomach grumbled, so I walked to the front and served myself a pile of food, then scanned the faces around me. There were two girls sitting together at a table, both listening to music through headphones. One was reading a magazine and bopping her head to the beat much like Charlie had when he'd played yesterday. She was pretty, with light-brown skin and curly brown hair—clearly of Chinese and Scandinavian heritage. After a long career of matching couples and witnessing their spawn, I could tell. I walked over and sat down next to her. She stopped bopping.

"Hello. I'm True," I said.

She leaned away from me, sliding wary eyes in my direction. I picked up one of the doughy sticks, dipped it in the vat of maple syrup I'd been provided, and took a bite. My eyes almost rolled back. Nirvana. "What *is* this?"

The girl tugged her earphones from her ears. "Um . . . french toast sticks?" Her voice was a squeaking whisper.

"It's heavenly!" I replied, shoving the rest of the stick into my mouth and reaching for another.

"You must be really hungry," she said, eyeing the pile of food on my plate.

"I've found that eating and drinking keeps the headaches at bay," I told her, munching. She stared. "So what's your name?"

"I'm Marion," she replied. "Marion Garvy."

Syrup dripped down my chin and onto the front of the overalls. Marion dipped a napkin into her water cup, then held it out to me. I smiled. A kind lover of music who was clearly so timid she didn't have it within her to stalk anyone.

"Marion Garvy," I said, taking the napkin. "I have a proposition for you."

CHAPTER TWENTY

Katrina

"I know I usually harsh on lunch, but these cheese tots are frickin' awesome," Raine said, spearing a mound of potatoes and cheese with her fork. We were sitting at a picnic table near the edge of the quad, soaking up the sun like every other fifth-period luncher at the school. It was way too nice out to be inside.

"Lemme try," I said, opening my mouth and angling toward her.

"No way, dude." She slid the tray away. "Get your own!"

Lana and Gen laughed, and I rolled my eyes. Out on the street the white Goddess Cupcakes van rolled by, followed by a few cars, then a big Barnes & Noble truck. Ugh. The very thought of books made me want to curl into a ball and die. When I'd agreed to go back to honors English, I knew I was going to have to read more books and write longer papers, but the threat of Mrs. Roberge's first assignment had kept me up half the night. What the hell did public speaking have to do with English class?

I heard a familiar engine growl, and Ty's black Firebird pulled up at the foot of the stairs. The brakes squealed as he slammed to a stop. Everyone stared as he got out wearing a Hawaiian print bathing suit and a white T-shirt. His flip-flops slapped noisily as he walked toward our table.

"Hey," I said, getting up. "What's with the beachwear?"

He leaned in for a kiss, and he smelled like beer. I winced, but kissed him anyway. Hopefully he'd only had one. "Get your stuff, baby. We're going down the shore."

"I'm in!" Lana said, shoving her iPod into her purse.

"No one invited you," Ty said with a sneer. Lana sat back down again with a pout. Ty had a mean streak when he drank. So maybe it hadn't been only one. He picked up my bag and slung it over his shoulder. "Let's go. The guys are already up at the rest stop waiting for us so we can caravan."

"Ty, I can't," I said under my breath. "And should you even be driving?"

"Number one, don't tell me what to do," he snapped. Then he laughed and headed for the car. "And number two? Of course you can."

I pressed my lips together, holding my ground. Already I could feel people starting to stare, and I looked down at my feet, letting my hair cover my face.

"Katrina," Ty said through his teeth.

His nostrils flared, and sweat prickled the back of my neck. When I still didn't move, he glanced around, self-conscious. I saw a couple of footballers quickly focus on their lunches, pretending they hadn't been looking. This was going nowhere good. Ty already thought the "loser jocks" at LCHS judged him for dropping out. Me saying no to him in front of them would get right under his skin. And the beer would only make it worse.

"Why not?"

"I can't blow off half the day, Ty," I said pleadingly, reaching for his hand in an attempt to save the situation.

"God, Katrina, why don't you just go?" Raine said. "If someone came in here right now and invited me to the shore, I'd already be slapping on the sunscreen."

Great. Way to have my back, BFF.

"I've got English this afternoon," I told them. "It's important."

"And I'm not?" Ty took a step back, still wearing my bag, and lifted his chin. His fighting stance. I wanted out of this moment so badly I could taste it.

"I didn't say that. Don't be mad," I begged quietly. "I don't want to—"

"So let me get this straight." His voice boomed through the courtyard. "I'm good enough for when you need a place to crash, but you can't take half a day off to hang out with me and my friends?"

The sun was like a spotlight searing my skin. All around me, smiles were hidden behind hands, girls leaned across tables to whisper, I heard giggling and a few real laughs. Hot tears filled my eyes, but as hard as I tried, I couldn't think of a thing to say. I trusted Ty. He knew everything about me. Including how much I hated to be the center of attention. And here he was, humiliating me in front of the entire school.

I thought he'd let me crash at his place because he cared about me. Because he wanted me around. Not because it would mean I owed him something.

Tell him off, I thought. *Grow a pair and tell him to take his own drunk ass to the shore.* But it was like my mouth was pinned shut. I was too terrified to speak. So instead, I turned around and ran.

I had made it maybe three blurred feet when Ty's fingers closed around my bicep, the tips almost touching.

"Whoa, whoa, whoa. Where do you think you're going? We're not done talking yet." His grip was so tight I winced.

"Let go of me, Ty," I whimpered.

"Oh, no. I'm not gonna be the only loser there without his girl-friend."

"Let her go!" a girl's voice shouted.

Time seemed to stop. Through the haze of tears I saw vomit girl storming toward us, her blue eyes on fire. True. Right. Charlie had said her name was True. She dropped her tray of food on our table, stepped on the bench next to Gen, walked right over the tabletop, and jumped down next to me, her sneakers slamming heavily into the packed dirt and grass. She was wearing overalls that were a size too big and had her long hair woven into two braids down her back.

"Who the hell are you?" Ty asked, looking at her like she was a crazy person. "Super Lesbian?"

A couple of guys laughed. My jaw dropped and my face burned even hotter. Had he really just said that?

"Very original," True said, unfazed by my boyfriend's total bigotry. "Let go of her."

Ty shot me a look like, *Is she serious?* I had no idea what to say or do. My arm throbbed inside his grasp.

"Make me," Ty said finally.

True shrugged. "Okay."

She lifted her elbow and brought it down in the center of his forearm with a crack. "Ow! Sonofa—"

He let go. My skin was marked with the white stamps of his fingers. But True wasn't done. She grabbed his arm and twisted it against his back, getting behind him and bending him forward. Ty's face contorted with pain. A few kids lifted their phones, recording the whole thing.

"Let him go!" I cried. "He didn't mean anything."

"You won't be grabbing her again, right?" True said to Ty.

He grunted, turning his head to spit on the ground near my feet. *"Right?"*

Apparently True twisted even harder, because Ty let out a screech.

"No! Fine! I won't!" he muttered.

True let him go and he flung himself away. "You're a psychotic bitch!"

"That seems to be the consensus today," she replied.

Finally, two of the school security guards came jogging over in their white shirts, gray pants, and cheesy silver badges. The whole incident had taken about thirty seconds, but I was exhausted. Exhausted and hurt and humiliated.

"What's going on here?" the skinny one asked.

"Are you a student?" the chubby one demanded of Ty, heaving for breath.

"Lucky me, no," Ty replied, already backing off.

"If you're not a student here, you can't be on campus without a pass from the office," skinny guy said.

Ty raised his hands. "I'm already gone."

He shot me a disgusted look, then jogged down the stairs. With one dramatic rev of the engine and another loud peel-out, he was gone. I bit my lip, hoping I was wrong about the alcohol, or if I wasn't, that he would drive home instead of to the shore—that he wouldn't put anyone, including himself, in danger.

Meanwhile, every single pair of eyes in the courtyard was now focused on me. The security guards hovered at my sides like I was tonight's lead story on TMZ and they were protecting me from the paparazzi.

"Are you okay?" True asked, her startling blue eyes wide with concern.

I ducked my head, wondering if it was possible to die of embarrassment.

"You should've just gone with him," Raine muttered under her breath.

It took everything within me to hold back a flood of tears.

"I have to go to the bathroom," I muttered, shoving past the security guards. That was when I saw Charlie standing in the doorway to the cafeteria, holding his tray between his hands. He'd clearly seen everything, and his pity was written all over his face.

CHAPTER TWENTY-ONE

Charlie

I felt sick. I felt like I wanted to punch something. Preferably the asshole who was currently wheeling his way to the beach. But mostly I wanted to follow Katrina and see if she was okay. I wanted to tell her that she didn't deserve to be treated like that. She had to see that, right? If she didn't, I had to make her see it.

But who the hell was I? I'd talked to her exactly three times, for two seconds each time. Her friends were the ones who should have been running after her, but they were too busy whispering to each other. The door to the hallway swung closed behind Katrina. Screw it. I dropped my tray on the nearest table.

"Charlie! Wait!"

True jogged to catch up with me. I waited for her, but my toes were bouncing beneath me. Katrina was probably on her way to a bathroom somewhere. A bathroom I wouldn't be allowed inside of. One I probably couldn't even find, since I hadn't figured out the maze of hallways yet. I saw that girl from my first day, Zadie, dash into the hall, and hoped that at least she was going to check on Katrina.

"Hey," I said to True. "Are you okay?"

Her brow knit. "What? Me?" Then she seemed to realize what I was talking about. "Oh, yeah. That was nothing. I'm fine. But there's someone I want you to meet."

I was already looking past her at the door, as if Katrina was about to reappear.

"I'm sorry. What?"

True took my arm and started dragging me toward a small table in the shaded area of the courtyard. One where a girl sat alone, her curls nearly covering her face. I saw that her nails were painted black, the polish chipped, and that she had earbud wires dangling toward her bag.

"Charlie, this is Marion. Marion, meet Charlie," True said, with a completely confusing, proud smile on her face.

Marion's eyes darted to my face. Her curls shivered. I think it was her way of saying hello. Or possibly, *Go away*. I stared at True.

"Is this . . . what I think it is?" I asked.

She turned her palms out. "What do you think it is?"

"Another setup?" I whispered, turning away from Marion's huddled shoulders.

"Yes! You said you wanted to find love! I'm finding it for you!" True exclaimed.

"With a girl who doesn't speak?"

"She's into music, and she's sweet!" True whispered, leaning toward my ear. "And she's very reserved. There's no way she's going to send you two hundred seventeen texts in one night."

"True, look at her," I whispered. "She's literally trying to fold herself into an accordion. Did you even ask her if she was interested in me, or did you tell her she was?"

"Huh. You make a decent point. But I'm sure she—"

Right then, Josh, Brian, and Trevor burst out of the cafeteria with their trays, a big wall of blue-and-white varsity jacket. A few people scurried out of their way, which seemed the best strategy. Somehow those guys took up more space than everyone else. Josh looked over at me and did a double take.

"Dude," he said, joining us. "What're you doing over here?"

"We were just talking," I said.

"In no-man's land? No," Josh said, hooking his arm around my neck and dragging me toward his table in the sun. "We don't hang out in no-man's land." I had that squirmy feeling in my gut. That feeling that I'd been caught doing something wrong, not knowing the ins and outs of this school yet. But whatever no-man's land was, Josh wasn't harping on it. He straddled a chair and sat. "You coming to the first football game Friday night?"

I glanced over my shoulder at True. She just stood there. Glowering. Marion, however, seemed relieved. I knew I was right about her. She looked like the kind of girl who wanted to be left alone.

"Um, sure. I guess." I'd never gone to a game by choice before. Only to support my brothers in big play-off games and stuff. I sat down in the seat where Josh basically deposited me. Veronica, Darla, and a few other girls were already eating their salads.

"You have to come," Trevor said, taking a big bite of burger. "And bring your dad so he can see where the real talent in Lake Carmody is."

"You know it." The guys high-fived over the table.

Suddenly True dropped my tray in front of me with a clatter. My face burned. She looked pissed. And after what she'd just done to Katrina's boyfriend, I didn't like the idea of True pissed. I cleared my throat and pretended she wasn't there. It wasn't my fault she felt some need to find me a girlfriend. And it definitely wasn't my fault that she kept choosing the wrong girls.

"You could sit with us at the game," Darla said, smiling at me from across the table. The breeze tossed her dark hair forward so that it perfectly framed her face. "The student section is always packed, but I could save you a seat."

I stared at her. So did True. Was Darla flirting with me? She was one of the hottest and most popular girls in school. The kind of girl who formerly would never have considered speaking to me. Even Josh raised his eyebrows in what looked like intrigued surprise.

"Um, sure," I said, pressing my sweaty palms into my thighs. "That'd be cool."

"Cool," Darla replied.

"Are you gonna stand there the whole period?" Veronica asked True snottily, flicking a piece of lint off her tight short-sleeved sweater.

"I wasn't planning on it," True replied. "But I need to talk to Charlie."

I glanced around the table. Josh pointedly turned his head toward Veronica and Trevor. Brian stared straight ahead as he shoveled fries into his mouth. Darla widened her eyes while picking at her salad. None of them wanted True here. These people were actually starting to accept me—they were even flirting with me!—but clearly, they were nowhere near accepting True.

"So talk," I said through my teeth, feeling squirmy. True was cool. Outspoken, badass, and oddly chivalrous. And I didn't want to be rude to her, but . . . I wished she would walk away. Just for right now.

"Are you just going to ignore Marion?" True asked me.

Darla and Veronica looked over at Marion's table. She was sitting there, silent and still.

"I told you, I don't think she's interested," I replied quietly.

"You just need to get to know her!" True protested. "Give her a chance."

"Who? Marion the mouse-girl?" Veronica said with a laugh, flipping her thick blond hair over her shoulder. "She hasn't talked to anyone since the second grade."

"Why? What happened to her in the second grade?" True asked, her expression concerned.

Veronica made a disgusted noise in the back of her throat. She picked up a piece of lettuce between two fingers and bit into it like it was a chip. "Like I care."

"Well, she talked to me this morning," True shot back.

Veronica's blue eyes flicked over True, her nose wrinkling. "Why am I not surprised?"

"True, can you just let it go?" I asked, avoiding eye contact.

"No! I cannot let it go!" True said. "You said you wanted to find love, and I'm going to find you love!"

The entire courtyard fell silent. Her words hung in the air around us. Everyone was staring at me, and something inside of me snapped. I got up and walked away from the table, knowing True would follow. Once I was halfway to the hall where Katrina had long since disappeared, I turned on her.

"What's wrong with you?" she demanded.

"Why do you have to be so weird?" I hissed through my teeth.

She pulled her head back, shocked but not offended. "What do you mean?"

I sighed. "Look, I'm actually making friends here. For the first time in my entire life, I have people to hang out with at lunch. People who like me. People who want me to come to their parties and their games and be part of their teams. You can't keep hanging around me and spouting weird stuff about love and the universe and all that crap. Please. Let it go."

"I'm trying to help you," True said flatly. "If you would come talk to Marion, I know you would—"

"Stop!" I shouted, bringing her up short. I felt bad for yelling at her, but there was no taking it back now. I wanted to get back to my table and hope everyone would forget about this. "Please, just leave me alone."

I walked away, this time praying she wouldn't follow me. As I took my seat, the two security guards who had stepped in on the fight walked up behind her.

"Are you True Olympia?" the skinny one asked.

"Yes," she snapped.

"The vice principal wants to see you."

Prayer answered.

"He'll have to wait," True replied, crossing her arms over her chest.

"*She'll* see you *now*," the chubby guard said in a pretty convincingly menacing voice. He hiked up his pants, but they fell right back to where they'd been.

True heaved a sigh and rolled her eyes. "Fine. Apparently I'm not wanted out here anyway."

As she walked off in front of the security guards, the entire courtyard exploded in applause. True had definitely put on a show. I pushed my hands into my thighs again, drying the sweat that had pooled there, and glanced at the door to the hallway one last time. Still no sign of Katrina. I hoped she was okay. Wherever she was.

CHAPTER TWENTY-TWO

True

The vice principal's office was about the size of one of those phone booths that had anchored every street corner back in the last century. I'd once hidden inside one to watch the couple I'd just united make out under an awning in the rain. It had been one of my most uncomfortable half hours on Earth. Linz, Austria, Valentine's Day, 1974. But the couple was still together today, and the woman had given birth to three children, all of whom were happily wed.

And they say I'm no good at my job.

"Miss Olympia, I'm Vice Principal Austin." The vice principal had thick light-brown hair pulled back in a tight bun, and wore a brown suit and orange shirt. She did not look like a happy woman. "Have a seat."

She gestured at a wooden chair as the security guard closed the door behind me. If I had to guess, I would have said we had about five hours' worth of oxygen in the room before we both passed out. I sat down. The round white clock above the door loudly ticked off each passing second.

"What's this about?" I asked. I wanted to get this meeting over with as quickly as possible so I could get back to Charlie and Marion. I could make something out of that pairing. I was certain of it.

Ms. Austin paused halfway into her seat, her hands under her butt as she smoothed her skirt. "It's about your behavior today, Miss Olympia."

I laced my fingers together in my lap. She stared at them. "My behavior?"

Ms. Austin hit a few buttons on her keyboard and glanced at her computer screen, which cast an unattractive green glow over her skin. In my mind's eye I saw that red sand slipping through the hourglass on my desk. My skin felt prickly and warm, and I glanced at the one small window in the room. It was shut tight, locked. The clock continued its infernal ticking.

"Apparently this morning you destroyed the cell phone of one of your fellow students."

"He took a picture of me without my consent," I replied succinctly.

Ms. Austin blinked. She seemed confused by me, though I had no idea why. "Even if that is the case, it doesn't warrant you destroying someone else's property."

"Well, he called me a bitch," I replied. "Is that merited?"

Ms. Austin cleared her throat. I stared at the window lock, wishing I had my powers so that I could whip it open and get some air in here. *Tick, tick, tick.*

"I'll have a chat with him about his use of language, but your infraction is still far greater," Ms. Austin told me.

"Fine," I said. "I'll get him a new cell phone."

Her lips flicked toward a smile, but didn't exactly land there. "Precisely the solution I was going to propose. Except the boy would like the money necessary to buy his own new cell phone. It seems he'd like to pick it out himself."

"Fine," I said again, unclasping and reclasping my hands. My underarms were beginning to prickle, and my nostrils widened with each breath. "How much?"

"I'll put you in touch with the student." She tapped a few more keys on her keyboard, and I heard a *ding*. "There. I've sent his e-mail address to your school-assigned e-mail address."

"I don't have a computer," I told her. My eyes kept traveling to the window. My pulse was beginning to accelerate. What was my body doing now? I had thought I'd figured out its new, human peculiarities. I felt each tick of the clock at the top of my spine.

Ms. Austin's face went slack. She leaned back in her leather chair, the springs squealing. "Is that a joke?"

"I don't see what's funny about it," I replied, my nostrils widening farther as I breathed in. I resisted the urge to blow out through my mouth, though it was overwhelming. There was movement in the hallway, and I saw Katrina pass by with a tall man, his bushy eyebrows his most prominent feature. A door nearby closed, and I heard him talking in low tones in the next office.

"You don't have a computer? No tablet, no cell phone?" she asked, incredulous.

I shook my head, growing impatient with this useless line of questioning. It was getting warmer by the second in this tiny cell of a room, and lunch was practically over. If I didn't get out of here soon, my chances of getting Charlie and Marion to speak to each other were gone. Another day, wasted.

Tick, tick, tick.

"No means of retrieving an e-mail at all?" she said.

"No." I angled my knees toward the door. "Can I go now?"

Slowly Ms. Austin looked me up and down. She sat forward again, resting her arms atop the desk blotter. "Miss Olympia, if you

don't mind my asking . . . do you have the means to pay this boy
back?"

My jaw dropped. How insulting. "Of course I do! Just because I
don't choose to carry around one of those infuriating, soul-sucking
devices doesn't mean I'm destitute! How dare you imply such a
thing?"

"I'm sorry! I'm sorry! Forgive me!" She raised her pink palms
in the air. "You may use the computers in the computer lab or in the
library to retrieve your school e-mail."

"Fine." I rose from the awful chair, flinching now with each tick
of the clock. "Is that it?"

"No. It's not," she said, standing as well. "There's the small matter of an assault you just perpetrated in the courtyard."

I groaned. "An assault? That Ty person was the one who
grabbed one of your students. I was simply defending her."

"Violence is not the answer to violence," she said, leveling a
glare at me. "Next time, please report any incidents to school security. We wouldn't want you getting hurt."

"Fine," I said again. "I'll do that."

I yanked open the door and stepped out into the hallway. The
whoosh of cool air brought my blood pressure down instantly. The
security guards hovered at the end of the hall, keeping a sharp eye
on me. I turned in the opposite direction to take the long way back
to the courtyard, but at that moment, the bell rang.

I leaned back against the wall and kicked it as hard as I could
with the sole of my sneaker. Pain radiated up my leg and jarred my
kneecap. I bit down on my lip as the hallway flooded with students.
Gods, I hated this place and its narrow halls and its tiny rooms and
its hordes of shrieking students. I hated this body and its insane
limitations. I had to get out of here. I had to get back to Mount

Olympus and Orion. But I was no closer to achieving that goal than I had been this morning.

The door to the next office opened and Katrina stepped out, her face hidden behind her hair.

"Are you okay?" I asked.

Katrina looked up at me, startled, then angry. "Why does everyone keep asking me that? Why can't you people just leave me alone?"

As I watched her storm off, I started to wonder if Zeus had been right to give me that C in psychology. Maybe, when it came to the human heart and mind, I really was clueless.

CHAPTER TWENTY-THREE

Katrina

I am not.
I am nothing.
I can't live without you.
No one knows.
No one cares.
No one wants to see through.

I tore the page out of my poetry notebook and crumpled it as quietly as I could. Even though I had spent the entire period sitting in the back corner with my hair over my face, writing, I knew everyone in the room was staring at me. The same way they had last year after my father had died and his picture had run on the front page of the paper. Poor little Katrina, the girl whose dad died in a freak accident.

Except now they were thinking, *Poor little Katrina, the girl whose boyfriend abused her in front of the whole school. The weird girl who was so pathetic she had to be defended by an even weirder girl.*

At least that's what Dr. Krantz had called it when he'd scurried me into his office earlier. Abuse. He'd said that if someone grabbed me hard enough to scare me, it was a "reportable incident," and he asked me if I wanted to press charges. Against Ty. I almost laughed in his face.

It was one arm grab. One time. It just happened to take place in front of a hundred people. Ty was everything to me. He was my family. He was my home. He was the only person left on this earth who gave a crap about me. He just didn't like not getting his way.

In the aisle closest to the wall, True sat with perfectly straight posture, staring at the clock. Charlie was right next to her, tapping a quiet beat against the edge of his desk with his fingers. He'd tried to get my attention a couple of times, I think. I'd seen a hand wave through my hair about five minutes into class. But I'd chosen to pretend it wasn't there. I was too humiliated to look him in the eye. And besides, I didn't want to get him in trouble with Stacey again.

I looked down at my phone under the desk. Five minutes left. Only three more classes to go in this awful day. I couldn't wait to get the heck out of here. I was going to practically sprint to the library to blubber on Mrs. Pauley's shoulder. Thank God I had a shift this afternoon.

"Well, we've only got a few minutes left, so it's time to put you out of your misery," Mrs. Roberge announced.

My heart stopped. I looked up at her through my bangs. She hovered at the front of the room in an unattractive violet top and black skirt, a Ziploc bag full of paper scraps in her hand. Oh God. I had totally spaced on the project. Today was the day she was going to assign the first chapters.

"If I call your name, please come to the front of the class."

Please don't call my name, please don't call my name, please don't call my—

"Katrina Ramos! You're going to be our first presenter on *Great Expectations*!"

I swear I would have thrown up if I'd eaten anything today. My eyes automatically flicked to Charlie. He gave me a bolstering look, which only made me want to heave even more. Yesterday I thought he maybe kind of liked me. Even just as a friend. Today he thought I was a special case. A loser. Someone in need of bolstering looks.

"Miss Ramos? Come on down and get your assignment," Mrs. Roberge called out happily.

I pushed myself out of my chair. My knees shook as I navigated around the bags in the aisle, leaning up against chairs or dangling from chair backs. At the front of the room, I took a wide step over Stacey's outstretched leg, which I could have sworn hadn't been there a moment ago. Mrs. Roberge held out the assignment to me.

GREAT EXPECTATIONS: CHAPTER ONE
Some points to consider for your lecture.

Lecture? She expected me to lecture?

"We're looking forward to having you lead our class on Monday," Mrs. Roberge said with a huge smile.

That was all it took. My whole body flushed with heat and my eyes stung. I was going to throw up anyway, even with an empty stomach. The assignment crumpled in my hand as I flung myself out into the hallway, letting the door slam.

Giving everyone one more reason to talk about me.

CHAPTER TWENTY-FOUR

True

I walked into the house that afternoon and, shockingly, found my mother at the kitchen table. She sat with her legs splayed, her back bent, her eyes unfocused and staring. She wore nothing but a fuzzy blue bathrobe and gray socks. Her blond hair was matted and slimy, and her skin looked tired and baggy. The bath was a discovery she'd not yet made. I slammed the door, and she nearly jumped out of her skin.

"Is that necessary?" she asked with a groan.

"I've had a bad day," I told her, walking to the stainless-steel refrigerator and grabbing a bottle of water. I took a long drink from it and licked my lips. "Where's the money?"

"What money?" she asked.

"The money," I repeated, sitting down at the end of the wood table. "I assume Zeus sent us here with some cash. Where is it?"

Aphrodite laughed, the sound filling the modern kitchen with its sarcastic tone. If it had been any louder, the untouched cooking utensils would have quivered in their ceramic container.

"You give Zeus too much credit," she said. "There is no money."

"What?" I blurted, a bit of water dripping over my bottom lip.

I wiped it away with the back of my hand. "But I have to buy some cretin a new cell phone. And according to the unusually handsome librarian at the school, it would benefit my studies greatly to have my own home computer."

Aphrodite turned her narrowed eyes on me slowly, a glare that had stopped thousands of mortal men cold over the last few thousand years.

"Then I suggest you procure a job," she said. "In fact, I insist upon it. Because once we consume the food provided, I'm not entirely certain it's going to reconstitute itself." She gestured toward a garbage can full of empty green bottles. "I know the wine hasn't been so kind."

"You went through the entire wine cellar?" I demanded.

She shrugged. "A goddess must do what a goddess must do."

"So why don't *you* get a job?" I asked, pushing myself up from the table. The chair teetered and fell back on the red tile floor with a clatter. "Isn't that what the parent is supposed to do? I'm kind of in the middle of an important mission here."

My mother heaved a grand sigh as she rose to her feet. "You forget, my dear daughter, that I'm not the one who had us banished. Now if you will excuse me, I must situate myself before the television, where an enthusiastic woman has promised to inform me on how to shed sixteen pounds in sixteen days."

Then she turned, lifted her imperious chin, and swept out of the room. I threw my water bottle after her, but it bounced off the intricate molding around the door and landed with a thud in the hallway, then rolled back in my direction as if mocking me. My hands curled into fists at my sides and I drew in breath after breath, trying to calm my ire. How I wished Orion were here. What I really needed was a bow and arrow and a run through the woods with my love at my side. A good, sweaty hunt followed by a nice, long, adrenaline-fueled kiss. I needed to blow off some steam.

But there was no time for that. And it appeared that Ms. Austin's suspicions about me had been correct. I didn't have the means to pay Darnell Lockwood back for his insidious phone. I was not only a human, I was a destitute human.

"Not for long," I said through my teeth.

Part of me wanted to run upstairs to check the sand timer to see how much time I had left, but an even bigger part of me didn't. I grabbed the blue band jacket off the hook near the door as I stormed outside. It was time for this goddess to get a job.

Approximately forty-two frustrating minutes later, I found myself inside the Lake Carmody Public Library. I'd gone door-to-door from business to business, but so far, no one had been hiring. Not the small Italian catering company that smelled so good it made my mouth water, not the gift shop with the ridiculous ceramic cats, not even the funeral parlor, though they had kept me there for fifteen minutes, grilling me on why I wanted to work in the mortuary. As I stepped into the hushed, airy lobby of the impeccably kept library, I felt my muscles begin to uncoil.

Peace. Peace and quiet and words. I could definitely spend some time here.

The walls of the grand foyer were hung with muted works of art, watercolors of covered bridges, secluded streams, and fields of wildflowers. A closer look at the placards near the paintings and I discovered that they were the work of local artists, donated to the library this past spring. As the foyer opened up to a large circular room, I saw a small partition wall made entirely of cork, the words STUDENT POETRY pinned across the top in cardboard letters. There

were a couple of pedestrian pieces written in pencil by second grad-
ers, a missive about love penned by a girl named Carrie in seventh
grade, and a poem about a motorcycle by twelve-year-old Zeke.
But right in the center was a short haiku, and the name at the bottom stopped me short. It was by Katrina, aged sixteen.

> *She the sun and moon*
> *He the earth the sea and life*
> *Torn apart. We die.*

It was so mournful. I realized in an instant that it was written by
the Katrina I knew. The kind girl with the awful boyfriend who'd
taken pity on me in my time of need. She was still suffering from
the death of her father. That much was clear. Was that why she
stayed with that horrid troll of a male? Because she was in need of
a father figure? Or was it something more?

Powers. If I could only read her, I'd know.

I heard hushed voices on the far side of the first row of shelves
and found a wide, gleaming oak desk marked CIRCULATION. Behind
it two women talked urgently, their heads bent close together. I took
a step toward them, and the younger one glanced up. It was Katrina.

She looked better than she had when last I'd seen her, running
out of English class that afternoon when her skin had been positively
gray, but I could tell by the tightness of her lips as I approached that
she wasn't happy to see me.

"Can I help you?" the other woman asked politely.

Her brown hair was cut into a bob, and she wore an autumnal
striped sweater over brown corduroys. Her smile was friendly.

"I hope so," I replied. "My name is True Olympia. I'm looking
for a job."

The woman opened her mouth to reply, but Katrina cut her off. "We're not hiring."

"Katrina," the woman hissed in admonishment. She reached out a hand to me. "I'm Olivia Pauley," she said. "It's nice to meet you."

"It's nice to meet you, too," I replied, giving Katrina's glower a sidelong glance. We shook hands and her skin was soft and warm. If I'd had my powers, that one touch would have told me every last thing about her, from her shoe size to the number of times she'd had her heart broken. But today, nothing. Not even a zip of emotion.

I suddenly felt very, very tired.

"But I'm afraid Katrina is correct," Olivia told me. "We're not hiring right now."

"Okay," I said, my shoulders slumping. "Thank you for your time."

As I turned to walk away, I heard Katrina whisper, "That's her—the girl who humiliated me today."

My face flashed with anger. I turned right back around again, standing up straight. "Excuse me, but I don't believe I was the one who humiliated you. I helped you."

"Please. I would have been fine," Katrina whispered harshly. "Ty's my boyfriend. He loves me."

"People who love you don't hurt you," I shot back.

Olivia's eyes widened with concern. "Katrina? Did he hurt you?"

"He grabbed her. Hard," I told the librarian. "And from where I was standing, it didn't look like he had any plans to let go."

"Well, you don't know him like I do," Katrina replied, her face flushed with color. "And you didn't have to attack him."

"I don't believe this!" I cried. "You should be thanking me!"

"Thanking you? I've never been so embarrassed!" Katrina whispered. "Everyone was talking about me the rest of the day."

"But I—"

"Girls!" Olivia hissed, leaning her hands into the desk. "Both of you calm down." I set my jaw and crossed my arms over my chest. Katrina stared at her copy of *Great Expectations*, which lay closed in front of her. Beneath it was a black spiral notebook with frayed corners. "Katrina, it sounds like True here only meant to help you, not humiliate you," Olivia continued. "You were just trying to be a friend, right, True?"

"Right," I replied.

"So maybe you can see a way to forgive her, even if she embarrassed you in the process?" Olivia suggested.

Katrina took in a deep breath and blew it out. "I guess."

"Good. Now why don't you two apologize to each other and move on?" Olivia suggested, gesturing between us.

"I have nothing to apologize for," I protested. "I didn't—"

"Eh! Yes, you do," the librarian said.

I shifted from one foot to the other. It wasn't every day I took orders from a human. But this Olivia person seemed wise, and kind. And she clearly had Katrina's best interests at heart. It was always nice to see humans caring for each other.

"Fine," I said finally. "I apologize if I embarrassed you or that Ty person."

Katrina looked up at me through her thick eyelashes. "I'm sorry I got mad at you for trying to help."

"Apology accepted." I glanced at Olivia. "Are we done here? Because I really have to go find a job."

"We're done." Olivia smiled at me and seemed to be on the verge of a giggle. "Thank you, True Olympia. And might I say you have quite the poetic name?"

"Thank you," I said. "I chose it myself."

Then I turned my back on her curious expression and headed for the door. When I got to the sidewalk, I heard someone running up behind me. I whirled around, set to defend myself, but it was only Katrina.

"Hey," she said sheepishly, her hair falling forward over her cheeks. "I thought you'd want to know I saw a 'Help Wanted' sign the other day. I'm not sure if it's still there, but—"

"Where?" I asked.

Katrina turned and pointed up Main Street, where dozens of bright awnings and sale signs and colorful flags waved in the breeze. Pedestrians dotted the walkways, carrying paper shopping bags and sipping at iced coffees. I saw the mail carrier who'd seen me through my window the other morning, and when he spotted me, he dropped the mail he was flipping through all over the cross-walk.

"See the pink-and-brown awning? That's Goddess Cupcakes," Katrina told me. "They're hiring."

I smirked as I zeroed in on the business in question. "Goddess Cupcakes?" I said. "Perfect."

As I turned up Main Street, I passed by a small French restaurant called Pourquoi Pas?, where the waiter was setting up a few outdoor tables for that night's meal. The linen tablecloths and gleaming crystal glasses brought me right back to Valentine's Day earlier this year and a little thrill warmed my heart. It was the day my existence had changed forever.

· · ·

My toes were so cold they'd gone numb, so I imagined them warm as I turned away from the window of Coatstown, Maine's, finest eatery and walked through a packed parking lot. I smiled as I passed by a compact car where Sandy Luongo and Leanna Chen were sharing first love's kiss, thanks to my golden arrow.

Every year my mother sent me to Earth for Valentine's Day. She told me it was to give me an opportunity to glimpse the fruits of my labor up close, but really I think she wanted to force me to walk past cardboard images of the "God of Love," depicted as that bulbous male baby. I think she got a good laugh out of it.

Still, I often enjoyed these little sojourns, watching lovers share intimate meals or nuzzle noses under icicle-hung eaves, witnessing the more elaborate declarations of love like fireworks displays, messages stomped into the snow, or a path of deep-red rose petals leading a loved one to the diamond ring of her dreams.

This year, however, I felt bored by it. Even with success stories like Leanna and Sandy to my credit. With a sigh, I turned my thoughts inward and tried to figure out why I felt so melancholy. Nothing was amiss in my life. My mother was happy with her latest consort, which meant fewer tirades for me, and fewer evil divorces on Earth. My brothers were hermited away in their marble palace, striking fear and terror in random parts of the world at will, while Harmonia tried as hard as she could to sweep up after their messes. Everything was normal. Everything was fine.

I blew out a cloud of steam and looked up at the clear night sky. Orion hung directly overhead, and suddenly I couldn't breathe. I felt Orion staring down at me, and even as I realized how ridiculous a notion that was, the center star in his belt seemed to wink.

I narrowed my eyes. A sizzle of possibility warmed my fingertips. I had always felt a tad guilty about what had happened to Orion, knowing that on some level, Artemis was right. If I hadn't struck them with my golden arrows, they never would have been together and he never would have died that awful death. With a glance around, I determined that I was, in fact, alone. Aside from Sandy and Leanna, there was no one outside on this frigid night, and those two were otherwise occupied. For fun, I lifted my hands to the sky, pressing my wrists together for added power, and imagined Orion's laughing face the way it had been when I'd last seen him alive, at the Feast of Persephone on Mount Olympus. He'd been one of few mortals allowed to attend as the guest of Artemis.

"Orion," I whispered. "Come to me."

There was a brief absence of sound. Not just a hush, but a complete silence. The world went still. The branches overhead ceased their creaking. The wind stopped howling. The traffic along Main Street, three blocks down, halted. And then, a power like nothing I had ever felt before vibrated inside my bones. It boiled my blood and seared my skin. Suddenly white-hot electricity shot from my hands into the night sky. I was blasted back into the ground and my skull was slammed against the concrete. It took a long moment for my vision to clear, but when it did, I still couldn't believe what I was seeing.

A body. The limp, lifeless body of a man. Careening toward Earth.

I jumped up, but there was nothing I could do. Within seconds he had collided with the ground at my feet, yet aside from the fact that his eyes were closed, his figure limp, he looked none the worse for the fall. He was wearing the exact same clothing he'd worn the day he died those thousands of years ago. Silver breastplate, red cape, leather leggings, leather sandals. The only change was the small white scar where the gaping wound in his head had been.

"Orion," I whispered.

I dropped to my knees. This wasn't possible. I was a lower goddess. I was not supposed to have the power to do such things. I reached my hand out to touch his lifeless shoulder. The skin was warm. My eyes turned to the sky, and there were the stars of the Orion constellation, still bright in the winter sky. Still winking at me like they knew something I didn't.

Suddenly the world awoke. The wind whipped my face. The traffic whizzed by. Somewhere, a screen door slammed. And I was kneeling in a parking lot next to a corpse.

I glanced desperately around. As a lower goddess, I had no means of returning to Mount Olympus on my own. My mother would summon me at midnight and I would appear in her chambers to give my report on my day. For now, I was not a goddess. I was a human being in a very real world with very real consequences for murder.

I had to hide the body. At least until Aphrodite summoned me.

I shoved my hands under his arm. His head lolled forward, and he groaned.

"Orion?"

I dropped his weight in surprise, and his skull bounced against the hard ground.

"Ow." He winced and reached his arm back to touch his head.

"You're alive?" I asked, sitting down next to him, so stunned I forgot how cold the blacktop would be.

"Of course I'm alive, you idiot," he replied. "You made it so."

"You saw me?" I asked.

Orion sat up. He rolled his head around on his neck and blinked a few times.

"I see everything," he said. "For two thousand, nine hundred sixty-four years, I've seen everything."

"Wow," I said. "That's a lot to process."

He looked at me then, and our eyes met for the first time. I was

172 · kieran scott

astonished by the shade of blue. They were the exact color of the Aegean Sea at dusk.

"Hi," he said with a small smile.

"Hello," I replied, breathless.

A car engine revved. Headlights flashed. Brakes squealed. My hands flew up to cover my face as a car stopped mere feet away.

"What the hell are you kids doing sitting in the middle of a parking lot?" the driver shouted out the window.

I yanked Orion to his feet and we stumbled out of the way, under the boughs of an old elm tree.

"That was close," I said under my breath.

"What do we do now?" Orion asked.

I looked down. His hand was clasped around mine. Suddenly I wondered who else was watching us. Aphrodite? Zeus? Artemis?

Dear gods, let her and her awful brother not be watching. They had tried countless times over the last two thousand years to do what I'd done with one quick meeting of my wrists. To say they would be enraged was an understatement. To wonder whether they'd exact revenge, an act of folly. The moment those two discovered that Orion was alive and well, they would come for him, and they'd slaughter anyone who stood in their way. Namely, me.

Suddenly I felt Artemis's fingers digging into my neck, felt the life draining out of me. It had been the most terrifying moment of my existence. I couldn't give her the motive to finally finish the job.

"We'll find you someplace to stay. Someplace no one will find you," I told Orion. "At least not until I figure out what the hell is going on."

"Hey! Watch it!"

A couple of skateboarders parted around me on the sidewalk,

and I realized I'd been walking blindly for the past five minutes as I daydreamed. Luckily, I'd walked myself right to my destination, Goddess Cupcakes, where the windows gleamed, the tables were jammed with customers, and the bell at the door trilled merrily whenever someone entered or exited.

I took a step toward the door, and a handsome, bulky, raven-haired boy in jeans and a flannel shirt held it open for me on his way in.

"After you," he said with a smile.

I grinned. The day was looking up.

CHAPTER TWENTY-FIVE

True

"Any questions?"

I smiled at Dominic Cerlone, the manager and head baker at Goddess Cupcakes, and the first human I had recognized in Lake Carmody. I had matched him with his current wife back when they were in high school in Brooklyn, New York, and they had been together ever since. There was nothing better to bolster my mood than to see my successful work in progress, and to know that high school sweethearts could still make it, especially considering where I was concentrating my efforts these days.

It was Thursday afternoon, my fourth day on Earth, and the day of my first shift as an employee of Goddess Cupcakes, where I had been hired after yesterday's brief interview. Dominic had just given me the general tour of the shop, including its impressive kitchen, from which emanated the sweet scent of baking cupcakes, the large stockroom, the small bathroom and break room for employees, and the garbage Dumpster out back. He'd run through the twenty-two cupcake flavors the eatery currently offered, as well as the five specials of the day, and laid out his theories on coffee.

"We don't do fancy," he'd told me. "You want nonfat, half-caf, extra foam with room? Go to Starbucks."

I did remember liking him back in the day.

Behind the counter, the register dinged and the till slid open with a bang. The pretty, bespectacled girl working there, Tasha, handed change to a large woman toting a bag full of cupcake boxes.

"Yes. When do I get paid?" I asked.

Dominic laughed heartily. "Every Friday," he said. "Except you won't get paid this Friday because you've only got one shift this week, so it'll be rolled into next week's pay. Okay?"

My heart sank. Darnell had been a tad irritated this morning when I'd told him I couldn't pay him back yet, and I knew a week's delay wasn't going to please him. But what was I going to do? I couldn't ignore him or I'd risk expulsion from the school, and if that happened, I'd never complete my mission. I had to earn money, and I was grateful to Dominic for giving me a chance, with no work experience whatsoever (other than the countless years of sparking love between unsuspecting humans, including himself). I knew better than to complain.

"That's fine," I told him, smoothing the front of my white apron. On it was printed the establishment's logo—a pink-iced cupcake wearing a white toga-style dress instead of a cupcake wrapper, silver stars dotting the icing, and a gold halo hovering over its pink peak. It was more of an angel than a goddess, but I understood the appeal. "What should I do now?"

"You're on bussing for the rest of the day." He stepped behind the counter and came out with a pink rectangular bin. "Go around and remove empty plates and cups, clean up used napkins and whatnot. If someone still has food on their plate, make sure you ask if they're done. Okay?"

"Okay. I'm on it," I told him as he headed back to the kitchen. "Thank you!"

With a sigh, I turned toward the jam-packed dining area. In less than a week I'd gone from lounging on a cloud with Harmonia and our friends to cleaning up garbage. I would have to learn to keep my temper in check from now on, but even then, frustration burbled up inside me. I was stuck here for four hours. That was four hours away from my mission. Four more hours of sands slipping through the hourglass. Four hours closer to Orion's doom.

Trying not to dwell on the many reasons to race from the building, I walked to the nearest table. Two girls in private school uniforms chatted over coffee and empty cupcake plates.

"So he totally broke up with her," one girl said to the other, checking her cell phone for texts as I removed her dish. "I swear you two are getting back together."

"You think?" the other girl asked hopefully. "Should I call him?"

"No. Absolutely not. Let him call you. You must play this cool."

I dropped their plates into the bin and turned to the next table. A guy in a Lake Carmody High School jacket leaned back on two spindly legs of his chair, sipping soda through a straw casually, while the girl sitting across from him sniffled.

"But we're still going to homecoming, right?" she asked tearfully.

He lifted one shoulder. "I dunno. Maybe. I gotta leave my options open."

I scowled and grabbed his plate, which still had half a cupcake on it, dumping it upside down into the bin. Ass.

In the corner, a pack of girls chatted over coffee.

"You should ask him out!"

"No way! I couldn't."

"I swear. He's too shy."

"She's right, Becks. He'll never do it himself."

I paused behind their table, a light, airy feeling filling my chest. Slowly I smiled. When I had walked into Goddess Cupcakes yesterday, practically begging for a job, I hadn't realized what I was lucking into, but now I took a moment to really survey the place. Packs of kids from half a dozen different schools were crowded around every table. The private school girls in their maroon-and-gray uniforms. A handful of LCHS guys sporting their royal-blue-and-white jackets. In the corner, a pair of boys in green-and-yellow sweatshirts chatted up girls wearing red-and-black cheerleading uniforms. And there were dozens more with no discernable loyalties who could have been from anywhere.

Goddess Cupcakes was a matchmaker's dream.

The bells above the door tinkled, and Darla traipsed inside with two of her friends trailing behind her—no sign of the awful Veronica. She was laughing until she saw me, and then her face fell.

"Oh," she said, her purse dangling above her elbow. "Hi."

"Hello."

I watched her closely as she found an empty table near the window with her friends and they settled in, perusing the menu board behind the counter. A tiny inkling of a thought took root in the back of my mind, then slowly grew into a sapling. Yesterday at lunch, Darla had flirted with Charlie. And he hadn't shied away from it. She wasn't the nicest person I'd ever met, but she was by no means the worst, and she was better than vile Veronica. Besides, Charlie had said it himself—he wanted to fit in at this school. What better way to fit in than to have a girlfriend in the so-called popular crowd that he clearly wanted to be a part of?

I walked over to Darla's table. "Hey," I said. "Can I talk to you?"

She glanced at her friends, both of whom appeared shocked and appalled by my presence.

"About what?" Darla asked, picking at the front of her cashmere sweater.

"It's about Charlie."

Her eyes widened ever so slightly. She was intrigued. "I'll be right back," she told her friends.

I led her into the nearest corner. "Do you like him?"

She pursed her lips. "Why would you say that?"

"You were flirting with him yesterday at lunch," I replied. "So do you like him, or were you just bored? Because I know him pretty well, if you want some pointers."

Darla looked at me like I was crazy. "Why would you help me? We're not friends."

"I have my reasons," I replied, thinking of the hourglass, of the look on Orion's face as I'd been ripped away from him.

Darla's knees bounced beneath her as she considered. "Okay, fine," she said finally. "What do I need to know?"

I smiled. Bull's-eye. If I played this right, Charlie and Darla would be a couple before the end of the week, and Charlie would never know I had anything to do with it.

CHAPTER TWENTY-SIX

Charlie

"Our first big project of the year is going to teach you how to be adults," Mr. Chin explained, pacing the front of my econ classroom on Friday afternoon. "At least, that's its goal."

Outside the windows, rain poured down in buckets. Cross-country practice was definitely going to be canceled, but I was sure the football game would be played tonight, rain or shine. Was Darla still going to show up in this weather? And more important, did she really want me to sit with her, or was she taking pity on the new kid?

I held my pen at its center and waggled it, tapping each end against the desk rapidly. Behind me to my left, Katrina sat at her desk, writing in a black notebook like her life depended on it. She hadn't so much as looked at me today, but I couldn't stop staring at her. At least True hadn't come at me with some new and wild hookup scenario. Maybe she'd given up on me. After the way I'd treated her the other day, I wouldn't have blamed her.

"Today you will be filling out this questionnaire to help me decide on your mock careers," Mr. Chin continued, walking along the aisles and handing each of us a set of stapled papers. "On Monday I will let you know what your jobs and salaries will be. Then, on Tuesday, you'll be taking a compatibility test, and on Wednesday, you will be matched up with partners so you can embark on an entire semester of wedded bliss."

My heart skipped a few beats, while everyone around me groaned. We were going to be pretend-married to someone? I glanced over my shoulder at Katrina. She was still writing.

"Together with your partner you will scour Craigslist for apartments, you will make a list of monthly expenses and a budget, you will keep a working checkbook and, in October, each of you will proudly welcome a bouncing baby doll into the world."

Mr. Chin lifted a well-worn, life-size newborn doll out of a box and held it up. More groans.

I suddenly couldn't stop smiling. Wedded bliss. Apartments, budgets, checkbooks, babies. Whoever I was hooked up with, I'd be spending crazy amounts of time with that person for the entire semester. I stared down at the career questionnaire, my heart pounding, and started to fill it out. What if Katrina and I got matched up together? Then she'd *have* to look at me.

Before I knew it the bell had rung. I handed in my paper at the front of the class. Katrina slipped out the door in front of me. I was opening my mouth to say hi, when suddenly Darla was all up in my grill. She smelled like strawberries and looked like she was on her way to a club, not eighth-period gym.

"Charlie! I have to talk to you!"

Behind her, Katrina disappeared into the crowd.

"What's up?" I asked, leaning one shoulder into the wall.

"Listen, I was thinking . . . about the game tonight—"

Here it came. She was going to politely tell me she didn't really want me to sit with her. Not that I cared. Really. Who wanted to sit in the bleachers and get drenched while watching a bunch of meat-heads battle it out over a ball? I clenched my teeth and told myself to take it like a man.

"I don't really want to sit outside in this, do you?" she asked.

I glanced out the window across the hall. Lightning flashed. "Doesn't seem safe," I replied.

She laughed, and my face warmed. "Exactly! So I was think-ing . . . maybe we could hit Moe's Diner instead? They have the best pie, you have no idea."

I blinked. Had I heard her right? "What about your friends?"

"Oh, they'll go to the game anyway," she said with a wave of her hand. "But can I tell you a secret?" She leaned in super close to me, and I forced my eyes to gaze at the window and away from her cleavage. "I kind of hate football."

"Me too!" I said.

Darla's smile widened. "So then it's a date?"

I grinned back.

"Definitely."

"Cool. I'll get your number from Josh and text you the info," she said, turning around, her skirt twirling out around her. "Bye, Charlie."

"Bye," I said, half-dazed as I lifted my hand.

I glanced around as the hallway buzzed with activity, waiting for the punch line. Had one of the hottest girls in school really asked me out?

I was starting to think this place was different after all.

CHAPTER TWENTY-SEVEN

Katrina

I am not.
I am nothing.
I am nothing to you.

I stared at the rain from under the small overhang in front of the library on Friday afternoon, clutching my books. My shift had ended half an hour ago, and my mother was supposed to pick me up and take me for my annual checkup at the doctor. It was on the calendar. As out of it as she'd been lately, she'd never forgotten anything that was on the calendar. But clearly not even the calendar mattered anymore. Before long she was going to forget I existed entirely.

I checked my phone. Thirty-five minutes late. I envisioned myself stepping out into the rain and walking home, but in this deluge I'd be soaked through in five seconds and my books would be ruined. I stared at Ty's face on my home screen. I hadn't spoken to him since Wednesday, but who else was there to call? Raine didn't have a car, and things had been weird between us anyway, since she'd kind of turned her back on me during my argument with Ty. I'd purposely shown up to school late the last two mornings to avoid our bathroom ritual, and I'd spent my lunch periods in the library, eating with Zadie while she read novels and I prepped for my English presentation on Monday. Aside from sitting next to Raine in the two classes we had together, I hadn't seen her.

Thirty-seven minutes. I held my breath and hit Ty's name. He picked up on the first ring.

"Hey," he said flatly. "I thought you were never gonna speak to me again."

My heart slammed over and over and over again. "I thought *you* were never gonna speak to *me* again."

We both laughed. "So what's up?" he asked.

"I'm kind of stranded at the library," I said, wincing over needing a favor after the silence of the past two days. "Is there any chance—"

"I'm right down the street," he told me. "I'll be there in five."

He hung up. I sighed and leaned back against the gray brick wall next to the automatic door. At least he wasn't mad at me. Or at least he wasn't so mad he'd turn me down. But there were still nervous butterflies buzzing around my chest. Where was my mom? Had she really forgotten about me, or was it something worse?

Taking a deep breath, I told myself to chill. I was just more on edge lately than usual because of this English project. And because of the fight with Ty. But this rain felt ominous, portentous. What were the chances that both a person's parents could end up in devastating car accidents in the course of one year?

Ty's car pulled to a stop in front of the library. I pushed away from the wall. At that exact moment, my mother came trudging around the corner of the building, huddled under an umbrella.

"Katrina! There you are! I thought you were meeting me at the doctor!"

Ty got out of his car and jogged over, holding his denim jacket up over his hair. My throat closed over as my mother saw him.

"Mrs. Ramos," he said. "You're here!"

"You don't have to sound so shocked," she replied. "She's still my daughter."

"The calendar said to pick me up here," I told her quietly. "I never could have walked to the doctor from here in time."

"No. It said 'Katrina, doctor, five p.m. I've been sitting in that waiting room worried about you for half an hour. Why didn't you call me?" she demanded, her eyes flashing.

Because I'm terrified to call you, I thought, starting to tremble. *Because you always yell at me when I call you.*

"I—"

"Oh, I see. You'd rather call him!" my mother said, throwing a hand toward Ty but not bothering to look at him. "You'd rather your knight in shining armor come to your rescue."

My fingers curled into fists. I couldn't believe I was getting yelled at. Again. I'd done nothing wrong. I almost never did anything wrong and she was always, always yelling at me.

"I *just* called him five minutes ago," I told her. "After you didn't show up!"

"Don't you take that tone with me, young lady!" my mother thundered. "This is not my fault!"

"Katrina, maybe we should go," Ty said.

I took a step toward him, realizing I had to get out of this argument. Feeling very much like I was about to explode.

"What makes you think she's going with you?" my mother demanded.

"Maybe because she's actually welcome in my house," Ty replied sarcastically.

My mother's face went slack, then turned purple. "How dare you? My daughter is always welcome in our home. It's not my fault she chooses to avoid it at all costs."

Unbelievable. *Not my fault.* Nothing was ever her fault.

"Then whose fault is it?" I demanded, rain dripping from my hair, my nose, my eyelashes.

"What?" my mother gasped.

"Whose fault is it, Mom?" I asked, shaking from head to toe. "At least I know Ty loves me. I can't say the same for you."

"Katrina!" my mother gasped.

But it was too late. I'd already taken Ty's hand, the same hand that had clasped my arm so hard on Wednesday afternoon, and we walked toward his car.

"Katrina! You'd better not get in that car!" my mother yelled through the rain. "Get back here right now!"

Ty opened the door for me, and I dropped into the low seat. As soon as the door closed, I couldn't see my mother anymore. She was nothing but a blur of tan coat distorted by the raindrops. Ty got in and I tried to stop my lip from quivering.

"Wow. That was intense," he said.

"Can we go, please?" I asked, my voice cracking.

Ty looked at me, breathless. "Move in with me."

My jaw dropped. "What?"

"Screw her," Ty said. "Move in with me full-time. I'll even clear off a shelf for your books."

I laughed, a tear slipping down my face. I knew that we had to talk about what had happened at school on Wednesday, and somehow, someday I'd find a way to bring it up. But now was not the time. Now he was being more romantic than he'd ever been in his life.

"Seriously?" I said. "The guys won't mind?"

"Who cares?" he said. "I pay most of the rent anyway. They'll suck it up."

I leaned over the center console and kissed him. "Thank you," I said. "I'm in."

"Good. Now let's go get something to eat." He slammed the car into gear and pulled into traffic. "Because it's payday and after that performance, my baby deserves a steak."

I took a deep breath. The last thing I felt like I could do at that moment was eat, and steak was really my least favorite food on earth. But I knew how much he loved Longhorn and at that moment, I didn't want to argue. What I wanted was to pretend the last five minutes had never happened.

CHAPTER TWENTY-EIGHT

Charlie

The finish line was dead ahead. I could see my mom and dad standing a few yards away. When my father spotted me, his jaw dropped. I knew the feeling. Was it really possible that I was winning this? How could I be winning this?

Behind me, footsteps pounded. The ground was still wet from yesterday's rain, and my legs were dripping with slick mud. The back of my blue LCHS tank was a sweat rag. My lungs burned with effort. The finish line was five feet away. Two. One. And I was across.

The small crowd exploded in applause. I leaned forward, bracing my hands above my knees as Brian and my other teammates caught up with me.

"Dude! Way to turn on the speed!" Brian gasped. "We came in one-two-three!"

I slapped hands with him and with the other LCHS runner, Carlos. Some big dark-haired kid with a camera came over.

"Smile for the yearbook!" he said, and snapped our picture, our arms loosely draped around one another. Then, out of nowhere, Darla flung herself into my arms. I was so stunned, I nearly fell over and took her with me. Luckily, Brian was there to stop me.

"You won!" Darla cried, bouncing up and down. She was wearing a blue-and-black-plaid miniskirt, a low-cut white tank top, and a skin-tight blue cardigan. Half the guys from the other teams were eyeing her as they got their water. "Can you believe you won?"

"Not really, no," I said as my mother and father joined us.

"Great run, Charlie!" my dad said, clapping me on the back. He'd come straight from a St. Joe's JV football game and was still wearing his SJP colors. My mother, ever the supporting wife, also wore a green-and-yellow scarf around her neck as she enveloped me in a hug, her brown hair back in a loose ponytail.

"You were amazing!" she said, releasing me quickly. She looked down at her fingers. "Sticky, but amazing!" she joked.

I blushed deep red and looked at the ground, avoiding Darla's eye. "Thanks a lot, Mom!"

"I'm sorry! Your brothers are usually the sweaty, dirty, guy's guys," she said. "I'm still getting used to the idea of you as an athlete."

Great. This kept getting better and better.

"Who's your friend?" my dad asked.

"Oh, sorry. This is Darla Shayne," I said. "Darla, these are my parents."

"It's so nice to meet you, Mr. and Mrs. Cox," Darla gushed.

"You as well," my mother said, casting a discerning eye over Darla's outfit. "You were the girl Charlie went out with last night?"

"Guilty," Darla said with a laugh.

I smiled as our eyes met. We had gone to Moe's and ordered twelve different kinds of pie so that I could try each one, and Darla had tasted most. She had joked that she'd brought me there for selfish reasons. Apparently Veronica never stepped foot in the place because she said she "gained ten pounds just from inhaling." It was nice to see that Darla wasn't always deferring to Veronica. And that she liked to eat.

"Thanks for that," my dad said. "That apple pie he brought home was delicious."

"Oh, well, Moe's is the best diner in North Jersey," Darla said. "You would have found that out eventually."

"We were going to take Charlie out for a late breakfast slash early lunch and then go buy him his varsity jacket," my mother said, looping her arm around Darla's and steering her away. "Why don't you show us how to get to this Moe's place?"

"I'd love that!" Darla said, glancing back at me. "As long as it's cool with you, Charlie."

I smiled. "Yeah. Of course."

Suddenly Coach Ziegler appeared in front of me and my dad, grinning from ear to ear. "That was a stellar run, Charlie," he said. "Absolutely stellar. No one on our team has beaten Brian in the last year."

"That's fantastic, son," my father said, his blue eyes wide.

"David Cox? It's a pleasure to meet you," Ziegler said, offering his hand. "Thanks for not turning your son here into a football player. I've never been happier to have a transfer student join our team."

"Looks like he finally found his sport," my dad said, shaking hands with the coach.

"He certainly has," Coach said. "You two have a good day. We'll meet in the gym before school on Monday morning to go over the race with the team, okay, Charlie?"

"Sounds good." I nodded.

"He seems to really like you," my father said, following me to the bleachers to grab my stuff. I was kind of dying for a shower, but my mom and Darla were already halfway to the parking lot. It looked like I was going to have to throw on a hat and a sweatshirt and deal.

"He barely knows me," I replied, swiping some of the mud off my legs with a towel from my bag.

"Yeah, but you're a winner now," my father said, shoving his hands into his pockets and rolling up on his toes. "And everybody loves a winner."

I smiled, but something about the way he'd said that made my insides curdle. You're a winner *now*.

"So, tell me about this Darla girl," my father said, reaching around my back and squeezing my shoulder as I stood up. "And what happened to Stacey? You becoming a heartbreaker on me too?"

I looked down at my feet as we walked. My sneakers were covered in mud. I slipped out of my father's grasp.

"You know what, Dad? I think I'm gonna run inside and shower," I said, my stomach clenched.

"But your mother and Darla are waiting," my father told me.

"I can't sit and eat with them like this," I said, backing away. "It'll be five minutes."

Without waiting for him to reply, I turned and jogged off toward the locker room, my legs quivering beneath me from the strain. I couldn't get away from my father fast enough.

What the hell was wrong with me? My entire life I'd been salivating for my father's approval. And for him to get off my back about football. And now here I was, making him proud. Plus, I had a hot girl throwing herself at me, and I was going to a party this Friday with some of the most popular kids in school. For the first time in my nomadic existence, everything was falling into place.

But all I wanted to do was keep right on running.

CHAPTER TWENTY-NINE

Katrina

"Calculate the value of the cosine in the following triangle. . . ." I read under my breath, chewing on the end of my pencil. "Okay, with the Pythagorean theorem that would be—"

The numbers blurred in front of me, the back of my skull feeling foggy and gray. I was exhausted after a sleepless night, listening to Ty and his friends smack-talk over the latest version of Madden football on the big screen in the living room. As little sense as trigonometry made to me on a good day, it made much less when I couldn't stop yawning. But I had to get this done. I needed as much time as I could buy myself to go over my lecture for English class tomorrow. A thought that made my heart sink so fast I felt dizzy.

Tomorrow. How was I going to make it through tomorrow? My body hit me with a huge yawn, and I shook my head. How was I even going to stay awake until sixth period?

I put my head in my hand and closed my eyes, listening to the wail of a drill in the garage. It was nice of Ty's uncle Gino to let me study in his office while Ty worked, but it wasn't that conducive to the occasional power nap. I folded my arms and laid my head down. In about two seconds I felt myself start to drift off, and in that odd haziness between being awake and being asleep, I saw Charlie. He was sitting under a tree in a blue-and-white varsity jacket, yukking it up with Stacey Halliburn, Josh Moskowitz, and Veronica Vail. Then True walked by, and they laughed even harder.

Why was Charlie even friends with those people? He was so nice. So normal. Why did he have to get sucked in by the popular crowd?

Suddenly the dream changed, and now Charlie and I were back in the band room, facing each other. Except this time I leaned in and kissed that dimple. And this time, he turned his head and kissed me back.

A huge crash inside the garage scared me half to death, and my head popped up. Blinking, I looked at the dingy window over the desk, which I could barely see through, thanks to the dozens of yellowing *Non Sequitur* comic strips taped to the glass. Chubby, balding Gino Rivello of Gino's Auto Body screamed at Ty and his two buddies, letting out a string of curses that actually made me blush. He started for the office, kicking an oilcan against the wall as he came. I quickly sat back down in his ancient cracked-vinyl chair and pretended to be concentrating.

Gino flung the door open and froze. "Oh, Katrina. I'm sorry. I forgot you were in here," he said, putting his hands on his hips. He looked at the floor as if ashamed of himself. The bare top of his head gleamed under the fluorescent lights. "I suppose there's no way you didn't hear that?"

My heart was still pounding, but I smiled at him. "Hear what?"

He laughed and closed the door behind him. His gray overalls were streaked with grease and spattered with paint. He grabbed a beer out of the mini-fridge next to me and sat down at the other desk.

"Trig, huh? I was always good at trig," he said, swinging the chair around to face me.

"Want to do it for me?" I joked.

He laughed. "Not your thing?"

"I don't hate it," I said with a sigh. "But it's not easy. I didn't exactly pay attention in geometry last year."

"Well, you had a rough year," he said plainly.

My heart pinched. Sometimes I forgot that every living person in Lake Carmody knew what had happened to my dad. "True. But the trig book doesn't care."

Gino smiled sympathetically. There was another, smaller, bang out in the garage and he closed his eyes, breathing in deeply. "Isn't there someplace quieter you could be studying?"

I shook my head. "The library closes early on Sunday, and I'm supposed to have lunch with Ty anyway, so . . ."

Suddenly my phone beeped and my heart hit the floor. I hadn't heard from my mom since our argument on Friday, having snuck into our house to get most of my stuff when I knew she was on shift. I'd left her a note saying I was moving in with Ty full-time, and I kept waiting for her to call or text or show up at Ty's door, but so far, nothing. And this text was from Raine.

WHERE ARE YOU? WE'RE GOING TO THE MOVIES!

My whole body felt heavy. Apparently I'd been right all along. My mother really didn't care about me.

STUDYING. SORRY. TTYL?

UGH! LOSER!

I turned the phone off and shoved it into my bag.

"Bad news?" Gino asked, seeing my face.

I shook my head, laughed shortly. "Bad friend."

I didn't even realize that I truly thought that until I said it. But

Raine hadn't called me to find out why I hadn't shown up at our pre-homeroom hangout for two days. She hadn't asked me, in the brief moments we'd seen each other in class, what was going on with Ty. She was always so caught up in her own thing, her other friends, what she wanted to do, that sometimes it felt like she didn't remember I existed.

You could call her and tell her what's going on too, a voice inside my head said—the voice that sounded like my dad's. And that was true, of course. Which sparked the question . . . why hadn't I?

Then the office door opened unexpectedly, clattering against a metal filing cabinet. Ty wiped a dirty rag across his forehead.

"Hey, Kat," he said.

"You ready to go?" I asked, my stomach already grumbling.

He shook his head. "Not gonna happen. We had kind of a setback out there, and we're gonna have to stay late. You wanna run down to Bellissimo and get me and the guys some Italian subs?"

"Oh." I tried not to look disappointed. "Sure. Let me finish this one problem."

"They're kind of starving now," Ty said, holding out a wad of folded bills. "Could you please just go?"

"Tyler," Uncle Gino said in a warning tone.

"What?" Ty's face was pure innocence. "I said please."

"It's fine," I told Gino, closing my book. "I'll go. I'm hungry anyway."

"Are you sure?" Gino asked, giving Ty an admonishing look.

"Positive." I was touched that he cared. The thing was, he didn't know how much I owed Ty. He was giving me a place to stay so that I didn't have to deal with my mother. He paid for half my meals and drove me everywhere. Making one food run was nothing compared to what he had done for me. It was the least I could do.

I stopped next to Ty on my way out the door and gave him a kiss, trying to ignore the streak of grime across his cheek.

"I'll be back in ten minutes," I told him.

I trudged out the back door and walked down the cold, shadowy alleyway to the street. As soon as I stepped out into the sunshine, I had a fleeting memory of the dream I'd had in the office, and my skin warmed. Charlie. Thinking about him brought a smile to my face.

At least he would be there tomorrow when I headed up the class discussion on *Great Expectations*. That was a good thing. Or it would be, if I didn't make a fool of myself in front of him. Again.

Something slammed behind the garage doors, and I saw Ty staring out at me. I swear it was like he knew I was thinking about another guy, however innocent those thoughts were. I ducked behind my hair and speed-walked up the block toward Bellissimo.

CHAPTER THIRTY

True

I bit into a strawberry cupcake on Sunday afternoon, and my taste buds hummed with happiness. This job was the best thing that had happened to me since arriving on Earth. Not only had it gotten me out of the house and away from my self-pitying mother on a day when I otherwise would have had nowhere to go, but I was also surrounded by potential match-ees on a day when I otherwise might not have encountered a soul. And today I was working a full shift, which meant that by Friday I'd have enough money to buy Darnell a new soul-sucking cell phone of his choice. But the best part was the cupcakes. I'd been on break for ten minutes and I'd already eaten four of them. They were perfection in a mini cake.

I was going to have to thank Katrina for sending me here.

I took another bite, and as if my thoughts had conjured her, Katrina walked into the shop, carrying a heavy plastic bag with an Italian flag stamped across the front. She placed an order at the counter, then turned and spotted me. The magnitude of her grin was surprising.

"Hi," I said as she approached my corner table. "You look happy."

"I am," she said. "Guess what? Ty asked me to move in with him."

"Oh." Somehow, I couldn't muster her level of enthusiasm. "Really?"

"Yeah. I was spending half my time over there anyway, so it made sense," Katrina said.

"And your mom is okay with that?" I asked dubiously.

Katrina's face hardened. "She works a lot, so . . . Yeah. I think it's good for everyone. Now she can have her own space."

Even without my soul-reading powers, I didn't believe that positive spin for a second, but I nodded anyway. "Okay. Well, good then."

"Ramos? Your order's up!" my coworker, a gangly guy named Torin, called from behind the counter.

"See you at school," Katrina said.

I watched her go, wishing there was something I could do to make her see how very not-made-for-each-other she and Ty were. But I had a feeling that my advice wouldn't exactly be welcome. Besides, I was here to bring couples together, not break them up. I finished off my strawberry cupcake and reached for my milk. Out on the sidewalk, Darla appeared, peering through the window until she saw me. Her face lit up, and she practically flung herself at the door.

Excellent. People were really excited to see me today.

"You're here! Good!" She yanked out the chair across from mine and sat, wearing LCHS sweatpants, silver flip-flops, and a barely-there white tank top. "Thank you *so* much for hooking me up with Charlie. He's so yummy!"

I sat up straight, my spirits rising considerably. Had I finally done it? Had I finally made a real match? "Really?"

"Totally," Darla said, checking some messages on her phone. "I mean, he totally fell for that 'I hate football' thing, so we hung out on Friday, and then yesterday I went to his race and even met his parents. You were *so* right! Being interested in the stuff he's interested in and *not* in the stuff he's *not* interested in totally worked! And he is *so* sweet and polite and mature. I swear he is *almost* perfect. I can't wait till he—"

I blinked. "Wait a second. Did you say *almost* perfect?"

Darla shrugged and shoved her phone back into her minuscule purse.

"Well, yeah," she said, resting an elbow on the table. "I mean, he could bulk up some, and maybe wear something that's not from a signature line at Kmart. Plus, does he have to carry those drumsticks around *everywhere* he goes? Like, what? A drum set is going to suddenly appear out of nowhere in the middle of the movie theater and he'll just have to play it?"

She laughed, and I felt like I was going to vomit. Which was something I never, ever wanted to do again.

"No, no, no, no, no," I said, regretting that last cupcake. A lot. "Charlie is amazing! He's sweet, he's chivalrous, he's musical, athletic, smart. He's awesome the way he is!"

Darla rolled her eyes hugely. "Whatever. If he's going to take me to homecoming, he's gonna have to step up his game. I mean, am I really gonna go out with a guy who's in band? Not likely. Veronica would *die*."

I gripped the edge of the table with both hands. If I had my usual strength, I would have cracked it in half and hit her over the head with it. Both sides.

"Anyway, listen, since you've been so cool about this Charlie stuff, I think there's something I should tell you," Darla said, lowering her voice and leaning across the table. Her long glossy hair fell forward into the crumbs from my first cupcake—tiramisu—and I didn't tell her. It was the tiniest act of revenge, and it made me feel very slightly vindicated. "Or maybe I should show you."

She took out her phone, hit a few buttons, and laid it in front of me. On the screen was a picture of me, taken from the side, without me knowing. It looked like it had been shot on the first day of school, when I'd worn those painful cowboy boots. The title across the top of the page read, "True-ly Awful!"

My skin seared. Darla touched her fingertip to the screen and flicked to the next picture. It was me on vomit day, wearing the band jacket over the long, gauzy dress and jeans, a photo I was fairly certain Veronica had taken. Then me in my overalls on Wednesday, that itchy plaid vest I'd sported on Thursday, and finally the purple sweatpants and striped shirt I'd worn on Friday.

"Sorry. I thought you should know," Darla said, with a sympathetic click of her tongue.

"Who's taking these?" I asked, furious. "Who's posting them?"

"Honestly? Whoever started the website made it so anyone can post. There are, like, a hundred pictures from farmer day," she said. "Plus the video of when you kicked Ty Donahue's ass."

Something inside me snapped. I reached for the phone, but she tucked it into her purse and under the table. She was smarter than she looked. If she hadn't acted, her phone would have gone the way of Darnell's, and I'd have had to work another week to pay it off.

"The good news is, I can help," Darla said, her brown eyes wide. "You know that boutique up the street? My Favorite Things? Well, I work there! If you come in, I'm sure I can get you a discount." Her eyes flicked over my gray button-front shirt and apron. "We even have bras!"

I crossed my arms over my chest, then quickly dropped them, annoyed over feeling self-conscious. I was a goddess, for Zeus's sake! There wasn't a human on Earth who could touch my beauty. Except for my mother, of course. And as for bras and underwear, those things were purely archaic. The human body was not meant to be so constricted.

I glared around the room and, for the first time, noticed several people glancing from their phones to me, then back again. A pair of boys in green jackets laughed behind their hands. A girl with a million braids in her hair gave me a look so disgusted it was like she was eyeing a pig in slop. I stood up, shoving my chair back so hard it slammed into the wall and shook the framed cupcake art behind me.

"Evil trolls!" I shouted.

Everyone in the shop laughed.

I could smite each and every one of you, I thought, my fists like rocks. *When I get my powers back, I will smite each and every one of you.*

But for now, there was nothing I could do. I turned on my heel and stormed into the kitchen, through the baking area, and into the back room, slamming the door behind me.

At least I thought I slammed it. I didn't recall touching it, but that was probably fury blackout.

"Are you okay?" Dominic asked, opening the door tentatively and sticking his head in. Flour streaked his long nose, and a swipe of red icing decorated the front of his apron.

"I'm fine," I said, pacing the room from end to end, trying to work off my anger.

"This is what I get for hiring teenagers," he said under his breath. "Look, I need you back out on the floor in five. I'm gonna have Torin train you on the register."

"Great," I blurted. "Fantastic. I'll be there."

He shook his head and closed the door quietly. I glared at it, wishing like hell I were anywhere but here. This day couldn't possibly get any worse. Katrina was moving in with Ty, I was the school jester, and Darla and Charlie were clearly a mismatch.

I sat down on the plush couch that took up one wood-paneled wall and hung my head in my hands. This was a nightmare. Clearly, I couldn't make one match without my powers, let alone three. I was never going to get this right. Never.

Orion was doomed.

CHAPTER THIRTY-ONE

True

The sun was sinking behind the shingled rooftops and towering spires of downtown Lake Carmody as I walked home from work that evening, my eyes trained on the ground. Normally, dusk was my favorite time of day on Earth. A time when colors were muted, sounds seemed less harsh, friends met up with friends, and families gathered together again after a long day apart. It was the time of day when more first kisses happened than any other time. But today I couldn't have cared less. Today I hated Earth and everything that came with it.

The kids at school were picking on me. Me. Eros. The Myth. The Legend. The Goddess of Love. No one was ever going to want to be friends with me now. No one was even going to want to be seen talking to me. Darla, bless her weak little heart, had taken a huge risk even sitting down with me today, but who knew if she would ever do it again unless I hit her boutique and bought myself some underwire. Not that I had any money to do so.

If no one wanted to talk to me, it would be a cold day in the underworld before I coupled anyone. As if that mattered. I'd been talking to Charlie ever since I got here, and all I'd managed to do was find him three inadequate candidates.

I took a deep breath and looked up. Somehow, I had walked myself to the corner of a square park near the center of town. A twentysomething couple sat on a bench nearby, smooching over milk shakes. I felt like spearing them both through the chest.

Why couldn't Charlie have that? He was such a great guy. So handsome and accomplished and mature. There had to be someone out there who would love him for him, not for the him he could become with a few tweaks. Why was this so hard?

I turned my back on the couple and walked up the pathway toward the center of the park. Never in my entire existence had I felt so defeated. Even when I'd been banished, when I'd had Orion ripped away from me, I hadn't felt this desperate, because I'd known I was going to find my way back to him. I'd known that I could and would complete the task set before me. But now, my heart felt heavy and sick. I was failing him. With each slipping sand grain of the hourglass, I was failing him. Just as I had once before. . . .

"He's suffering," I wailed at Harmonia, kneeling at the edge of my Earthen window. "He's suffering and it's my fault."

Harmonia put her hand on my shoulder as we watched Orion, who lay on a cot in a small, sparsely furnished cabin. He was curled up like a frightened child, mewling, crying, thrashing in his sleep. I'd had only the time to find him shelter before Aphrodite called me back from Earth. My envy for the upper gods and their powers always burned inside me—a small, irritating flame in my gut—but it now overtook everything. I had to get to Orion, but as a lower goddess, I couldn't go to him without the help of an elder.

"Is there nothing you can do?" I asked Harmonia.

"I've done the best I can, but I can't control his dreams," Harmonia

told me, kneading her fingers before her. "He's seen endless destruction and misery, suffering and pain . . . you must have expected this."

"I didn't expect anything!" I ranted, unfairly taking out my frustration on her. "I didn't even mean to bring him to Earth. Not really. I was just fooling around. I never thought it would work."

Orion let out a guttural wail, and Harmonia and I clasped hands as he spun on the mattress, clawing at the sheets. I was glad I had chosen to trust her with this, my greatest secret. There was no way I could have dealt with the consequences of my actions alone, and I knew that my sister was loyal to me above all else, as I was to her. No matter what, we would always keep each other's confidence.

"He's not equipped to deal with the atrocities he's seen, as we are," Harmonia told me. "Mortals can't process such things as we can. If Artemis knew what she'd done to him—"

"She must never know," I told her, squeezing her hand. "Promise me."

"Of course," she replied. "No good could come of it. Even I know that."

Orion screamed so sharply it pierced my heart.

"You must go to him," Harmonia said, breathless.

"I can't. I've tried. You have no idea how many times I've tried," I whispered.

A stiff, warm wind swept our hair across our shoulders, and my mother appeared on the far side of the window. My heart stopped beating.

"So try again," Aphrodite said calmly.

Harmonia and I exchanged an alarmed look. "What?" I asked. "Do you even realize what I've done?"

"I do," my mother said, with an eerie sort of calm. "It seems you have developed some new powers, Eros."

I scrambled to my feet as Aphrodite strolled around the rim of the window, her white robes sweeping behind her.

"I didn't—How did you—?"

"Did you think I wasn't watching you? Did you think I wouldn't mark what you'd done?" she asked.

She was calm. Too calm. And an unmistakable anger sizzled within her words.

"You are not supposed to wield that kind of power," she said, looking down her nose at me imperiously. "How did you, Eros? Did you make some sort of deal with Zeus? Because deals with Zeus do not come without consequences."

"No!" I replied as Orion let out another soul-shaking wail. "I didn't—"

"Who then? Please tell me it wasn't Hera," she said with a sneer.

My mother's feelings about Hera were well known, although she managed to hide them whenever we were in the royal court. Barely.

"No! Mother, I made no deals. I was shocked when it worked," I told her. "Truly. I don't understand how it happened."

My mother studied me for a long moment, and finally her features softened. I let out a relieved breath. She must have decided I was telling the truth. "Well then. Let us see what else you can do."

She stepped aside, opening a pathway to the window. I looked down at Orion uncertainly. "What do you mean?"

"Go to him," she replied.

Harmonia raised her shoulders. "She's tried."

"Too hard, I'm sure," my mother said with a knowing smirk. "What were you thinking about when you returned him to Earth?"

"I wasn't thinking about anything," I replied. "It was just for fun. I was playing."

"Then relax." My mother put her hands on my shoulders and steered me to the edge of the window. Her hands were warm, and I felt calmer suddenly. Like nothing was wrong. Like everything was possible. *"Don't think about anything other than what you want."*

I looked over my shoulder at her, wondering if this was some sort of trick. Was she trying to get me in trouble? Everyone knew that lower gods and goddesses were not permitted to come and go as they pleased. If any of the upper gods caught me, they could take me right to Zeus for punishment. He could banish me to Mount Etna, or worse, rob me of my powers.

"Don't worry," she told me. "I will cloak you both. No one will be the wiser."

"What?" I asked. "Why would you do that for me?"

"Sheer curiosity?" she replied, her eyes glittering with mischief. "Let's see what you can do, my daughter."

She took a step back and nodded at me. Instantly I was bathed in a cool pink cloud. I glanced at Harmonia. Her forehead lined with concern as she gazed without focus at the spot where I'd been. The cloak was working.

"I'll be right here," she said, unable to meet my eyes.

I knew what she meant. She would keep an eye on my mother and make sure Aphrodite didn't betray me.

I took a deep breath and concentrated on Orion, my arms flat at my sides, as I'd seen many upper gods do before they traveled to Earth. Orion cried out in anguish.

"Orion," I whispered, gritting my teeth. "I wish to go to Orion."

Nothing happened.

"It's not working!" I said, looking at my mother.

"Relax," she told me. "Relax your body, your mind, your soul. Think only of where you want to be."

I took another breath. I felt my muscles relaxing. I tried to quiet my brain. I opened my fists, relaxed my jaw, softened my elbows and knees. I closed my eyes and saw myself at Orion's bedside.

"Orion," I whispered.

Suddenly I felt my hair lift off my shoulders. My skin prickled, and with a blast of heat, I burst into a million tiny pieces. I cried out, anticipating the pain, but it never came. The sensation, instead, was like a pleasant tickle in every inch of my body. And then, just as suddenly, I was whole again. I felt the solidity of the floor beneath my feet. The scent of raw wood filled my nostrils. I opened my eyes. Orion lay before me.

"It worked," I breathed, looking up at the heavens. "Mother, it worked!"

I imagined Aphrodite watching me, laughing at my reaction, but the joy lasted only a moment as Orion gripped his pillow and screamed. I fell to my knees and reached for him. His skin was on fire, and he was bathed in cold sweat.

"Orion, wake up," I said gently, laying my hand against his cheek. "Wake up. It's all right. Everything's all right. You're safe."

With a jerk, Orion's hand darted up and grabbed my wrist. He sat up straight and turned, twisting my arm like he was turning the screws on a torture victim. His eyes were crazed.

"Orion. Please, stop," I told him calmly, resisting the divine instinct to defend myself even as my fingers hummed, ready to smite him. "It's me. It's Eros. You're alive and all's well."

"Eros?" he breathed. He looked down at his fingers and, as if stunned, released me. He turned and drew his legs up on the bed, resting his face in his hands. "I was having this dream . . . this awful, violent dream."

There was a small kitchen against one wall of the cabin. I went to the sink and wet a towel, then returned and pressed it to his forehead. He reached up and touched my hand, holding it against him as if afraid to let go.

"Do you want to talk about it? Tell me what it was about?" I asked. Orion shook his head. "I don't want to think about it."

I knelt at his bedside, considering Harmonia's theory, that Orion would be haunted by all the earthly crimes and wars and genocides he'd witnessed.

"I'm here now," I told him. "And I'm going to help you."

"How?" he asked, taking in a broken breath. "How are you going to help me?"

"I don't know yet," I admitted. "But I'll stay as long as it takes."

A pair of cawing crows brought me back to Earth, and I found myself standing at the center of the park, at the foot of a marble statue—a tribute to war heroes long gone. I sat down on one of the wide steps and sighed, wishing that Orion's nightmares were still my biggest problem. Dotted around the grassy, shaded area were groups of friends and couples, gathered on picnic blankets or sitting on benches near the monument. A pair of girls I vaguely recognized from school sat smoking cigarettes and paging through a magazine. Pathetically, when I saw them, it made me think of how nice it must feel to have a friend.

I needed help, but I couldn't even tell anyone who I really was or why I was here. And Aphrodite clearly had no interest in being of service. Not these days. The woman didn't even eat anything unless I brought her a tray, and if I heard her say it was my fault we were here one more time. . . .

What I would have given to speak to Harmonia right now. Even for a minute. She always knew the best advice to give. Always.

A cool autumn breeze tossed my hair back, and a piece of paper came flying toward me—an advertisement for ten-dollar pies at some place called Pizza City. It flattened against the statue behind me and I stared at it, feeling a small spark of recognition inside my gut. In a rush, it hit me.

"Of course!" Suddenly I was on my feet. "The center of town!"

Harmonia had led me here. I was sure of it. This was where her powers were most potent, at the epicenter of a town or city, the traditional meeting place of the people. I quickly dug in my bag for the small notepad and pen I'd taken from the shop's office earlier today and scribbled a note to my sister.

Harmonia,

I am in desperate need of your advice. Working without my powers has proven near impossible. How do I connect with these people when they have no desire to connect with me? Please send help if you can, and word of Orion.

Your loving sister,

Eros

I tore the note from the pad. Now I needed to burn it so that the winds could take the message to her.

"Hey! Do you have a match or a lighter I can borrow?" I asked the smoking girls.

They looked up from their magazine and one of them paled. "Hello, Vomit Girl."

My stomach turned. Right. That was why I knew them. They'd been in the bathroom that morning I'd thrown up. When Katrina had saved me. They were Katrina's friends. Or not, considering how they'd avoided intervening in her sparring match with Ty the other day. That girl had a hard time noting the true colors of the people around her.

"Vomit Girl, Farmer Girl. What other incredibly original nick-names are going around?" I asked.

The girl with the orange hair smirked. "Darnell calls you psycho-bitch."

"Ah. That's right. I think I like that one the best." I held out my hand. "So. Lighter?"

"Sure." The girl with the huge eyelashes shrugged and handed over a black lighter.

"Thanks."

I walked back to the monument, held the note over the marble, and lit the bottom corner. An unusually large flame flashed, and the paper burned rapidly. I held on to it as long as I could without singeing my fingers, then let the rest of it fall and stamped out the ashes.

The acrid scent of the smoke still curling through the air, I closed my eyes and said a prayer. "Please answer me, Harmonia," I whispered. "I will patiently await your reply."

Then I handed the lighter back to the two bewildered girls and headed for home.

CHAPTER THIRTY-TWO

True

Waiting patiently was not my strong suit. I had sat at the window most of the night next to that awful sand timer, which was at the halfway mark and seemed to be moving faster with each passing day. Unsure of what form Harmonia's message might take, I'd kept watch on the sky until my eyes had finally closed and my head had hit the desk. Painfully. Unwilling to risk further injury, I'd crawled into bed and passed out, still sporting the gray shirt and brown pants I'd worn to work. When Monday morning dawned and I'd heard nothing from Harmonia, I found I couldn't lift my head from my pillow. Outside, cars whooshed by. I heard the rumble of the school bus, the squeal of its brakes. Someone laughed. A dog barked. The bottom of the sand timer was almost two-thirds full. I turned my face into the cool cotton and groaned.

This wasn't Earth. It was Hell.

When the doorbell rang, I was so startled I nearly fell out of bed. I gripped the sheets, hoping my mother would actually lift herself off her beautiful ass and answer it, but then it rang again. I screeched in frustration, knowing she would hear, and trudged down the stairs.

When I yanked open the door, I found a ridiculously handsome guy with cocoa-brown skin in a sleek, chrome-wheeled wheelchair looking up at me with merriment in his dark-brown eyes. He had a duffel bag in his lap and another latched to the handles on the back of his chair. A large flat package wrapped in plain brown paper was tucked into the mesh pocket on the seat, wedged securely in place by the second duffel.

"Hey, E!" he greeted, wheeling himself inside and narrowly missing my black-socked toes. "Heard you're having some kind of breakdown, so I've come to put you out of your misery."

"I don't remember inviting you in," I snapped, still standing near the door.

"Oh, come on! Is that how you treat your old friends?" he asked.

My brow knit. "I'm sorry, but who the hell are you?"

"You don't recognize me?" He spread his arms wide, his brown leather jacket opening to reveal a black T-shirt with some sort of crazy skull art on the front. He wore red mesh gloves, black wristbands, and cobalt-blue nail polish. "I'm crushed."

There was a creak at the top of the stairs, and we both looked up. My mother hovered a few steps down, wearing a flannel nightgown, her blond hair in a million knots. It was clear by the stunned look on her face that she did recognize our visitor.

"In the name of Mount Olympus, woman!" the boy barked. "What have you done to yourself?"

"Hephaestus?" she intoned. "What are you doing here?"

"Harmonia sent me to help you two ladies get your shit together," he said with a laugh. "Imagine my surprise when she told me that between Eros and Aphrodite, you couldn't even manage to earn a proper wage."

"Hephaestus!" I cried, recognition flooding through me. I hadn't seen the god in several centuries, but if memory served, when last he'd been banished from Mount Olympus he'd been sniveling and half-mad and not this attractive. In fact, he'd been flung from Mount Olympus so many times, his legs had been permanently damaged, so that when he did come back he'd had to use a set of crutches he'd fashioned for himself, which, I supposed, was the reason for the wheelchair on Earth. As the divine craftsman, Hephaestus was always working with fire and metals. When last I'd seen him, his skin was constantly caked with grime and smelled of sulfur and melted steel. Now he smelled of leather and something spicy, and it was pretty clear he hadn't sniveled in decades. "You look so different."

He lifted one shoulder. "I put on some muscle, got myself a style going." He adjusted the lapels of his jacket, clearly pleased with himself. "Unlike you two," he said with a wrinkle of his nose.

"You're in communication with Harmonia?" my mother demanded, descending the rest of the stairs. "How?"

He wheeled himself farther into the living room, his expression guarded. "We've found our ways," he said vaguely, wisely choosing not to trust us. "The point is, she knows I've been here long enough that I've learned how to play the game." He turned his wheels to face us. "So consider me your new professor."

"In what course?" I asked dubiously.

"Life on Earth 101," he replied. His discerning gaze quickly flicked over the two of us, my mother in her ankle-length gown, the buttons misfastened, her hair a rat's nest, me in my frosting-stained work clothes—the baggy gray shirt, the ill-fitting pants. "And lesson number one will take place on a field trip. Get yourselves together, ladies. We're going shopping."

"But we have no money," I told him.

Hephaestus reached into the side pocket on his chair, drew out a wad of cash that could have purchased a hundred Darnell-approved cell phones, and grinned.

"Leave that to me."

CHAPTER THIRTY-THREE

Katrina

You're not tired. You're fine. You're fine and your notes make perfect sense.

I stared at the pages of notes in front of me on Monday afternoon, the moment I had dreaded all night and day finally here. Mrs. Roberge had set up a podium for me to stand behind at the front of the classroom, which made me feel less exposed, but also more official. Like I was supposed to say something that actually mattered. As the students filed into the classroom, they looked more awake than usual. More interested. It was like they were excited to see me crash and burn.

Cara and Stacey walked in together. Stacey sneered as they passed me by, but Cara paused.

"Break a leg," she said, almost shyly.

I tried to smile. "Thanks."

"I'd die if I had to go first," she added, biting her lip.

And suddenly I felt like I really had to pee, even though I'd gone right before class.

"Are you ready, Katrina?" Mrs. Roberge asked, taking a seat front and center as the bell rang. Her wide shoulders dwarfed everyone else in the first row.

I glanced at the seats normally occupied by Charlie and True, which were empty. The only two semi-friends I had in this class, and they'd both deserted me in my time of need. Butterflies rioted inside my chest. Every time I breathed in, they scattered again, filling my ribs and choking my throat, then reconvened around my heart to make it pound even harder.

No. I'm not ready, I thought. *I will never, ever be ready.*

Then the door opened, and Charlie slipped in wearing a brand-new varsity jacket, the white leather sleeves so bright they were blinding. As he dropped into his chair and shot me a smile, he looked exactly like he had in that dream I'd had yesterday afternoon. Okay, so maybe it would have been better if he hadn't shown, because now I was seriously going to throw up.

"Um . . . I guess," I said.

"Good." Mrs. Roberge nodded curtly. "You may begin."

I cleared my throat. The printed pages in front of me blurred.

"*Great Expectations*, chapter one," I said.

"Can you speak up?" Stacey asked. "I can't hear you."

My heart constricted and I reached for the sides of the podium. I stared at the pages. "Sorry. Yeah. Chapter one." My raised voice sounded like a shout to my ears. "In chapter one we meet Pip, who never knew his father or his mother."

"Because his father died, right?" Stacey said loudly.

"Stacey!" Cara admonished under her breath.

I froze. My eyes flicked up and I stared at her. How could she say that? *Why* would she say that?

"Miss Halliburn! Inappropriate," Mrs. Roberge snapped. She shifted in her seat, straightening the lapels of her blue jacket. "Continue, Miss Ramos. And there will be no more asides from the class until the question period at the end."

I tried to breathe, but my breath came in broken. My eyes stung and fogged over. My face felt tight. I was never going to make it through this. I was going to get an F and get booted back to my old class. At least Raine would be excited. She'd have someone to cheat off again.

Breathe, mija, I heard my dad say in my ear. *Breathe.*

But somehow, hearing his voice right then made everything worse.

"Miss Ramos?" Mrs. Roberge said delicately.

I gripped the podium. I saw myself gathering my notes and walking out the door. I felt my feet start to turn. Then there was a loud rap. Someone had knocked on their desk like they were knocking on a door. Everyone glanced around, wondering where it had come from. My eyes caught Charlie's. He gave me this look. This mischievous look. And when the class turned to face me again, he held up a notebook. On it, in black pen, he'd written:

All you have to do is get through the next 40 minutes.

He flipped the page.

No one in this room is as smart as you are.

I blushed. He flipped the page again.

Also, every last one of us is naked.

I laughed through my nose, and my hand fluttered up to cover it. "Any time, Miss Ramos," Mrs. Roberge said with a sigh. I had a feeling she was seriously reconsidering the sagacity of letting students run the class. I looked at Stacey, imagining that she was not only naked, but covered in nasty boils. Somehow, it calmed the butterflies. A tiny bit.

"In chapter one of *Great Expectations*, we meet Pip, who never knew his parents," I said again. "This is the single most defining aspect of his character, and will be a part of every decision he makes from page one on."

Mrs. Roberge's lips flicked into a smile. Charlie gave me a double thumbs-up. The clock behind me ticked. Forty minutes. Maybe, just maybe, I could get through this. Maybe it would even turn out okay.

CHAPTER THIRTY-FOUR

Charlie

I didn't get a chance to talk to Katrina after English. She bolted right to the bathroom and didn't make it to econ until after the bell. I was already sitting next to Darla, and Katrina stared at the floor as she passed between us on her way to the back of the room. I hoped she was okay and not worried about her presentation. Because as I had written on my last note to her toward the end of class—she was awesome.

"These are the jeans I was telling you about yesterday," Darla told me, slipping a square catalog onto my desk. On the cover was some shirtless guy in jeans, sitting on a rock at the beach, staring blankly into the distance. "Check out page ten. I think the Ramones are totally you."

"Everyone grab a seat, please!" Mr. Chin shouted from the front of the room. He yanked a stack of papers out of his black briefcase and held them up. "I have here your careers!"

I idly flipped through the catalog. Every guy inside was half-naked. It was like soft porn. I shoved it into my bag as Mr. Chin arrived at my desk.

"Charlie! Congratulations. You're a music teacher!" He

dropped the two stapled pages on my desk as a few people around me laughed. Apparently, teaching music wasn't the most coveted job. But my salary was $52,000 a year. Not bad.

"Katrina, your test pegged you as an author, so I gave you the benefit of the doubt and made you a bestseller. Congratulations, you're the second-highest earner in the class."

Katrina's face lit up. She was so beautiful it made my heart hurt.

"Who's the highest earner?" Veronica asked.

"That would be Darla," Mr. Chin announced. "CEO of a major international fashion corporation!"

Darla squealed and clapped her hands. "NYC, here I come. Bring on the penthouse suites, Mr. Chin."

"Not so fast, Darla," Mr. Chin said, wagging his finger. "Even someone on your salary has to come up with a solid budget and live within their means. Which is what we'll be talking about today."

He distributed the rest of the careers and headed for the board. I saw that there was one handout left and realized True had never shown up today. I wondered what career she'd landed. Matchmaker? I hoped not.

I glanced at the empty chair in the room and realized I sort of wished she were there. Even though she'd been totally off the mark with Stacey and then Marion, I was curious what she'd think about me and Darla as a couple. I'd never even been interested in a girl like her before. But after hanging out with her most of the weekend, I could sort of see us together. She talked about Veronica a lot, but it made sense since they were best friends. Aside from that, she liked music and she was smart and she laughed at my jokes. Plus, she was pretty and my parents liked her and she was friends with my friends. Or the people who seemed like they were going to be my friends. It made sense to go out with her.

But still. I felt like running the idea past someone for some reason. Someone with an actual opinion. And it wasn't like I could talk to my dad, who was already 100 percent onboard. Or my brothers, who were too busy to care. Or Josh, who would probably tell me to shut up and stop thinking like a girl. True, I realized suddenly, was the only friend I had around here. The only person in this town I could really talk to.

And the last time I'd seen her, I'd yelled at her to leave me alone.

"Don't worry about your little job," Darla whispered to me teasingly. She lifted her pages so I could see her salary. "I'll take care of you."

I smirked, but something inside me twisted. Because even though Darla and I made sense on paper, I wished I was sitting next to Katrina.

CHAPTER THIRTY-FIVE

True

"I can't believe those jeans didn't fit," I grumbled as I slipped a light-gray dress over my head.

"That's what happens when you eat a dozen cupcakes a day," Hephaestus called out. Someone in a nearby dressing room guffawed.

"So you're telling me I can't drink *or* eat?" I replied, shoving my arms into the sleeves. Back home I could have eaten five dozen cupcakes a day, plus a roasted pig, a vat of potatoes, and fifteen chocolate-dipped strawberries, and not one millimeter of my body would have ever changed. "I hate this place."

Hephaestus laughed. "Let's see the dress. It's more you anyway."

I checked the mirror. Hephaestus was right. The soft cotton fell half an inch below the knee and cinched in at the waist, the sleeves puffing slightly and the eyelet neckline framing my face. I shook out my freshly conditioned hair—Hephaestus had taken me to a salon that had done wonders—and smiled.

"Are you going to show it to me or what?" Hephaestus asked.

I opened the slatted door and stepped out. Hephaestus eyed me appreciatively. "Add a leather belt and you may have something there."

"It's quite comfortable compared to everything else I've worn here," I said, turning back and forth in front of the three-way mirror. "I had no idea how binding earthly clothes could be."

Hephaestus widened his eyes at me. I could practically feel the woman in the next dressing room listening in. I rolled my eyes and snatched a sweater off the discard rack. It was red—my favorite color next to white—with an open weave and a high neckline.

"What do you think?" I asked, holding it up to my chest.

"That'll look great with the tan cargoes," he replied, backing his chair up a bit as the other shopper emerged from her room, a pair of jeans slung over her forearm. I couldn't believe she'd been in there for even longer than we had and had only found one suitable pair of jeans. Being human really was a trial. "Grab everything from the yes pile and let's go find your mom. I'm sure she's out there terrorizing some poor unsuspecting Gap girl."

The moment we'd arrived at the mall, Hephaestus had sent my mother off to try to find a job, telling her to tell anyone who asked that she was a single mom, recently divorced, who'd never worked but suddenly found herself in need of an income. She'd been so distracted by the display in the window of the YSL store that I was fairly certain she hadn't heard a word of it. Hephaestus was right. We had to find her soon, or who knew what kind of mess she'd get herself into? Hera had probably invited the upper goddesses over for a viewing party to watch her navigate the job search. I imagined them eating grapes together, their heads thrown back in laughter at my mother's expense.

The thought sent an awful, terrified chill down my spine.

"Hephaestus!" I hissed. "What if Zeus is watching us right now? He can't be happy you're helping us."

"Don't worry," Hephaestus replied. "No one up there has paid any attention to me in centuries. Besides—"

"But they are paying attention to me," I replied as I quickly changed back into my velour sweatpants and zipped hoodie—an outfit Hephaestus had approved before we left the house. "What if they—"

"Besides," Hephaestus said pointedly, "Harmonia said she figured out a way to cloak my actions. If they are watching you right now, as far as anyone up there can tell, you're shopping by yourself."

I opened the dressing room door. "How? Harmonia doesn't have that kind of power."

"I don't know how, but if she says she figured out a way, we have to trust her."

He turned away from me, effectively ending the conversation. Unfortunately, it continued right on in my mind. Were Harmonia's powers growing like my own? Or had she sought the help of an upper god? Not my father, surely. Hera? Harmonia did have a special relationship with the queen, regardless of the rivalry between her and our mother. But my sister knew better than to trust Zeus's wife with something as huge as this. Right?

"Don't overthink it," Hephaestus said over his shoulder. "Everything's gonna be fine."

"Easy for you to say. The love of your life isn't on the line," I muttered.

We made our way to the register. My arms were laden down with comfortable but stylish pants, flowy skirts and dresses, colorful sweaters, and a few basic T-shirts. I had found jeans to be far too constricting in general and promised myself I would never ask Orion to wear them again. If I ever saw him again. As I laid everything on the counter for the woman to scan, Hephaestus took out some bills and started to count.

"Where did you get all this money?" I asked.

"I've been working for a long time now," he replied, casting a warning look toward the saleslady.

"Doing what?" I asked, fingering a beaded bracelet on one of the counter's displays. I slipped it onto my wrist and admired the way it caught the light.

"I work on cars," Hephaestus told me. "Bringing wrecks back to life, tricking out old rides. It's my specialty."

"Sounds about right," I said, adding another bracelet to my arm. Back home Hephaestus had been one of the most artistic gods I knew, aside from Apollo. He could forge anything out of metal, and everything he made had a unique beauty unparalleled by anything man had ever created. He'd once made an intricate cup for Harmonia that looked as delicate as glass but was as strong as steel. She kept it by her bedside to this day.

"I landed a new job yesterday when I got into town, down at Gino's Auto Body?" He raised his eyebrows at me, like I was supposed to be familiar with such an establishment. I shrugged. "Gino's a cool guy," he said, eyeing the numbers as they flashed across the register's screen. "But his employees are a bunch of idiots."

The woman behind the counter laughed. Hephaestus shot her a winning smile, and she blushed.

"Anyway, I figure I'll go to school with you tomorrow, see what's up, and try to help you turn things around."

"Thank you, Hephaestus. I can't tell you how much I appreciate you're being here," I said. "I'm honestly starting to think that I have no idea what I'm doing."

"Did you say something humble?" Hephaestus teased.

"This place has changed me," I admitted, sliding a third bracelet onto my wrist. "I thought I was up for the challenge, but . . ." I sighed, my heart pounding with nerves. There was something

I wanted to ask him, but I was terrified of the answer. I screwed up my courage and leaped. "Did Harmonia say anything to you? About Orion?"

The teasing look in Hephaestus's eyes died.

"That'll be seven hundred fifty-five dollars and ninety-eight cents," the woman said as she started to pack my new things into paper bags.

Hephaestus drew several bills out of his roll and slid them across the counter. The saleslady did a double take but quickly entered the bills into her machine.

"Hephaestus, what?" I asked. "What did she say?"

Hephaestus twitched his head, telling me to lean closer. "He's alive. Confined, but alive," he whispered in my ear, sending chills right through me. "Zeus, however, is none too pleased with your lack of progress, and you know what he's like when he's frustrated."

My jaw clenched. I stood up straight. I knew exactly what Zeus was like when he was frustrated. He took it out on every undeserving being in sight. Starting, I was sure, with Orion. I missed him so much. I couldn't stand the thought of him being subjected to Zeus's whims, not after how far he'd come. . . .

I sat at Orion's bedside, his sleep marred only by the occasional twitch. It was four weeks into my visit, and Orion was slowly improving. When he awoke, his blue eyes locked on mine, and he smiled.

"I've already made your tea," I said, rising from my chair.

I had cozied up his quarters over the last two weeks, bringing in warm blankets and thick rugs, an intricate iron guard for the fire, and a painting of a whaling boat from the last century, which I often found Orion staring at when he thought I was busy cooking or baking. Yes, I had basically become a housewife, but it suited me, at least for the moment. *It wasn't something I could imagine doing forever, but for him, for now, I was loving it.*

"You don't have to do this anymore, you know," he said as I poured his Earl Grey. "I'm sure there are far more important things you could . . . you should . . . be doing."

I hesitated, an unpleasant and unfamiliar sensation clawing at my gut. Was this his way of saying he didn't want me here?

"Such as?" I asked, turning to him with a smile.

"Such as matching couples from the heavens, wielding those legendary golden arrows of yours," he suggested, swinging his legs over the side of the bed to accept the steaming cup. "Insuring the perpetuation of true love?"

For some reason, my heart skipped at his last two words. "The world is doing fine without me," I assured him. "When I return to Mount Olympus, I'll double my workload."

Orion sipped his tea, watching me with a pensive expression. When his brow furrowed this way, he looked like a different person. In his first life, he was never serious. Always laughing or mocking or focused on the hunt, but never serious.

"Why do you linger here?" he asked, glancing around at the fresh bread on the counter, the fire crackling in the fireplace. "Why lower yourself this way? You are a mighty goddess. You should not be playing housemaid."

"I linger here because I'm responsible for you," I replied, an edge in my voice. "I brought you here. I made you mortal again. I'm not going to desert you to fend for yourself in the modern world. What kind of goddess would I be if I—"

"I apologize," Orion said, placing his strong hand gently on my arm. "Please, forgive me my queries." He set the tea aside. "I simply don't remember you being this kind."

His eyes were teasing.

"Is that so?" I asked.

"You did match me with Artemis as a joke, did you not?" he asked, raising his eyebrows. "Because she had claimed that loving a mortal was beneath her?"

"How did you know that?" I asked.

"One hears things," he said, for the first time in this millennium flashing that cocky grin I had once known so well. Somehow, I knew it was Apollo who had told him. I had no idea why he had done it, but he had.

"Do you still love her?" I asked.

Orion's jaw clenched, and he stood up to walk to the window, which overlooked the hills of our pretty island, now green with the first buds of spring, and the rooftops of the small village on the water down below. "I haven't loved her since the day she took my life."

"She didn't mean to do it," I told him, clueless as to why I was defending her. "She was tricked."

He turned halfway, barely glimpsing me over his shoulder. "But she knew what she was doing when she hung me with the stars. And for that, I will never forgive her."

A flutter of nervousness warmed my stomach, and I looked at the floor. I felt the blush lighting my cheeks and couldn't believe I was reacting this way. Excited by the mere possibility that Orion's heart was free. I could have read his thoughts, his desires, his needs a thousand times over, of course, but I refrained, feeling somehow that it would be a violation to do so without permission. After everything he'd been through, after what I'd done to him, I felt he deserved his privacy.

"There's one other thing I didn't remember about you," Orion said. He stepped up to my chair, his knees almost touching mine. I looked up, and our eyes met.

"What's that?" I asked, breathless. The fire warmed my face and I felt suspended, as if at any moment I could either drop to the earth like a stone or float weightlessly into the clouds.

Orion reached out, the side of his calloused thumb barely grazing the skin of my warm cheek. "I didn't recall the depth of your beauty."

"Here's your change."

I blinked, startled, as the saleslady slid a few bills and coins across the counter to me. I grabbed them and turned to storm out. The memory of Orion had rattled me, as well as the thought that the gentle, loving, trusting guy I loved was being subjected to untold tortures right this very minute. Thanks to me.

"Wait! Your bags."

The woman hefted two heavy bags up onto the counter. I grabbed them and started, again, for the door.

"Wait!" she shouted again.

"What?" I snapped back.

"Were you going to pay for those bracelets?" she asked, her eyes flicking judgmentally toward my arm. I groaned and looked at Hephaestus.

"Have I mentioned I hate this place?"

Hephaestus handed the woman two more bills. "Keep the change," he said with a wink.

"Oh, no. I couldn't. It's against store policy to—"

"Oh, I think you can," he said.

He shot her one last grin as he rolled toward me, taking one of the bags and hanging it from his chair as we made for the door. I walked right over to the closest bench and sat, hanging my head in my hands.

"How do you do it? How do you live here?" I demanded as

Hephaestus caught up with me. "The clothes don't fit, you have to pay for everything, when you take what you want people take offense. It's impossible."

"You get used to it," Hephaestus said with a laugh.

"I don't want to get used to it," I told him as a woman pushed two screaming babies past us in a stroller. "I want to complete my mission and get the hell back to Mount Olympus. And back to Orion."

"So that's what you'll do," Hephaestus said simply, smiling at a pair of women who blatantly checked him out as they strolled by in their ridiculous high heels. "Tomorrow everything will start to turn around. You'll see."

"What makes you so positive?" I asked.

"After a couple hundred years living on this Earth, you realize there's no surviving it without a good attitude."

"I did it! I secured a job!" Aphrodite was striding toward us with a triumphant grin. I hadn't seen her look so awake, or so upright, since we'd been banished here. She'd consented to a shampoo and haircut, and her shiny blond locks now swung around her cheekbones. Every man in the immediate vicinity drooled as she swept by. One of them even tripped over a potted plant. "You said it was not possible, but I've proved you wrong," she declared, lifting her chin haughtily at me.

"I'm duly impressed," Hephaestus said. "Where is it?"

"It is at a very brightly lit establishment called . . . Perfumania," Aphrodite said, reading from the name tag in her palm. "It smells putrid, but the women working there are universally beautiful, so it was the only place I felt comfortable."

"Well, this is fantastic," Hephaestus crowed. "A new beginning for everyone."

I reached for Orion's arrow and hoped he was right. Because the timer was running low, and my heart couldn't take much more uncertainty. I had made Orion a promise, and with Hephaestus's help, I might finally figure out a way to keep it.

CHAPTER THIRTY-SIX

Katrina

I jogged down the stairs toward Ty's car on Monday afternoon, feeling about ready to skip. It was over. My English presentation was over. And according to that last note from Charlie, I'd done great. In spite of Stacey. I thought I'd bounced back from that pretty well. Thanks to Charlie. Cara had even caught up with me in the bathroom afterward and congratulated me. It was like I was my old self again.

Honors English. I was doing it. I was really turning things around. I felt as if the sunlight on the back of my neck was actually my dad smiling down at me.

"Hey, Ramos!"

I paused at the sound of Raine's voice. Even as my heart slammed a nervous beat, I gave her, Lana, and Gen a big smile.

"Hey! What's up?" I asked.

"Where've you been?" Raine asked, glancing past me toward Ty's car. "It's like you've dropped off the face of the earth."

"Is it true you moved in with Ty?" Lana asked excitedly.

"I . . . how did you hear about that?" I asked.

"Raine told us," Gen said, popping her gum.

234 · kieran scott

I narrowed my eyes at Raine. "How did you hear about it?"

"Not from my best friend," she said coolly. "Ty came into Pizza City the other day. He told me about it while he was having a slice."

"Oh. He didn't tell me he saw you," I said, feeling this icky sourness inside my stomach.

"I guess he has secrets too," Raine replied, crossing her arms over her chest. "So why have you been avoiding me?"

Ty leaned into his horn. I jumped inside my boots. "I haven't been avoiding you," I replied. "I've been really busy. I had this huge fight with my mom, and then I had an English project due today. I haven't had time—"

"For your best friend?" she said, making Lana and Gen squirm. My heart felt sick.

"Yo, Katrina! Let's go!" Ty shouted.

"Looks like you don't have any time now, either," Raine said, lifting a shoulder. "Guess you're too good for us with your honors classes and your live-in boyfriend."

She turned and started back up the stairs, the other girls trailing behind.

"Raine!" I called after her. "Look, I'll meet up with you guys in the bathroom tomorrow. I'll bring the doughnuts."

Raine paused. She turned slowly and looked down her nose at me. "Don't bother. In fact, don't bother coming again. It's not like we have anything in common anymore anyway. Have fun hanging out with the dorks again."

I was still processing what she'd said when she and her friends disappeared over the hill. She didn't want to be friends anymore. Raine had dumped me. In front of Lana and Gen. She didn't care about me or how I felt. And at that moment, I started to wonder if she ever had. Would she have done for me what Charlie had done for me in class today? I almost laughed trying to imagine it. But she was always cheating off my tests, getting me to bring her food, criticizing my opinions and decisions. Suddenly I felt like a complete idiot. For eleven years I had been friends with someone who only cared about what I could do for her.

Ty leaned into his horn for a good thirty seconds. My eyes hot with tears, I tromped down the stairs toward his car. But I refused to cry over Raine. She was right. We didn't have anything in common anymore.

"Hey," I said brightly as I got into the car, trying to regain my good mood. I leaned toward Ty for a kiss, ready to tell him about the presentation, but he didn't turn toward me. Feeling awkward, I kissed his cheek anyway.

"Hey," he said flatly.

"What's wrong?" I asked.

He gunned the engine and peeled out, almost running over a herd of cheerleaders on their way to a bus. I sunk down farther in my seat.

"Gino hired some new dirtbag in a wheelchair who now thinks he's running the place. He showed up for his shift at two o'clock and started changing everything," Ty said, his jaw working as he took a corner like we were in the middle of a NASCAR race.

"Ty, what're you doing?" I asked. "You're gonna crash."

"Don't tell me how to drive!" he barked.

I held on to the door handle, news images of my father's accident flitting through my mind. "I'm sure it'll be fine," I said, hoping to calm him into slowing down. "Gino wouldn't hire someone who wasn't cool, right?"

"Yeah. That's what I thought," he said. "Until the asshole looked at the sixty-seven job and said we had to do it over again. And Gino agreed."

The light up ahead had been yellow for half a minute, but Ty wasn't slowing down. "Ty! Stop!" I shouted.

"What?"

He flew right through the intersection as the light turned red.

"You just ran that light!" I blurted, glancing back over my shoulder.

"Don't shout at me when I'm driving!" he said through his teeth. "God! Do you know how dangerous that is?"

I was putting us in danger? Was he kidding? And had he totally spaced on the fact that I'd lost the most important person in my life to a car accident?

After a few seconds, he finally started doing the speed limit. I gritted my teeth and sat back. Tears stung my eyes, so I stared out the window. Clearly, now was not the time to tell him about my honors English triumph. He wouldn't care and I'd feel worse. I'd learned my lesson after calling my mom with the news of my moving up last week. After Raine's reaction to my switching classes. Sometimes it was better to keep my mouth shut.

I reached into my bag, fiddled with the spiral on my poetry notebook, and thought of Charlie. I saw his messages to me, his big smile, his double thumbs-up, and felt a flutter in my chest as I remembered him turning to that last page in his notebook, the huge letters scrawled across the page.

You were awesome! it had read. A smile tugged at my lips as I leaned back in my seat. *You. Were awesome.*

CHAPTER THIRTY-SEVEN

True

For the first time since I'd arrived on Earth, no one was staring at me as I made my way to the front door of the school on Tuesday morning. They were staring at Hephaestus, who had moved into the first-floor guest room at the house yesterday, unpacked his meager things, and declared himself "home sweet home." Aside from a few stacks of trendy clothing and some manly toiletries, all he had with him was a large mirror with an elaborate metal frame. It looked like something he would have forged back in his Mount Olympus days, with its delicate interweaving vines and leaves and flowers, hewn of metals that varied in texture and color. The piece was stunning. When I asked him where it had come from he'd shrugged and said, "Antique store somewhere." And then he'd promptly changed the subject, which, I assumed, meant he was lying. I wasn't sure why he'd felt the need to fib about furniture, but for the moment, I didn't care. All I cared about was the fact that he was pulling attention away from me. A welcome relief.

Unlike my mother, I'd never been a glutton for the notice of others, and now that I was dressed "like a normal human being" as Hephaestus had put it, and was wingmanned by a gorgeous guy, the onus was off me. As I yanked open the front door so Hephaestus could wheel through, I actually saw one of Darnell's friends lift her phone to snap my picture, but she hesitated and looked crestfallen. Guess she couldn't find fault with the red sweater and tan cargoes. Success was mine.

"The office is down here," I told Hephaestus as we entered the main hall.

A woman was pinning a notice to the bulletin board and dropped a stack of papers right in front of me. I kicked a few out of the way and opened the office door for Hephaestus. When I looked back, both he and the woman were staring at me.

"What?" I asked.

Hephaestus narrowed his eyes. "Sorry. My friend woke up on the blind side of the bed this morning."

He reached down and gathered what he could of the papers, handing them back to her. She smiled and thanked him, then shot me an unreadable look as she bent to pick up the rest. Hephaestus shook his head as he joined me.

"What?" I asked again.

"Nothing," he said lightly.

Inside, a line of three kids waited at the desk in front of Mrs. Leifer. I groaned. We didn't have time for this. I wanted to introduce Hephaestus to Charlie before first bell. I walked up to the desk.

"My friend needs to register," I told Mrs. Leifer.

She barely glanced up. "One minute, hon. It's a bit busy this morning."

"Yeah, and I was here first," said the girl at the desk. She looked familiar.

"Weren't you the one who called me Vomit Girl the other day?" I asked.

"Yeah? So? That doesn't mean you get to cut the line." She glanced back over her shoulder at Hephaestus. "No matter how hot your friend is."

I rolled my eyes.

"True, it's fine. We'll wait," Hephaestus said, angling his chair behind the last kid in line, a guy with spiked blond hair.

I groaned and sat down on the vinyl couch next to the line. It took forever for Mrs. Leifer to sort out whatever these kids needed her to sort out. My foot bounced beneath me and I sighed, watching the clock on the far wall ticking its way toward first bell.

"All right, new student?" Mrs. Leifer said, glancing at Hephaestus.

I stood up, slapping my hands against my thighs. "Finally."

"Watch the attitude, Miss Olympia. I'm doing the best I can," she said.

"Clearly you need to set higher goals," I muttered.

"What?" she snapped.

"Here are my transcripts," Hephaestus interjected, lifting a brown folder toward Mrs. Leifer. "My name is Heath Masters. I'm a senior. Moved here from California over the weekend." He gave her one of his smiles and she was so startled by it, she snorted.

"Oh, well." She opened the folder and looked it over. "Excellent grades, Mr. Masters."

"Thanks," he said smoothly. "I do what I can."

I rolled my eyes.

"Well, we'll need to take your picture for your ID and get your schedule together. You'll probably spend first period in the office, I'm afraid, since we had no advance notice of your coming." She quickly tapped a few buttons on her computer. "And we'll have to set you up with a senior guide."

"Oh, thank you, but I don't need a guide," he said. "I'm pretty good at navigating my own way."

"Good luck with that," I said under my breath.

"Well, it's school policy," Mrs. Leifer told him. But her tone lacked conviction. Wait a minute. Was she going to cave?

Hephaestus angled his chair so he could lean his arms over on the edge of Mrs. Leifer's desk. "Mrs. Leifer," he said in a low, charming voice, "take a good, long look at me. I have no parents. I'm moving in with my cousin and my aunt. I support myself by working a full-time job, on top of getting straight As in every one of my AP classes. Do you really think I'm the kind of guy who's going to let someone else lead him around like a puppy dog? Do you think I'd be comfortable with that?"

Mrs. Leifer stared into his eyes for a good fifteen seconds. "No. No, I don't." She cleared her throat. "Okay, then. I think we can make an exception this once."

"Ha!" I blurted.

She was clearly annoyed with me as she bustled to the end of the counter. "Come on over and we'll take your picture."

Hephaestus struck a pose, then wheeled back over to the couch to wait for his schedule. I sat down next to him, my jaw hanging open. "How did you do that?"

"That woman clearly hasn't had sex in about ten years, plus she has a soft spot in her heart for people who triumph over adversity," he said, nodding at her desk. For the first time I noticed that her wall calendar was from the Special Olympics. Next to it hung a colorful thank-you card handwritten by about a dozen kids. It read, *Thanks for coming to read to us in the children's ward at St. Mary's!*

"I never noticed those things," I said flatly.

Hephaestus tilted his head, considering me. "You know, for

someone whose entire job revolves around understanding the human condition, you are entirely clueless."

My face burned. "I never had to notice these things before!" I whisper-shouted. "I could always read people's hearts. I knew everything about them in a snap. Do you know what it's like to suddenly not have that ability to rely on?"

"Then I suggest you start honing your powers of observation, and fast," Hephaestus replied through his teeth. "That is, if you still want to save Orion."

"Of course I do," I replied, reaching up to touch the silver arrow hanging from my neck.

"Good. And you're also going to have to work on your social graces," he said, crossing his arms over his chest. "Because your problems at this school go way past your fashion faux pas."

"What do you mean?" I asked.

"I mean, I've been here five minutes and you've already completely ignored a woman in need, tried to cut a line, and treated Mrs. Leifer like a piece of dirt," he replied. "You need to accept that you're not a goddess anymore, *True*," he said pointedly. "You're not special. You're not entitled. You're going to need to learn to treat these people as equals."

The bell rang, and the hallway outside the office flooded with students. I watched them go by, the shrieking, texting, chest-bumping, moping, chatting, gossiping mass of them, and gritted my teeth.

Hephaestus laughed under his breath. "And we're also going to have to do something about that sneer."

CHAPTER THIRTY-EIGHT

Katrina

"Miss Ramos?"

I froze at the sound of my name. Mrs. Roberge handed me a piece of paper, folded at the center. She smiled. "Nice work yesterday."

Cara and Stacey stared from their seats in the front row. I ducked my head. "Thanks."

I didn't open the paper until I was seated, safe in the back of the class. I definitely hadn't expected to get my grade back this fast. I held my breath and unfolded the page.

PREPARATION: A
DELIVERY OF MATERIAL: A
PUBLIC SPEAKING: B
OVERALL GRADE: A–

Holy crap. An A–! I couldn't believe it. A huge smile broke across my face as I folded the paper again, then unfolded it to make sure I'd read it right. I'd gotten an A– in honors English. On the project I'd been terrified of from the moment it was assigned. Not only was it over, but I'd aced it!

I glanced around the room, wanting to tell someone, wanting to scream, but there was no one there to tell. At least, no one who would care. Cara might, but she and Stacey were busy whispering and I didn't want to interrupt. Then Charlie walked in. He came right to the back of the room and hovered in the aisle next to me.

"Hey." His eyes widened when he saw my face, the paper in my hand. "Is that your grade?"

"Yep," I said with a grin.

His blue eyes were bright. "Well? What did you get?"

From the corner of my eye I saw True take a seat on the far side of the room. She looked over at us curiously and I was about to wave, but then Darla and Veronica walked in behind her. Darla shot me a look of death, and I felt myself shut down. First Stacey, now Darla. How many girls were in love with Charlie Cox anyway?

"It's no big deal," I said, folding the paper away.

"Are you kidding? It's a huge deal. What did you get?" he asked, sitting down next to me and shoving his bag under his chair.

At the front of the room, Darla and Veronica were now whispering too.

I bit my lip. "An A minus."

Charlie's whole face lit up. "I knew it!" He reached out and shoved my arm like we were old friends. "I told you you were awesome."

My heart felt like it was overflowing. "Thank you," I told him. "Honestly, I couldn't have done it without you."

At that moment, Darla arrived. She pressed the fingertips of one hand into my desk, the fingertips of the other hand into Charlie's.

"Couldn't have done what without him?" she asked with a sour smile.

"Nothing," I said, staring down at my desk.

"Oh, hey, Darla," Charlie replied. "I just helped her out with her English project yesterday."

"Oh, really?" Darla said. "That's so sweet! Isn't my Charlie so sweet?"

I hated her. In that moment I fully hated her. Because it was so obvious what she was doing, and the fact that she thought it would affect me meant she thought I was an idiot. I pulled out my phone and looked up at her. It took every ounce of strength inside me to meet her gaze.

"I think I'll text *my* boyfriend and tell him about my grade," I said pointedly. "He's going to be so excited."

Then I turned my back on both of them and did just that. Unfortunately, I was shaking so hard I had to type it three times over, but by the time I faced forward again, Darla was gone, class was starting, and I didn't dare look at Charlie.

"Are you okay?" he whispered to me as the latest victim of Mrs. Roberge's evil project took the podium.

"I'm fine," I told him, forcing a smile. "Thanks again. Really."

He looked like he was going to say something else, but then Mrs. Roberge shot us a glare and we both faced forward. I felt sick to my stomach. Like Charlie and I had been on the verge of something and now it was somehow ruined. But what could we have been on the verge of? I had a boyfriend and he clearly had a girlfriend.

Suddenly a folded note skittered across my desk. I grabbed it before it could fall off the other side. With a surreptitious glance at Charlie, I carefully unfolded it.

THIS TOOL IS NOWHERE AS GOOD AS YOU WERE.

I snorted and slapped my hand over my nose as the lecturer looked up.

"Sorry!" I whispered.

"You're doing great!" Charlie called out.

And then we spent the rest of the class period trying not to laugh.

CHAPTER THIRTY-NINE

True

"Hey, True."

Charlie caught up with me as I followed Hephaestus through the door into our econ class, the only class we had together aside from lunch, since he'd made himself a senior and I'd made myself a junior. Hephaestus wheeled over to Mr. Chin to show him his schedule, and I moved to a desk near the wall.

"Hi, Charlie," I said. "How are you?"

He seemed surprised I'd asked. "Good. So you're still talking to me? After last week?"

I blinked. "Right! Last week. Our . . . argument. Don't worry about it," I said. "I've had a lot going on. I've barely even thought about it."

"So you're not gonna try to set me up again?" he asked. "Because I kind of have this thing going with Darla. . . . You know, Josh and Veronica's friend? We spent the whole day together on Saturday and most of Sunday, too."

I hesitated. Little did he know he was with Darla because of me. And that she was totally wrong for him.

"Oh, yeah?" I asked. "How's that going?"

"Pretty good, I think," he said with a shrug. "She's cool." He angled himself toward me and lowered his voice. "You know her, kind of, right? What do you think?"

My eyebrows darted up. "You want my opinion? Really?"

He smirked. "Don't let it go to your head. But yeah, I guess I was curious . . . what my friends thought about it."

I grinned even as I couldn't believe how excited I was to be called his friend. And now I could tell him what I really thought. That Darla was okay, but shallow and superficial and totally blind to half his awesomeness.

But then I saw Hephaestus eyeing us over his shoulder and remembered this morning. Perhaps blunt wasn't the way to go. Charlie clearly liked Darla, so insulting her might upset him. But he wasn't gushing about her, so I didn't think I had to either.

"Well, she's pretty," I said carefully. "And nice." This was not a lie, considering how she'd warned me about the True-ly Awful website. "But she's a bit more into clothes and stuff than you, isn't she? Like always worried about how she—and other people—look?"

Charlie's face fell. "Yeah, maybe. She does keep asking me to come to her boutique and shop."

"Me too!" I said.

"Maybe she runs a secret makeover program for new students," Charlie said with a laugh.

"Maybe," I replied. "But anyway, if you're happy . . . I'm happy."

But you're not, so I'm going to find you the right person. I swear, I added silently. If I could possibly figure out who that person was.

Powers of observation, I thought, looking at Hephaestus. *Hone your powers of observation.*

"Well, thanks," he said. "That's really . . ."

Charlie was distracted as Katrina walked by us, clutching her black notebook to her chest. Her gaze was trained on the floor as she brushed by him, and I saw his muscles tense. He followed her with his eyes but didn't turn. There was something about that body language. . . . I felt a subtle tingle down my spine.

"Nice, I meant to say," he finished, chuckling at himself. "That's really nice. So, I'll see you after class?"

Then he turned and grabbed the seat next to Katrina's at the back of the room. She tucked her hair behind her ear and smiled, not exactly in his direction, but there was a definite darkening of her skin as he sat next to her. The tingling intensified. I felt like I was under some kind of spell, and I couldn't move lest I break it. Then Darla came in, saw where Charlie was sitting, and huffily took a seat in the third row.

"You all right?" Hephaestus asked, maneuvering his chair in next to me.

"I'm exercising my powers of observation," I told him. Slowly I lowered myself into the chair, keeping one eye on Charlie and Katrina as the bell rang.

"Listen up, everyone, today's the day!" Mr. Chin lifted a stack of papers from his desk. "These are your compatibility tests! You're going to spend today's class period filling these out, and tomorrow I will announce the names of your soul mates." He paused as he dropped a few of the papers on the first desk. "For the purposes of this class, anyway."

Katrina and Charlie exchanged a fleeting glance, and now Charlie's skin was the color of cooked lobster. Katrina wrapped the fringe on the end of her blue scarf around and around her finger. Darla glanced over her shoulder at Charlie and he froze, snagged. It was a split second, but I saw it. He was worried that Darla had seen him getting googly-eyed over Katrina, and he forced a smile.

Apparently that was enough for Darla, because she faced forward again, grinning. Charlie, however, reached across his desk and gripped the far edge like a marooned pirate clinging to a piece of driftwood for dear life.

This was great. This was *beyond* great. Charlie was interested in Katrina. Now if only Katrina would dump that brutish meathead she was living with and wake up and smell the adorable . . . Gods, this could really be it.

The boy in front of Katrina handed her a blank test.

Please let me get matched up with Charlie.

Katrina's voice. As clear as day. Inside my head. I almost fell out of my chair. Had I really *heard* that? Two weeks ago, when I had my powers, I would have had no doubt. Hearing the voices of the lovelorn was something I lived with every day of my eternal existence. It was something I could tune in to or out of intrinsically, with as much thought as I gave to breathing. But now . . . was it possible? Had I used my power?

I stared at Katrina and concentrated as hard as I could.

Say something, I begged silently. *Please, please give me something else.*

Silence. Awful, disappointing silence. It was as if a wall of ice had gone up between us. I tried Charlie, too, but the only sounds were pencils scratching on paper, and that relentless clock ticking above the door. I must have imagined it. The disappointment was deep, but I chose not to focus on that. For the first time since I'd been on Earth, I felt a match to my core.

Katrina and Charlie.

Charlie and Katrina.

They were both kind and mature. Both artistic. Both considerate.

Both in need of true friendship—true understanding—and looking for it in all the wrong places—Katrina with her so-called friends, who clearly didn't care about her and her clueless boyfriend, Charlie pursuing the popular crowd like being in with them would somehow make him whole.

But if they could get together, if they could be there for each other, they could make *each other* whole.

There were, of course, a few roadblocks. Katrina did have a boyfriend with whom she was currently living, but he didn't hold a candle to Charlie. And Charlie was with Darla, but that was four days old if anything, and he didn't seem particularly excited about it. I could do this. I could fix it. I could spark true love between them. I was sure of it.

Hephaestus had already taken out a pencil and started to fill out his test. I grabbed his arm, my fingers squeezing the hard leather of his jacket.

"Write Charlie Cox at the top," I hissed.

"What? Why?" Hephaestus asked.

I glanced back at Charlie, who was breezing through his test.

"I have an idea."

Hephaestus followed my gaze, then tilted his head. "If you say so."

He filled in Charlie's name and started in on the multiple-choice questions. I wrote Katrina's name at the top of my test and waited for Hephaestus to finish. Then, while Mr. Chin was busy reading, I grabbed Hephaestus's paper. I copied down his answers, making my answer sheet a duplicate of his save for two responses. Then I sat back to watch the clock. With three minutes left in the class, Mr. Chin looked up.

"Everybody finished?" he asked.

There was a general shuffling of feet, but no one said a word.

"I'll take that as a yes," Mr. Chin said. "Any volunteers to collect the tests?"

I jumped out of my chair. "Me! I'll do it!"

Mr. Chin's eyebrows shot up. "Thank you for your enthusiasm, True. Go to it."

I walked around the room, gathering the test papers, making sure to keep mine and Hephaestus's on the top. When I got to Katrina and Charlie, I put theirs on the bottom. Mr. Chin was still reading, and the students were starting to dissolve into conversation.

"What did you put for number three?"

"What was up with that question about the berries?"

"If I get stuck with Daniel DeMarco, I'll die."

My heart pounded as I approached the front of the room, Hephaestus watching me with interest. It was now or never. I "tripped" over Stacey's bag, and the papers went flying. Stacey and her friend gasped. Mr. Chin pushed his chair back. The room erupted in laughter and applause. The one day I wasn't being mocked for my clothes, and I'd gone and done this.

But it was a small price to pay. Before Mr. Chin could even get up from his desk, I folded Katrina and Charlie's papers into my pocket.

"I'm so sorry, Mr. Chin," I muttered as he knelt to help me.

"Accidents happen," he replied. "No worries."

I handed him my stack and he straightened it together with his own.

"You okay?" Mr. Chin asked kindly.

At that moment the bell rang. I smiled.

"I'm fine," I told him. "Thanks. I think this project is going to be very . . . useful."

His eyes narrowed. "I'm glad you approve."

Katrina was one of the first out the door. Charlie stopped to talk to Darla.

"What did you put for the last one?" she asked him immediately.

His eyes darted toward the hall. Longing for Katrina, I was sure. "Um . . . I don't remember."

I joined Hephaestus as he wheeled over the threshold.

"Got the tests?" he said under his breath.

"Yep," I told him, closing my fist around them deep inside my pocket.

"See? I knew you could do it," Hephaestus said. "You, my friend, are an evil genius."

I grinned back. "Only on my good days."

CHAPTER FORTY

True

Please let this work, I prayed the following afternoon, hoping Zeus actually *wasn't* listening in. *Please, please, please.*

Mr. Chin had already announced and "married" five couples, and Charlie and Katrina were still single. But so were Stacey and Darla and a dozen others. This could either go very right, or very, very wrong.

"Our next lucky couple is . . . Darla and Daniel!" Mr. Chin announced.

"Yes!" a scrawny boy in a plaid shirt cheered.

Darla sank in her chair before swinging her legs out into the aisle to join her betrothed. I breathed a sigh of relief.

"Quit worrying," Hephaestus whispered as Mr. Chin conducted his brief ceremony. "You got this."

"Congratulations!" Mr. Chin said to Dan and Darla. There was a smattering of applause, as there had been with each coupling, and Darla dropped back into her chair as Daniel loped toward his.

"Next up we have . . ." Mr. Chin consulted his tablet. "Charlie and Katrina!"

My heart leaped. They both beamed. Anyone in the room could

tell they were smitten. How had I missed this up until now? How had I not seen?

"Dude. Those two are cuter than a pair of YouTube kittens," Hephaestus said as they walked to the front of the room.

"I don't know what that means," I replied, my gaze trained on my latest project. Katrina grinned as she stared at the floor. Charlie rocked from his toes to his heels. He couldn't have stood still if he tried.

"Charlie Cox, Katrina Ramos, do the two of you swear to honor each other, work together, and hand in your assignments on time this semester?" Mr. Chin asked.

Katrina looked shyly at Charlie. Charlie grinned. "We do," they said together.

"Great! Then I now pronounce you seventh-period-econ husband and wife! Congratulations!"

I applauded loudly. So loudly that a few people turned to stare, so I shoved my hands under my butt and pressed my lips together. I'd done it. I'd paired up Charlie and Katrina on a project that would force them to spend hours together over the next few weeks. The two of them were going to fall in love. I was sure of it.

Mr. Chin matched up couples until only Hephaestus and I were left. He gave us a beady eye as he strolled toward our side of the room.

"Now to True and Heath," he said, lifting his chin. "I didn't seem to have test responses from either of you. What did you do during yesterday's class period?"

"Were we supposed to fill those out?" Hephaestus said with a huge grin. "Sorry. I'm new here."

A few kids laughed. Mr. Chin smirked. "Well, congratulations, you two. You're matched up due to mutual laziness." He shook his head. "Good luck in life."

More laughter. Then the bell rang, and we were free.

"Don't forget your first assignment as married couples!" Mr. Chin called after us. "I expect you to come up with your monthly net income by tomorrow and work out a preliminary budget so we can go over them in class."

"Do you want to get together after school?" Katrina quietly asked Charlie as they made their way to the door. Her shyness was so adorable, bringing a pleasantly pink hue to her skin.

"I've got cross-country. What about after that? Around five?"

"You're supposed to come to the shop!" Darla protested, catching up with them. She grabbed Charlie's hand possessively. "Remember?"

"Oh, right. Crap," Charlie said.

Darla's lips pinched like she'd tasted something sour.

"What about after dinner? Around seven?" I suggested. "The library's open late tonight, right, Katrina?"

The three of them looked surprised that I'd interjected, but I didn't care. This was it. This was going to be my first match. It had to work.

"Yeah. I can do that," Katrina said. "What do you think?"

We looked at Charlie. Darla's grip on his fingers tightened until he winced.

"Um, yeah. Okay. Seven at the library," he said. Darla glowered. Charlie didn't seem to notice. He was focused on Katrina's smiling face. "I'll see you then."

CHAPTER FORTY-ONE

Charlie

My hair was still wet from the postpractice shower when I walked up to My Favorite Things that afternoon. It was a small store on the bottom floor of an old house. Most of the mannequins in the window were girls, but the one male was wearing torn jeans and a preppy striped sweater. Darla was somewhere inside there, waiting for me. I looked over my shoulder. I didn't want to go in. I wanted to go to the library and wait for Katrina. I wanted to call her up and tell her to meet me. Now. But I didn't have her number, and I'd promised Darla I'd be here.

The door opened. Darla stuck her head out. "What're you doing? Come in!"

So that was that.

Darla took my hand and pulled me through the store. There was a tall girl with black hair behind the register. "Mira, this is Charlie. Charlie, Mira."

"Hi!" Mira said as I was yanked past her. "Darla's told me so much about you!"

"Um, okay!"

I didn't have much time to respond because I was practically flung into a dressing room. Hanging from a hook were several shirts. Three sweaters were folded on a gold bench. Next to them was a stack of jeans.

"I already picked some stuff out," Darla told me. "Hope you don't mind!"

Then she yanked the curtain shut. I glanced at the price tag on the first shirt, which was blue-and-burgundy plaid. It was seventy-five dollars.

"There's no way I can afford this stuff," I said.

"But I get a discount!" Darla reminded me. I could see her feet under the curtain. Her perfectly shined black heeled boots. "And you don't have to buy *everything*. Just try something on!"

"Okay, okay," I said with a laugh, trying to sound like I was having fun as I pulled on the first pair of jeans. They fit well.

"How did you know my size?" I asked.

"It's something I've always been able to do," Darla replied proudly. "Every year at the street fair I do that thing where I guess people's weight? Last year I earned over five hundred dollars for charity."

"Wow. Cool," I said, impressed that she volunteered. "What charity?"

"Oh, I don't know. Some kids' charity. Veronica's parents are on the board or whatever, so we always end up working it," she replied. "The town does it every year in the spring. You'll love it."

I yanked my sweatshirt off over my head and reached for the shirt.

"So how much does it suck that you got matched up with that Katrina girl?" Darla said.

I froze with the shirt halfway on, staring into its crisscrossed fabric. "Why?"

"Well, because we should have been matched up," Darla replied. "It would have been fun to work together."

"Oh. Yeah. I guess," I said.

"And besides, she's such a burnout," Darla continued.

My teeth clenched as I yanked the shirt down over my head. "What do you mean?"

"Her and her friends, they all hang out in the arts wing bathroom every morning and smoke. And they're so . . . anti-everything. Anti-school, anti-sports, anti-having-fun," she babbled. "No one hangs out with them. They're, like, total outcasts."

"Oh," I said quietly.

I buttoned up the shirt, remembering what True had said that afternoon—that Darla was kind of into appearances or something. Considering where I was standing, what I was doing, and every-thing I was hearing, I was starting to think that was true.

"What's up with her boyfriend?" I asked.

"Tyler Donahue? Exactly! What *is* up with him? He was, like, the star of the wrestling team until he dropped out a couple years ago," Darla replied. "It's like Veronica says, losers hang with los-ers."

I felt a twist in my heart area. Katrina wasn't a loser.

"I thought you defended her the other day. At lunch?"

"Oh yeah. I mean, she's *okay*, but . . . I just don't know. I just wish we'd gotten put together, that's all. Well? Can I see?" Darla asked.

I looked at myself in the mirror. The shirt was stiff, but the jeans were okay. I opened the curtain. Darla rolled her eyes at me.

"You don't button the shirt," she said, reaching for me. I froze. She stepped in really close and very slowly undid the buttons over my blue T-shirt. When she got to the bottom one, she stepped even closer, looking into my eyes. "There," she said, somehow making that one word sexy.

Wow. Tell me how you really feel.

"Now. Look into the mirror."

I turned, and suddenly I recognized the look she was going for. If it weren't for my blond hair and blue eyes, I'd be the spitting image of Josh Moskowitz. I think he even had that exact shirt.

"You look amazing," Darla said, tilting her head into the frame. "See what fashion can do for you? You can wear it to Josh's party on Friday!"

"I don't know," I said, feeling angry out of nowhere. I closed the curtain on her abruptly and yanked down on the shirtsleeve. "I think I should try something else."

CHAPTER FORTY-TWO

Katrina

"What's with you?" Mrs. Pauley asked as I leaned my elbows into the circulation desk that night. "You can't stop smiling."

I blushed down at the gleaming wood surface. I'd never felt my heart pound like this. Not even before my first date with Ty, which hadn't really been a date—more like a group hang. I'd changed my clothes three times before coming here, then felt guiltier than sin when Ty had dropped me off with a kiss and a wave.

But I couldn't help it. Charlie and I were about to spend a whole hour together. Alone. My palms itched at the very thought.

"I don't know," I told her, lifting one shoulder. "I guess I'm in a good mood."

She eyed me shrewdly, but smiled. "Well, I'm glad to see it."

"Thanks."

I heard the automatic doors open and close and used every ounce of self-control I had not to turn around. I could feel someone walking up behind me, though. Could hear the swish of jeans as his legs rubbed together against the silent backdrop of the library. I stopped breathing.

"Hey," he said.

I turned around. His hair was combed farther to the side, exposing his eyebrows for the first time since I'd met him. He wore another band T-shirt, this one heather blue, and it totally brought out his eyes. I gripped the desk behind me with both hands.

"Hey," I replied, biting my bottom lip.

"Oh," Mrs. Pauley said. "Now I get it."

"Shhh!" I replied giddily. "It's a library."

"So get to work then," she chided, picking up a stack of returned books. "I reserved the good table for you."

"Thanks," I told her, sliding my backpack onto my shoulder.

"You get perks around here?" Charlie asked as I led him around the desk toward the windowed alcove.

"I work here, so . . ."

"Oh really? Cool," he said. "You must really like to read."

I slid into one of the hard-backed chairs at the study table. There was, in fact, a small RESERVED sign at its center, and Alison Toshika was hunkered down at the next table over, glaring at me. She loved this table. She was here every day with her laptop and her intimidating private-school texts, grinding away. I tried to hold back a smile. It was nice to have perks.

"Yeah. I do," I replied, feeling self-conscious. Because, of course, liking to read made me a dork. To most people, anyway.

"Me too," Charlie said. "What do you think of *Great Expectations* so far?"

I grinned. "Well, I *loved* the first chapter," I joked.

Charlie laughed. My smile was so huge my cheeks ached. I'd made him laugh!

"But seriously, it's good. The imagery is amazing," I said, tugging out my econ text. "I'm glad the pressure's off, though."

"I'm jealous," he replied. "My name hasn't been called yet."

I was aware of this. Because I couldn't wait for him to go so I could return the favor and help him the same way he'd helped me. I was already trying to think of something good to write in a notebook to flash at him from the back of the classroom.

"So . . . wife," Charlie said with a laugh.

"Yes . . . husband?" I replied, giggling against my will.

He toyed with the cover of his text, opening it and letting it flap closed over and over. "What do you think we should do first?"

I hesitated, surprised by the question. "Oh, I . . . um . . ."

Heat crept up the back of my neck. Had it really been that long since anybody asked my opinion? It was like I couldn't even form a thought.

"I don't . . . sorry." I stared down at my book. "What do you think we should do first?"

Charlie whipped out a calculator. It was like he hadn't even noticed my extreme moment of awkward. The air-conditioning suddenly whooshed to life, and I thanked God and the building's architect for the vent we were sitting under.

"Why don't we figure out what our monthly income is?" he said. "Luckily, I was smart enough to snag me a wildly successful sugar mama."

I laughed. "And I snagged myself a guy who will be home to hang out with me every day after three and all summer long."

Charlie grinned. "Sounds like we're going to have the perfect life."

I smiled back. This couldn't have gone any better if I'd imagined it myself. "Sounds like it."

Then Charlie's phone rang. Alison scowled. He quickly fumbled it out of his pocket, cursing under his breath. "I forgot to mute it."

I couldn't help glancing at the screen and seeing Darla Shayne's smiling face. And her breasts. She'd taken the picture herself, holding it up above her face so that the angle would catch the best vantage on her cleavage.

Ugh.

"How do you turn it off without . . ." Charlie fumbled with the phone. His hands were shaking, and he was clearly mortified.

"Sorry, I guess I have to . . ."

He got up, turning away from me and whispering into the phone.

"Hey! Yeah. I'm here now," he said. "No, I know. I'm only here an hour. I'll call you later." There was a pause. "Oh, um, sure. I'll meet you there." Pause. "Yes, I promise."

"Shhhh!" Alison hissed.

I shot her a look and she sighed, shrugging one shoulder like I was some hopeless cause. And maybe I was. My heart felt like it weighed about a ton and a half. I reached for my own phone and hit a button to bring the screen to life. The wallpaper was a picture of me and Ty taken down the shore that summer. I stared at his smiling face, pressed up against mine.

This was good, this call from Darla. It was a clear reminder that Charlie was taken. And it forced me to remind myself: I was taken too.

Charlie's phone beeped, and he turned it off before shoving it into the depths of his backpack.

"So." He cleared his throat. "Monthly income."

"Right," I said, adopting his new business-y tone. "Monthly income."

It was time to get down to the reason we were here. We were partners in a school project. Nothing more.

CHAPTER FORTY-THREE

True

I would have killed to have been a fly on the wall of the library while Charlie and Katrina had their study date, but unfortunately, I was scheduled to work and Darnell still needed a new soul-sucking device. So instead of watching my work in action, and maybe helping it along, I was busy sugaring up the rest of the teen population of Lake Carmody and doing my best to keep from scarfing down an entire fresh batch of pineapple-mango cupcakes.

"Hi, True!"

My face lit up at the sound of Katrina's voice. She looked happy, standing there under the multicolored lights over the counter.

"Katrina! How was studying? How's Charlie? How did it go?"

She gave me an odd sort of look. My gaze darted over to Hephaestus, who was sipping black coffee in the corner and doing the math on our project. He'd agreed to take it on himself so I could concentrate on "completing my mission and learning to act like a human." His words. Now he gave me a slight head shake, a gesture that I was starting to learn meant that I had to "dial down the crazy." Also his words.

"I mean, did you guys get anywhere on your project?" I asked.

"Yeah. He's going to type it up and print it out when he gets home," she said. "I stopped by to pick up some cupcakes for Ty. He loves the triple chocolate. Can I get a half dozen?"

I experienced an unpleasant sinking in my chest. Where was the effusive gushing about Charlie? The doubts about Ty? What the hell was she doing here buying that oaf cupcakes?

The bells above the door rang and Darla traipsed in, tugging Charlie by the hand. The second they were through the door, he pulled her to him and kissed her. A for-real kiss. Not a mere peck on the cheek.

Hephaestus and I exchanged a dead-eye look. What was *wrong* with these people? I couldn't understand how Charlie could not see that he and Darla were utterly mismatched.

Putting aside the fact that a few days ago I'd thought they might be perfect together.

"True?" Katrina prompted.

"Sorry. A half-dozen triple chocolate."

I boxed up her cupcakes, took her money, and yanked on the strings of my apron. On my way out from behind the counter, I grabbed two more triple chocolates of my own.

"I'm taking my fifteen!" I shouted to Torin.

"Noted!" he replied.

I dropped into the chair across the table from Hephaestus and unwrapped the cupcake.

"I thought you were counting the cals," he said.

"Why bother? Orion's as good as dead and probably me with him." I took a huge bite. "Might as well die sugar-filled and happy."

"So you're giving up?" Hephaestus asked as Charlie and Darla found a cozy booth in the corner and perused the plastic menu, holding hands atop the table.

I grimaced and took another bite. "What am I supposed to do? They just spent an hour together, and she's buying cupcakes for that troll while he's over there rubbing skin with the girl who thinks he's almost perfect."

I stuck my tongue out and Hephaestus winced. "Ew. Table manners, girl."

"Whatever."

He laughed. "Well, at least you *sound* like one of them."

"I'm serious, Hephaestus!" I said, leaning back in my seat. "Tell me what to do. Please. Whatever it is, I'll do it."

Slowly he closed his econ text and snapped the screen of his laptop down. "Okay, so forcing them to hang out for an hour didn't do the trick." He paused and looked at me, like he was waiting for something.

"And?" I asked, frustrated.

"Of course it didn't do the trick!" he cried. "I've only been here a day and even I can see they're both insanely shy. Plus they're both taken and clearly not the type of people who go around cheating on their significant others. And besides, you, *Eros*," he whispered, "should know that true love is formed on more than a physical attraction."

"I know," I grumbled, picking at the now-empty cupcake wrapper.

"So what is it based on?" he asked.

He was testing me. Prodding me. Trying to get a reaction out of me. And I did feel a bit of defiance sparking up deep in my gut. But I wasn't ready to give him the satisfaction of yanking me out of my wallow.

"It's based on a deep understanding of each other," I said flatly.

"A connection of mind, body, and soul. An appreciation for the unique qualities each person can find in no one else on Earth, and an ability to fulfill each other's needs in a way that no one else can."

I knew the words well. I'd written them. I toyed with the second cupcake, spinning it slowly between thumb and forefinger.

"So," Hephaestus said succinctly. "What do you need to do?"

In the corner, Darla laughed. Suddenly I sat up. "I need to show them what they're not showing about themselves."

"Okay. That's a start," Hephaestus said.

My head felt fuzzy and light, warm and buzzing at once. "Ever since he got here, Charlie has wanted to be part of the popular crowd, but that's not who he really is," I whispered. "He's an artist. He's unique. But he's trying like hell to blend in. He needs someone to appreciate who he really is and show him it's okay to be that person."

"And Katrina?" Hephaestus asked.

"She's hurting," I said, swallowing hard. "She thinks no one sees her or cares about her. And on some level, she's right. Her dad died, her mom apparently couldn't give a crap that she moved out, that Ty jerk treats her like meat, and her friends are useless. She needs someone to make her feel special. To make her the center of their universe." I looked Hephaestus in the eye. "And I know . . . I know that if Charlie knew the real her, he could do that. He would do that. He's a good guy. So much better than even he realizes."

I looked over my shoulder at him. He gave Darla a quick kiss, then went up to the counter to place an order with Tasha. He pushed his thumbs into the back pockets of his jeans and drummed a beat against his hips with his fingers. Darla noticed this too and rolled her eyes.

Suddenly I realized something. I realized that I was hardly one to talk about not seeing what was right before one's eyes. Especially after the way that Orion and I had finally gotten together.

I whirled into my mother's chambers one night in mid-March and smiled as I breathed in the familiar scents of lavender and lilac. It felt as if I hadn't been home in ages. But my happy homecoming moment was short-lived. Aphrodite grabbed me by the hair and flung me to the floor. My face collided with the hard, cold marble and my vision jarred, the floral arrangements along the walls vibrating before my eyes.

"What in the name of creation do you think you've been doing?" she shrieked.

"It's good to see you too, Mother," I replied, sitting up and rubbing my jaw. I was used to my mother's sudden fits of violence. They often came out of nowhere and for no logical reason. She'd suddenly recall some slight from fifty years ago and decide to take it out on me. "What have I done this time?"

"You've been gone for close to a month!" my mother railed, her eyes wide. "All this time I have been forced to lie for you! To keep you cloaked from detection!"

"So why didn't you call me back?" I asked.

"Do you think I have not attempted it?" she hissed, her enunciation sharp. "You sent yourself there and only you can send yourself back. You or Zeus. Who thankfully had no idea where you were."

My brain was very slowly processing what she'd said. "Wait. You couldn't bring me back? You? The mighty Aphrodite?"

"I wouldn't mock her right now if I were you," Harmonia advised, appearing at my side. The sight of her sent a shock wave of joy right through me, and we leaned together for a hug. "It's good to have you home, sister."

"It's good to see you, sister," I replied.

She leaned back and arched her perfect brows, the difference in wording not lost on her.

"Where did you tell everyone I was?" I asked, plucking a sprig of lavender from one of my mother's favorite golden vases and holding it to my nose.

"We said you'd gone to Etna to seek out Apollo's advice on some earthly matter," Aphrodite told me, crossing her arms over her chest.

"Apollo?" My nose turned up. "I would never seek out Apollo."

"Can you think of anything else we could have said?" Harmonia raised her palms, her arms wide at her sides. "Any place else Zeus wouldn't bother to track you down?"

I tilted my head. "Good point."

"It's no matter now," Aphrodite said, lowering herself onto a red velvet settee. "Now that you have returned, we can put this whole experiment behind us."

"I trust Orion is well?" Harmonia said, running her fingers over my hair and fiddling with the curled ends. "You left him with all his faculties?"

"Oh, I didn't leave him," I replied. "I'm going right back. This is just a quick pit stop so I can match some couples to keep Zeus from getting suspicious. Then I'll return to him."

I had already started to walk out, headed for my own chambers, when every door and window slammed shut.

"Oh, no you won't!" my mother thundered, her fingers curling into the carved oak frame of her seat. "You dare not return, Eros! You have proven your power. You have done your duty by Orion. It is time to return to your post."

"But I can't just leave him," I replied, turning to face her.

"You must," Harmonia said, reaching for my hand. "You can't

keep this up forever. And if anyone discovers your new power . . ."

I pulled away from her, feeling betrayed. "I don't care! Let Zeus know. What does it matter?"

My mother laughed, a short, barking kind of laugh. "What does it matter?" she asked incredulously. "What does it matter?" She rose to her feet, her blond hair tumbling down her back, and I could see her legs were shaking. "This is not supposed to happen, my daughter. Powers do not suddenly heighten. Upper gods have certain abilities and lower gods have certain abilities. You don't obtain new ones. Not without striking a deal with Zeus or Hades."

"Well, clearly that's no longer true," I replied, lifting my chin.

"And do you have any idea what Zeus will do when he realizes there is something in this realm that has grown beyond his control?" my mother asked. "Do you have any clue what that will do to him?"

"I can't undo it!" I cried as tears filled my eyes. "And I'm not leaving Orion. I won't!"

"Why not?" Harmonia asked, raising a hand to stop my mother's next tirade.

"Because I love him!" I shouted.

Both my hands fluttered up to cover my mouth. My mother's jaw dropped. My sister reached for the nearest column to steady herself.

"You love him?" my mother breathed. "How? Why?"

"I don't know," I replied, my arms falling limp at my sides. "But I do."

"Does he feel the same way?" Harmonia asked.

"I don't know," I replied. "I hope so."

"Why have you not read his soul?" my mother asked.

I looked at her feet, ashamed. "Because. I'm scared."

"Well. Stop it!" my mother asked.

"Stop what?"

"Stop being afraid," she replied. "Go to him and uncover his true feelings."

"But, Mother, you just said—"

"I know what I said, but this is the only answer," she replied. "If he does not love you, you no longer have an excuse to stay."

"But if he does love her?" my sister asked.

There was a long pause. "If he does love her, of course she must stay."

My jaw dropped. "You wouldn't try to stop me?"

"Of course not." My mother was suddenly incredulous. "Not if it is a matter of true love."

I reached out and hugged her. "Thank you, Mother."

"Do not thank me yet," she replied, running one warm hand over my hair. "Find out what you need to know. Then we shall plan."

"So?" Hephaestus said again, bringing me back to Earth. "What're you going to do?"

I whipped my head around and handed him the second cupcake. "I'm going to make them see each other for who they really are." I jumped up, leaned over, and kissed Hephaestus on the forehead. "Remind me to thank Harmonia for sending you to me."

Hephaestus grinned as I ran back behind the counter, knowing I was barely going to be able to contain myself for the rest of my shift—for the rest of the night. I finally had a plan, a real plan, forming in the back of my mind, and I couldn't wait to carry it out.

CHAPTER FORTY-FOUR

Katrina

If you could see
If you could hear
What I really am
Would you smile
Would you stare
Would you still be here?

"What're you writing?"

I slapped my notebook closed as Zadie came up behind me. It was Thursday afternoon and I was killing time at the school library again, hanging out for half an hour until it was time for me to make the walk into town for my shift.

"Nothing. Just . . . a poem," I said, staring down at my hands atop the notebook cover.

"Oh, yeah? Are you gonna submit it to The *Muse*?" she asked, sitting down next to me.

I blushed and shoved the notebook into my bag. "Uh, no."

I let Mrs. Pauley post my stuff on the poetry board at the library, but that was only because no one I knew ever went to the library.

Or if they did it was for a specific reason, and they weren't pausing to read poetry on their way in or out. Plus, she only put the poet's first name and age on the pieces. Otherwise, there's no way I would have let her talk me into it. I wasn't about to let the staff of the school's literary magazine read my work.

"Why not? If it's good—"

"It's not. Trust me," I said. I tapped my pen against the tabletop and glanced at the door. True was headed straight for us.

"Can we talk about something else?" I whispered, tucking my hair behind my ear.

"Sure, but if you ever want me to read anything, I totally will," Zadie said, popping open her laptop. "I'm on the staff, so I can even submit it for you anonymously if you want."

That was intriguing. "Anonymously?"

"What're you doing anonymously?" True asked, arriving at my side.

"Nothing," I said.

"Nothing," Zadie backed me up, typing in her password.

True was clearly frustrated at not getting an answer, and I hoped she wouldn't pry. She stood there for a second, knocking her fist against her hip, and I noticed her dress for the first time. It was a long gray prairie-style dress with a lace-up bodice and gathered waist, which she wore over stylish riding boots. Her hair was pulled back on the sides, and the arrow she always wore around her neck glinted in the sun. Her style had definitely changed since last week.

"Okay, forget it," she said finally. "Do you have two minutes?"

"For what?" I asked.

"Come with me," she said, backing up a step. Her expression was desperate, but somehow excited at the same time, which made me both interested and wary. "Please?"

"Where?" I asked.

"It's a surprise. Come on. I promise it'll be worth it."

I let out a sigh. "Okay . . ."

True bounced on her toes while I gathered my stuff. Then she actually grabbed my hand and led me toward the door. By the time we turned the corner into the arts wing, I was starting to wonder if she was taking me to see my friends. My former friends. They sometimes hung out in the bathroom for a bit after school too. But I hadn't spoken to any of them since Raine had told me off on Monday. To be honest, I'd barely even thought about them. I'd been too busy with Ty, the library, my schoolwork, hanging out with Zadie at lunch, and daydreaming about Charlie.

My steps slowed as we approached the bathroom door, but True kept moving, rounding the corner toward the band room.

That was when I heard the music. Well, not music, exactly. Just drumming. A complicated, insistent beat coming from inside. True pushed the door open very slowly. The thumping rhythm filled the deserted hallway, and now I could hear there was piano, too, though it was mostly drowned out by the drums.

I peeked through the crack in the doorway and my heart caught. Charlie. He was perfectly framed in the opening, pounding away on the drum set in the corner, his head nodding with the beat. He had his eyes closed, and every so often the nod would turn into a wag or a shake as he really felt the music. My mouth was completely dry.

Charlie was a musician. A real musician. Seeing him like this . . . it felt like a privilege. It was beautiful, plain and simple. He was exactly where he was supposed to be.

Although, not technically. His varsity jacket had been tossed over a nearby chair, and unless it had been canceled for some reason, I was pretty sure he was actually supposed to be at cross-country practice right then. Clearly, though, that either hadn't crossed his mind, or it didn't bother him to be missing it.

I glanced sideways toward the piano. Mr. Roon sat at the keys, playing what I thought was a jazz tune and looking over at Charlie appreciatively. The word "jamming" came to mind. The two of them were jamming.

"Should we be here?" I asked True, breathless.

She closed the door and looked up at me. "I wanted you to see that."

My heart was pounding so hard, it was like it was trying to get my attention. "Why?"

True smiled, her gaze on my fingers. I hadn't even noticed my hand pressing into my chest.

"Because," she said. "It's what's true."

CHAPTER FORTY-FIVE

Charlie

It wasn't until I grabbed my varsity jacket off the chair that I looked at the clock. Sonofabitch. How had that happened? Cross-country practice would be winding up in five minutes.

I weighed my options. Run up to the field and plead my case, or sprint out front, grab my bike, and make a break for it. Deal with it tomorrow.

"Everything okay, Charlie?" Mr. Roon asked, organizing his sheet music over at the piano.

"Yeah. Fine. Thanks, Mr. Roon. That was fun."

"Anytime," he replied.

Out in the hallway, a locker door slammed. Shouting voices echoed down the hall. Guys' voices. Possibly my teammates' voices. My stomach turned. Tomorrow sounded like a good idea.

Shoving my arms into the sleeves of my jacket, I ducked into the hall, then out the side door and around the building. A couple of guys in varsity jackets hung out in the parking lot, but I didn't know them. Soccer players or football players. Who knew? But the sight of them made me feel like a bad jock.

It wasn't my fault, though. Fred's friend Scotty had been out sick today, which meant Roon had given me a shot at the kettle-drums during orchestra. When class was over, even Fred had been forced to give me an impressed look—grudgingly, but still. And I was on such a high that when Roon had asked me to work on a piece with him after class, I'd automatically said yes. But I couldn't believe we'd been playing that long. Time flies . . .

I turned the corner and ran for the bike rack. As soon as my lock clicked open, True appeared as if from nowhere.

"Charlie! You have to help me," she said.

I tripped backward in surprise, slamming my shin against a pedal. "What? What's wrong?"

"I'm late to meet Heath at the library to work on our project. Can you give me a ride?"

"I don't have a car," I said, confused.

"But you do have wheels," she replied, yanking my bike from its slot.

I raised my eyebrows. "I guess you could ride on the handlebars. But I've never tried it. You could end up maimed. Or dead."

True grinned. "I'll take my chances."

We both climbed on, and I very carefully made my way down to the sidewalk. It was wobbly at first, but eventually I figured out that if I stood up on the pedals I could see better and keep my balance even. By the time we got to the library, we were both laughing. True hopped down.

"You coming in?" she asked.

"Why?" I said. I'd already turned my nose toward the street.

"There's something I want to show you," she replied.

I narrowed my eyes. "Okay, but I only have a minute. I have to get home, eat, do homework, and be back here to meet Katrina again tonight."

"Or you could just meet her now," True said, starting up the stairs.

My heart thumped. "Is she working?"

True nodded. "Just come on."

I quickly locked up my bike and we went inside. I had the trembly, nervous, blood-rushing feeling I always did when I knew I was about to see Katrina. It was a feeling I never got when I was about to see Darla, but I tried not to dwell on that. Darla was cool. She liked me, even if she maybe did want me to dress more like Josh. We had fun together. And she also didn't have a boyfriend.

I was about to breeze through the lobby and over to the counter, but True stopped in front of a bulletin board.

"Damn. It's not here," she whispered.

"What's not here?" I asked.

Then her eyes lit up. "Oh, this is even better."

"Okay, what is going on?" I asked.

True grabbed me by the shoulders and positioned me in front of the board. Student poetry. Right in the center was a long, listlike piece.

"Read that," she directed.

I sighed. "Are we here to see Katrina, or—"

She grinned. Half laughed. "Just read that."

I rolled my eyes. "Fine."

This was what I read:

> *I am not me.*
> *Not without him.*
> *He made me.*
> *He saw me.*
> *And still*

He loved me.

More than anyone has.

More than anyone will.

It's pathetic.

It's sad.

It's the oldest cliché.

But it is

who I am

Now.

Without him.

—Katrina, 16

I stopped breathing. Then I read it again. By the time I'd gone through it a third time, my eyes stung.

"She wrote that?" I whispered.

"She did," True replied.

I turned to her. "This is what you wanted to show me?"

"Yep," she replied, folding her hands in front of her.

"Why?"

"Because," she replied. "It's what's true."

I turned and looked back at the board. I read the poem one more time. Suddenly I had to find Katrina. I wanted to wrap my arms around her and say nothing. I wanted her to not feel like this.

"Hey, guys."

True and I both turned at the sound of Katrina's voice. She was smiling, but when she saw my face, her eyes darted to the board and she realized. Then she turned gray and was gone.

"Katrina, wait!"

I caught up with her by the bathrooms. She'd stopped before going into the ladies' room, and she leaned back against the wall next to the water fountain. I glanced behind me, expecting to see True, but she hadn't followed.

"Are you okay?" I asked Katrina.

She hung her head. "I can't believe you read that."

My heart was so full that I was terrified of saying the wrong thing. I didn't want to feel it deflate right now. Which was what it would do if I screwed this up.

"It was . . ."

"Stupid? Awful? Sad?" she asked, her eyes shining.

"Awesome," I said. "I could never do that."

"Do what?" she asked. "Be so self-pitying?"

"Put myself out there like that," I corrected. "And it's not self-pitying. It's . . . how you feel."

A tear spilled out onto her cheek, and she swiped it away. I took a step closer to her. "But do you really think that? That no one will—"

I stopped short of saying it. *That no one will ever love you again.*

"I don't want to talk about this," she said, straightening up and sniffling.

I nodded. "Okay."

She flicked a smile. "I saw you. Playing. Today in the band room."

I did a double take at the conversation shift. "You did?"

"Yeah." She nodded. "You were awesome."

"Um, thanks." She was there? How? Why?

She pushed her hands into the front pockets of her jeans and lifted her shoulders. "Have you ever thought about, like, joining a band or something? Because you could. I mean, not that I know anything about it, but . . . I think you could."

I smiled, staring at my shoes. "Thanks."

Then, taking a chance, I turned and leaned back against the wall next to her. There was only a sliver of space between her and the door to the men's room, so our arms brushed. She didn't attempt to move away.

"My dad would probably freak," I told her. "He's never liked the whole drumming thing."

"Why not?" she asked.

"If you met him, you'd understand. He's much more of a sports guy," I told her. "When I made varsity cross-country, he freaked."

She nodded. "That explains it then."

"Explains what?" I asked, feeling, incongruously, offended.

"Why you tried out," she replied. Not judgingly, but matter-of-factly. "I get it. I would do anything to see my dad's face if I could tell him about that A in English. It's not cool, I know, but making him proud . . ."

"Feels good," I finished for her.

She looked over at me and nodded, smiling sadly. "Yeah." Her voice broke. "But now he's gone."

I reached out with my pinky and touched the side of her hand, right near her wrist. For a second, she froze. I held my breath. Every inch of my skin was on fire. Then, just when I thought she was going to turn and run, she slowly, ever-so-slowly, pulled her hand out of her pocket and hooked her pinky around mine.

I bit back a laugh. And for a few, perfect seconds, we just stood there. We held our hands down between us, half-hidden by our thighs, and just were.

"Katrina," I said finally.

"Are you—" she said at the same time.

We faced each other and laughed, pinkies still entwined. "Ladies first."

She smiled. "Are you—"

"There you are!"

Her boss—at least I think she was Katrina's boss—appeared at the end of the hallway. She was the same woman who had been here yesterday when we studied together. Katrina yanked her hand away from mine and stepped forward.

"Sorry. What's up?" she asked.

I hung back. My pinky finger throbbed.

"Somebody moved all the Lemony Snickets again," the woman said, raising her eyes to the ceiling. She tilted her head to see me past Katrina's shoulder. "We have a Lemony Snicket bandit. Whoever it is comes in here once a week and hides them on us. In the bathroom, in the basement, under the trees. But Katrina always finds them. She's like our very own book detective."

I attempted to smile, but secretly, I hated this woman for interrupting us.

"I'm on it," Katrina said.

She cast one forlorn look over her shoulder. At least I think it was forlorn. Kind of hoped it was. "See you later?"

"Yeah," I said.

And then she was gone, and I was left with one seriously warm pinky finger.

CHAPTER FORTY-SIX

True

Charlie and Katrina were starting to fall. Even from the far side of the room I could see it—I could *feel* it. Anyone could have. They were sitting right next to each other at the study table, thigh to thigh, practically pressed up against each other. Every once in a while their eyes would meet, and he'd laugh or she'd tuck her hair back and bite her lip. I had to concentrate to keep myself from standing up and shouting, *Would you two kiss already?*

Charlie glanced at me, and I refocused on my history text. Beneath my chair, my feet did a happy dance. It had worked. My show-and-tell that afternoon had worked. When Charlie had chased after Katrina earlier, it had taken everything within me to keep from spying on their conversation, but whatever had passed between them, it had pushed them over the next hurdle. They were starting to understand each other. Starting to appreciate each other. Growing closer. Falling in love.

This time, I didn't want to count my proverbial chickens before they hatched, but I could hope. Hope like hell that before long, these two would be happily coupled and that damn sand timer would turn over and give me a fresh start.

Charlie's pinky brushed Katrina's on the tabletop, and they both blushed. I missed Orion so much it hurt. But with every touch, every look, every smile between the two of them, I was getting closer to him. I had to have faith.

The automatic door wheezed open behind me. Katrina looked up. Her hand darted under the table and the color drained from her face.

"There you are!"

Ty, apparently unfazed by the universally accepted quiet rule in libraries, stormed across the room. His eyes were wild and his muscles seemed to bulge beneath his denim sleeves. I instinctively stood. This was an angry man on a mission.

"Where the fuck've you been? I've been texting you for an hour," he shouted at Katrina.

"What's wrong?" Katrina asked, standing up shakily.

"I just told you! I've been texting you for an hour!" he repeated, casting a suspicious look at Charlie, who was still sitting in his chair. "Who the hell is this dork?"

"I told you I was going to be here studying with my econ partner," Katrina said, gathering her books. From the tense look she was casting about the room, she wanted to get him out of here as quickly as possible before he could make even more of a scene. "What happened?"

"I just got fired, that's what happened," Ty blurted.

"What?" she gasped.

"Katrina?" Mrs. Pauley emerged from behind the circulation desk. "Are you okay?"

"Of course she's okay," Ty shot back. "I'm here."

"It's fine, Mrs. Pauley," Katrina said, grabbing Ty's hand and leading him gently, but firmly, toward the door. "Charlie, I'll text you later," she called over her shoulder.

Stunned, he lifted his hand in a wave.

"Gino fired you?" Katrina asked as they blindly moved past me toward the door. "Why?"

"That new kid. Heath," he said with a sneer. "Asshole told him I overcharged on the Porsche job and Gino believed him. Now I'm out on my ass and that jagoff is the new manager."

"You overcharged on a job?" Katrina asked as the automatic doors slid open.

"More like charged what Gino *should* be charging," Ty said snidely. "I mean, we're the ones who do all the frickin' work, anyway. Who the hell does he think he is, telling us what we're worth?"

His employees, I answered silently.

I didn't get a chance to hear what Katrina said in response, though. The doors had already slid closed. On the far side of the room, Charlie shook as he stuffed his books into his backpack. My heart went out to him. He was just making some headway with the girl he loved. To be interrupted, and that violently, by the girl's boyfriend . . . that couldn't feel good. He stormed toward me, clutching his backpack in one hand, his jaw clenched.

"Are you okay?" I asked.

"Sure. Fine. Why?" he asked, shifting around.

"Because of what just happened," I replied.

"What? That?" He gestured at the door. "That guy's always been an ass, you know that better than anyone. I just don't get . . ."

He trailed off and shook his head at the floor.

"You don't get why she's with a guy like that," I finished for him.

He blew out a sigh and pulled his drumsticks from his bag, gripping them alongside his hip like a saber. "You know what, forget it. If that's the kind of guy she wants, then screw it. I have a girlfriend anyway. One who actually wants to be with me."

He tromped by me and the doors slid open before him. My heart was in my throat. This couldn't happen. He couldn't give up. Not when I was so close.

"Charlie, wait!"

But he didn't listen. He grabbed his bike and zipped off into the waning sunlight without looking back.

CHAPTER FORTY-SEVEN

Charlie

I was messing around on my drums on Friday after dinner, waiting for Darla and her mom to come pick me up for Josh's party, when the door opened. I looked up, expecting my dad to tell me to keep it down. But instead I saw my brother Corey. His blond hair was clipped short, as always, and he had a cut under his eye. A football injury, no doubt.

"Hey, man," he said.

"What're you doing home?" I asked.

"Came for the weekend." He stepped tentatively down the two concrete steps and chucked his chin in my direction. "Sounds good."

I looked at my hands. "Yeah, right."

Corey blew out a sigh and crossed the wide garage, stopping right in front of the drums. "I wanted to clear something up with you, man."

"What's that?" I asked, still not getting up from my stool.

"Last week when you told me about cross-country, I wasn't trying to insult you," he said, pushing his hands into the pockets of his jeans. "I was just surprised."

I felt a flash of anger and dropped my sticks on the snare.

"Right. Because how could I possibly do anything athletic? Why even bother trying to be as good as you guys?" I got up and walked out from behind the drums to face off with him.

"No! That's not it!" he said. "I was surprised because you've always done your own thing. You never wanted to be like us. You never let Dad browbeat you into playing football. . . . I just never thought you would cave."

I pulled my head back. "I didn't cave."

"Come on. You're telling me Dad didn't talk you into it?" he said with a laugh.

"No!"

"Then who did?" he asked.

I paused, feeling suddenly stupid and completely clear at the same time. My dad hadn't talked me into it, but Corey was right. Someone had. "These guys at school," I admitted.

"Oh," Corey said, looking down at his feet. "Big guys?"

I laughed, shaking my head. "Yeah, but it wasn't like that. It's not like they threatened me or something. I just . . ." I sat down atop one of the unpacked boxes. "I guess I wanted to fit in."

I dropped my head into my hands and groaned. "God! Did I just say that?"

"It's okay," Corey said. "Happens to everyone."

"Not to you!" I said, looking up at him. "You guys always fit in everywhere you go. You never have to try."

Corey sat down on my dad's favorite fishing cooler. "Not exactly," he said. "College is . . . it's different, man. It's different from any school we've been to."

"Different bad?" I asked.

"No. But different hard." He kneaded his fingers in front of him. "But just so you know, I get it, Charlie. And I think it's cool that you're . . . diversifying," he said, and we both laughed. "Just don't forget who you really are."

We both turned to look at my drum kit. "I won't," I promised him.

"Can you keep a secret?" he said.

"Of course."

"Chris doesn't even know."

I blinked, stunned and flattered. "Damn. What is it?"

"I'm taking guitar lessons," he said.

My jaw dropped to the floor. "Seriously?"

He grinned. "Yep."

"Are you any good?" I asked.

"Nope." He laughed, scratching the back of his neck. "Not yet anyway. But maybe over Thanksgiving we can, I don't know, jam together or whatever?"

"Sounds like a plan." I reached out and we slapped hands.

Standing in the center of Josh's living room, I could tell something was wrong. Everyone around me was drinking and laughing, telling stories and checking out girls, but I was watching Fred. He and two other guys I'd never seen before were setting up their gear in the corner of Josh's massive, cathedral-ceilinged living room very, very slowly. One of the guys kept checking the door while he tuned his bass, and Fred looked pale, like he was about to throw up.

"I *know*!" Darla said suddenly, reaching her arm around me. "Don't you love his hair like this?"

She ran her fingers up into the back of my hair and smiled. Josh and Brian smirked. Veronica gave me the once-over. She was wearing a tight black dress that showed off her cleavage. Darla was wearing the exact same dress in blue.

"Okay, I'll admit it. You've done an admirable job with him, D," Veronica said, taking a sip from her red cup. "You picked out the shirt?"

"Yep. I think red is totally his color."

"Totally," Josh said, earning a laugh from Brian.

"What do you mean, an admirable job?" I asked Veronica, side-stepping as a pair of girls traipsed past, holding hands.

In the corner, a cymbal crashed to the floor. For a second everyone got quiet, but then the noise started right up again. Fred glanced around nervously, then picked up the cymbal and attached it to the stand.

"Dude, don't you get it? You've been extreme makeovered," Brian said with a snort.

I looked down at the shirt I was wearing, not the one I'd tried on the other day, but a different one that Darla had brought over when she'd picked me up for the party. It was red-and-black plaid, more my speed, and I was wearing my own jeans. But I *had* let her put gel in my hair. Which was now making my scalp itch.

I heard Corey's voice inside my head. *Just don't forget who you really are.*

Darla's phone beeped, and she released me.

"I'll be right back," I said, grasping my freedom while I had it.

"Where're you going?" Darla asked.

I didn't answer. I was already halfway across the room, annoyed that I'd let her mess with my look. Not that I thought I had a look, per se, but clearly that was a problem for her and her bestest friend Veronica. And I'd let her fix it because I didn't care that much what I looked like. Well, now I did. I reached up and patted my hair down in the front. My fingers came back sticky.

Gross. I wiped them off on the butt of my jeans.

I stopped with my back to the band, pretending to check out the pictures on the mantel. A row of smiling family portraits. Josh and his three older brothers and their parents. For a split second I felt like Josh and I were meant to be friends. I had barely handled growing up with two big brothers. I couldn't imagine three.

"'Where the hell is he?'" one of the guys in the band blurted under his breath. He had a scruffy beard and a huge Adam's apple. The worn Steve Miller Band tour T-shirt he was wearing was half tucked into his baggy jeans.

"All I know is he's missed school for two days," Fred replied, slowly unwinding an extension cord. "He said he'd be here, but ..."

"And he hasn't texted you?" the second guy—the bass player— asked. He was more clean-cut—slick hair, black T-shirt, black jeans.

"No. I know. Dude has bailed one too many times, but don't worry. He swore he'd be here." Fred pulled out his phone. His hand shook as he stared at the screen. "Shit."

"He's out?" Steve Miller Band asked, dropping his guitar strap over his shoulder and letting his ax hang.

"He's out."

All three of them looked over at Josh. And they looked scared. Like scared-for-their-lives scared.

"What do we do now?" the clean-cut guy said. "God! Doesn't he get we can't play without a drummer?"

I froze. Did he just say drummer?

"Can you do it?" Steve Miller Band asked Fred.

He wagged his head, looking at the floor. "You know I can't sing and keep the beat. I been working on it, but ..." He blew out a sigh and his head hung even lower. "I guess I gotta tell him. Get ready to run for it."

"Wait," I said.

Fred turned around. His eyes widened when he saw me.

I squared my shoulders. "I can do it."

"Seriously?" Fred asked.

The other two guys edged over. "You play?" Steve Miller Band asked.

"Yeah," I said. "What's your set list look like?"

Clean-Cut unfolded a piece of lined paper from the back pocket of his jeans. "Mostly classic rock covers, with some newer pop stuff mixed in. For the ladies," he added, lifting one shoulder.

I ran my eyes over the list. "I can do this."

Fred eyed me suspiciously. He was about to ask me something when Darla, Josh, and Veronica joined us. Darla looped her arm around mine and held on. Tight.

"You guys gonna get going anytime soon?" Josh asked, sipping his beer. He glanced at his phone. "'Cause I thought we said eight o'clock, and it's already eight fifteen."

"Sorry, man," Fred said. "We're down a drummer."

"Dude," Steven Miller Band said, gesturing at me.

"No, you're not," I said. "I'm sitting in."

Darla and Veronica exchanged an alarmed look. Darla's fingernails dug into my flesh.

"Why would you?" Fred asked warily. He'd been a jerk to me since day one, lording his seniority over me. I kind of liked that the tables had turned. That now I was in charge and I was helping him out instead of screwing him over—being the bigger man. At least that's how it would look to him. But really I just wanted to play with a real band for once. And okay, yeah, it was nice to help these guys out. They were so obviously terrified of letting Josh down.

"Because I want to," I replied simply.

"No no no no no," Veronica said, shaking her head. "You *cannot* play with them."

"Why not?" I asked.

Behind her, I saw True and her new friend Heath enter the living room, Heath slapping hands with everyone in sight. That dude had made friends quick.

"Because. They're, like, band geeks," Darla hissed, turning away from the others. Veronica laughed. My face burned. Had she seriously just said that to my face?

"Darla, I'm in the band."

"Yeah, but do you have to advertise it?" Veronica said loudly.

"Veronica," Josh said through his teeth. "Are you serious right now?"

"What?" Her blue eyes widened innocently. "I'm just saying what everyone else is thinking."

"Actually, you're not," Josh replied. "If he wants to play, he should play."

"Josh. Come on," said Veronica, who was turning a kind of awful shade of purple. "It's total social suicide."

Clean-Cut's eyes narrowed. "Thanks a lot."

"I'm just saying," Veronica said, ducking her chin.

"You ever think maybe you should just *stop* saying things?" Josh asked.

"No, man. She's right," Brian said, fiddling with the collar of his varsity jacket. He leaned toward me, talking out the side of his mouth like he was in some cop drama. "All the guys from the team are here."

"So?" I replied.

Brian lifted his shoulders with this face on, like the answer was obvious. "So, they don't know you're in the band."

"What's the matter with you people?" I blurted. "Can't I be a runner and a drummer? What's the big freaking deal?"

"It's just," Darla said, bopping her knees like she had to pee. "These guys are . . . you know . . . and you're . . ."

Everyone squirmed except Veronica, who was pouting. Clean-Cut and Steve Miller Band had gone from terrified to looking like they were about ready to throw-down.

"What?" I asked. "I'm what?"

She just stared at me, and suddenly it hit me. She didn't even see me. All she saw was the Josh clone she wanted me to be. And I had let her. I had let her try to turn me into him, the same way I had let my dad make me feel like crap my whole life for not being more like my brothers. Suddenly I was sick of it. I was sick of feeling bad for just being me. I was sick of not sticking up for myself. I was sick of caring what other people thought. Especially the wrong people.

"That's it," I said through clenched teeth. "Who has the sticks?"

Steve Miller Band fumbled behind the drum kit and came out with a pair of drumsticks. I grabbed them, holding one in each fist. It was the first time in forever I had left my own at home. Because Darla had asked me to.

"Let's do this," I said.

"You sure?" Fred asked.

"We band geeks gotta stick together," I told him, staring daggers at Darla. I climbed over one of the smaller amps toward the drum kit, and Fred smiled. I'm pretty sure it was the first time I'd seen his teeth.

"But, Charlie—"

I ripped off the plaid shirt and handed it to Darla, revealing the band T-shirt I wore underneath, a souvenir from this awesome show at SXSW I'd seen last year. I'd had to sneak out to do it, and it was the only time I'd ever been grounded, but it was worth it. And so was this moment. Worth it, I mean.

"You can keep this," I said. "And also, we're done."

Darla let out an indignant noise as I used one hand to mess up my hair completely, then sat down behind the drums. She turned around and disappeared toward the back of the house, and Veronica followed. Fred shot me an impressed look as he got behind the microphone.

"We are Universal Truth!"

I lifted the sticks and counted out the beat. "One! Two! Three! Four!"

It had never felt so good to take out my anger on a set of drums. And as it turned out, Universal Truth might have been a crappy band name, but they were actually a really good band.

CHAPTER FORTY-EIGHT

Katrina

I sat on the edge of the fraying faux-leather couch and stared at the food on the kitchen table. The whole roasted chicken. The bowl of cornbread stuffing, which was Ty's favorite. The fresh green beans I'd chopped and steamed myself. All of it cold and congealing.

The clock read 9:00. It had been three hours. Three hours since he'd seen it, snorted, and walked out with a "Thanks, babe, but I gotta meet some people. I'll be back soon."

I'd tried to do my trig homework, but I couldn't. I was too busy being pissed. Later I'd tried to do my chemistry homework, but I couldn't. I was too distracted by the slowly ticking clock, wondering where he was. Finally I'd attempted to outline my history paper, but I couldn't do that, either, because by that point I was shaking from anger, worry, and to top it all off, hunger.

So now I was just sitting. Sitting with my legs crossed tightly, my arms clamped over my chest, and my bag packed at my feet.

The door at the end of the communal hallway slammed, and I heard the jangle of Ty's keys as he approached the door. I started to sweat. I had to remember why I was doing this. Yesterday at the library, Ty had made me feel about two inches tall and even less significant in front of Charlie and True and, maybe worst of all, Mrs. Pauley. And still, I'd done all of this for him. I'd done it to make him feel loved and special and like everything was going to be okay. But did he even notice? Did he even care?

A few weeks ago, even a few days ago, I might have let it roll off my back, but not now. Now I knew I didn't have to feel that way.

There were other ways to feel. Like proud. Like special. Like smart and appreciated and *seen*.

My bag was packed at my feet, my backpack next to me on the couch. But as the key was shoved into the lock, I started to double-think my plan. I had thought that this was something that had to be done in person, but maybe I should just get through the night and text him tomorrow.

No, Katrina. Don't chicken out. You can do this.

The voice in my head sounded a lot like my dad's.

The door swung open. Ty's eyes were shot through with red veins. He looked at me, looked at the bag, and turned away with a laugh.

"You moving out?" he asked, throwing his keys on top of the bookcase. They slid right off the other side and hit the floor with a clatter. He shrugged out of his leather jacket and tossed it toward the hook, but it landed in a heap at his feet.

I stood up. My knees were shaking. "We should talk."

Ty slammed the door and stormed past me to the fridge, kicking the jacket aside. He cast a dismissive look at the table, then came back with a bottle of beer and downed half of it before replying.

"No," he said. "I don't think so."

"Ty—"

"You're breaking up with me? *You're* breaking up with *me*?" he shouted, sauntering toward me across the stained brown rug. "I defended you to your bitch of a mother! I took you in! And now, when I'm fired and have nothing to do and *need* you, *you're* breaking up with *me*?"

"You didn't exactly need me tonight when I made you dinner and you decided to ditch out and get drunk instead!" I blurted, grabbing my bag off the floor. My whole body trembled in fear, in disgust, in regret. I just wanted to get the hell out of there.

"Oh, it's always about you, isn't it?" Ty shouted, his face turning purple.

"It's not about me! It's about you, Ty. What you want, what you need," I replied, my voice cracking. "You didn't take me in because you loved me or wanted to help me. You took me in because it made you feel good to shove it in my mother's face. You don't care about me. If you did, you wouldn't come to my school and humiliate me in front of the entire courtyard! You wouldn't storm screaming into the library and tell off my boss! All you care about is yourself and your job and your friends."

"That's not true," Ty said, spittle forming on his lips.

I drew myself up straight. "Fine. Then tell me one thing you love about me. Tell me one thing you even like."

Ty's face softened as he looked me up and down, an appreciative gleam in his eye. "You're—"

"And don't say I'm beautiful or sexy or something," I interjected. "Something else. Something real."

He clenched his jaw and his eyes narrowed. He was pissed, because he'd been caught. And he had no other answer.

"I'm outta here," I said.

I shoved the door open and speed-walked down the hallway toward the stairs.

"Fine!" Ty shouted after me, needing to get in the last word. "Just go! I can do better than you anyway, you little—"

I could imagine what he said next, but I didn't hear it. The door to the stairwell had already slammed behind me, and I was gone.

CHAPTER FORTY-NINE

True

"This has to be their last song, right?" I said, clutching the handle on the back of Hephaestus's wheelchair. Charlie smiled as he pounded the drums, having the time of his life. I was happy for him. He'd stood up for himself and was feeling that high. Not to mention the obvious rush he got from immersing himself in the music. But even more importantly, he'd dumped the deadweight Darla. He was now free to find his true love. It was happening. It was finally happening. "What do I do? What do I say?"

"Will you just relax? It's a party," Hephaestus replied. "And your friend there is a pretty stellar drummer."

"I knew that already," I replied, sweat prickling under my arms. I glanced around at the laughing faces, the jostling bodies, the raised cups. "It's hot in here and there are too many people. And why isn't Katrina here? She should be here."

"First of all, Katrina doesn't exactly run with this crowd, in case you hadn't noticed. Or have you still not figured out how high school works?" Hephaestus checked out a pretty girl in a tight purple shirt as she sauntered by. "And secondly, you can't just sit

on your cloud and observe from afar anymore. Humanity is everywhere. Deal with it."

"Ugh. Maybe I won't thank Harmonia for sending you," I
replied.

The song came to a crashing, slamming climax, and everyone
in the room cheered. The fat kid behind the microphone leaned
in, his upper lip glistening. "Thank you! We are Universal Truth!
Good night!"

More applause. Then he grabbed the mic again. "Oh, and we're
available for sweet sixteens and bar mitzvahs. Please come up and
sign your name to our e-mail list for more information."

There was a loud peel of feedback that sent everyone groaning
until someone finally hit the power.

"I'll be right back," I told Hephaestus, pushing my way through
the crowd.

Charlie shook hands with the other guys in the band and chatted with the singer. When I got to the "stage," he turned around
and his whole face lit up at the sight of me. To my surprise, I felt
flattered. It was nice that he was so glad to see me.

"Charlie! You were incredible!" I told him, beaming.

"Thanks! They're not bad, huh?" He glanced over his shoulder
at the other guys, who were huddling in the corner now. "They said
they might have a spot for me. Apparently, the kid who was sick
tonight ditches all the time so . . . I guess his loss is my gain."

I grinned. "That's great. I'm really happy for you."

"Thanks." Charlie's eyes darted past me as Hephaestus arrived
at my side. "Is Katrina with you?"

I reached for Hephaestus's shoulder and clamped down hard,
hardly daring to hope. "No. Why do you ask?"

"I have to talk to her." He whipped out his phone and started texting, then shoved it back in his pocket. "Screw this, do you know where she lives?"

My hands clasped in front of my heart. He'd chosen not to text? I was so proud of him I felt like I could burst. "Yeah. She lives with that boyfriend of hers. Ty."

"Oh." Charlie's face drooped, but only for a second. He cleared his throat and shoved the drumsticks into his back pocket. "Do you know where *he* lives?"

"Unfortunately, no."

"Wait a minute, not Ty Donahue," Hephaestus said.

I squinted at him. "Yeah, I think that's his name."

"That's her boyfriend?" Hephaestus asked, rolling his eyes. "I can find out where he lives." His eyes flicked over Charlie appraisingly. "You sure you want to go there?"

"If that's the way it has to be, that's the way it has to be," Charlie said. "But we'd better go now, before the performance high wears off and I lose my nerve."

"My van's outside," Hephaestus said, backing up. "I'll drive."

CHAPTER FIFTY

Charlie

My heart was pounding, my throat was dry, and my palms were wet with sweat. I rolled the drumsticks between my hands, trying to stay calm, trying not to think about how thoroughly my ass was about to be kicked. Ty was twice my size and, from the look of him, probably a lot more street-smart. I glanced sideways at Heath behind the wheel of his modified van. He seemed pretty tough. And I already knew True could throw down. But I didn't want to have to ask them for backup. This was my fight.

I also didn't want to look like a wuss in front of Katrina.

Heath pulled the van to a stop at the front walk of a square gray apartment building just as Ty came storming out. I gulped.

"Stay in the car," I said, opening the door. "I can handle this."

"Good luck," True said. Somehow, those two words bolstered me. Because I guess she could have said, *Are you kidding?* or *Your funeral.*

"Hey," I said to Ty as my sneakers hit the sidewalk.

He did a double take. His eyes were watery and red, and his fist was clutching some kind of cloth. After a second look, I realized it was the blue scarf with the fringe—the one Katrina always wore to school. It took him a second, but he finally recognized me.

"What the hell are you doing here?" he spat, squaring off with me.

"Is Katrina here?" I asked, trying as hard as I could not to shake in my Converses.

Ty laughed. "Are you the reason she broke up with me?"

"She broke up with you?" True blurted, sliding open the back door of the van.

"Oh, great. The whole freak show is here," Ty said.

"Where is she?" I asked again.

"She went home," Ty replied, looking me up and down. "Which is where I'm going right now. To get her back. You can back the fuck off."

He turned and walked off toward his black Firebird, which was parked haphazardly at the curb a block away. I got back in the van and slammed the door. True slammed hers as well.

"I can't believe she broke up with him," she breathed. "It's all happening."

"What's she talking about?" I asked Heath. Ty peeled out, his engine roaring as he sped past us. He didn't flick his headlights on until he was blocks away. Then he took a right turn at a haphazard, wide angle.

"Ignore her," Heath said, throwing the van into first. "Want me to follow him?"

"Definitely," I replied.

CHAPTER FIFTY-ONE

Katrina

"Mom?" I called, closing the door behind me. My voice broke and my mother appeared at the top of the basement stairs, folding a pink-and-white scrubs shirt.

"Katrina?" She seemed shocked to see me. "Why are you crying?"

She didn't move toward me, but at that moment, I didn't care. I tromped right over to her, flung my arms around her, and just cried. After a second she put her arms around me, too. I could smell the fabric softener as the shirt pressed against my neck.

"I'm sorry," I said into her shoulder. "I just broke up with Ty and I didn't know where else to go."

"You did?" Her voice sounded hopeful, and it sparked something defiant inside me.

"Yeah, why? Are you psyched?" I asked, pulling away.

"If it means you're coming home, then yes," she replied, her dark eyes wide.

I turned away, wiping my cheeks with both hands. "Why? It's not like you want me here."

"Oh, please, Katrina. Not this again." She hung the shirt on the railing and crossed her arms over her chest. "It's you who never wants to be here."

"Why would I?" I shouted. "All you ever do is yell at me and criticize me!"

Her jaw dropped. "That's not true!"

"Yes, it is! You yell at me for making too much noise, for forgetting one time to go to the supermarket, for calling you with *good news*!" I rambled. "I don't do enough around the house, I don't get good enough grades, I don't give you credit for how much *you* do. You want too much from me! It's impossible, Mom! I'm just a kid!"

I started to sob then, my tears mixed with huge gulps of air, my hands clutching my shirt at my waist. Somehow, I hadn't even realized I felt that way until the words had popped out of my mouth. I'd spent so much time acting like I was fine, taking care of myself, feeling all grown-up and sophisticated when I moved in with Ty. But I was just a kid, still, wasn't I? Wasn't I supposed to be?

"I know Dad used to do all this stuff for you because you work so much, but I can't do it all," I continued. "And then there's school and work and my friends and Ty. . . . It's too much! And I miss him too, Mom. I miss him too."

By now I was on my knees on the floor. I felt as if I'd never cried before. As if every tear was being wrenched out of me right now and they would never, ever stop.

"Oh, Katrina," my mother breathed.

And then she was on the floor in front of me, her knees even with mine. She wrapped her arms around me awkwardly, and we leaned into each other. It took me a minute to realize that she was crying too, just as hard as I was.

"I'm so sorry, Katrina," my mother said, sniffling. "I didn't realize . . . I put too much pressure on you, I guess. I didn't know."

"It's okay," I said automatically.

"No, it's not." She shook her head. "I'm sorry. I—I'll take a few days off. Maybe we should talk to that man at your school. Dr.—"

"No. Not him," I said.

She blinked. "Okay, but someone. I know some people through the hospital. They offered me grief counseling last year, but I—"

"Didn't want to talk about it," we said at the same time.

We shared a wavering smile.

"I'm thinking that maybe wasn't such a great idea."

I nodded and wiped my eyes. "Maybe not."

Suddenly the front door opened and Ty stood there, his shoulders practically filling the doorway. He took one look at us and sneered. My favorite scarf, the blue-and-white one my dad had given me on my fourteenth birthday, was clutched in his fist.

"You've got to be kidding me," he said.

"What're you doing here?" I asked, scrambling to my feet.

"I came to take you home." He crossed the room in two long strides and grabbed my arm with his free hand.

"I *am* home," I replied, squirming from his grasp.

"Yeah, right." He latched onto me again, harder this time. "Let's go."

"Get off of her!" my mother shouted, trying to pry us apart.

"Don't touch me," he spat at her. "We're going."

"No, we're not!" I replied. "Let go of me, Ty."

The doorway darkened. I could hardly even wrap my brain around what I was seeing. It was Charlie, and he was staring at Ty's hand on my arm.

"You again?" Ty chuckled.

"Let go of her, man," Charlie replied.

Then Ty did let go of me. He dropped my scarf and took a swing at Charlie. I screamed as his fist cracked against Charlie's jaw. He fell into the couch, and I was just going to see if he was okay when he shoved himself up and hit Ty so hard in the stomach that Ty hit the ground.

"Charlie!" I shouted, stunned. My mother grabbed the phone and dialed.

Charlie looked down at his fist. "I—I didn't even know I was going to do that."

"*How* did you do that?" I asked.

His eyes were wide as he looked at me. "I guess I learned something growing up with two big brothers."

Ty pushed himself up to his knees, clutching his stomach. "You. Are so dead," he said between gasps.

"I'd rethink that if I were you," my mother replied. "I've already got the police on the line." She spoke into the phone. "Yes, my daughter's ex-boyfriend is here, and he's making threats."

"That's your cue to leave," Charlie said to Ty.

"I'm not going anywhere," Ty said.

My mother covered the receiver. "You want me to tell them you actually hit this boy? That you laid hands on Katrina?" she hissed.

"For the second time," Charlie put in, rubbing his jaw.

"What?" Mom blurted. "Katrina?"

I looked away. The last thing I wanted to do right now was try to explain what had happened at school that day.

"Get out of here now or I'm pressing charges," my mother told Ty. I'd never seen her look so fierce. Her teeth were clenched and her grip on the phone so tight it was like she was trying to strangle it.

Ty looked around at the three of us.

"Ma'am?" I heard a voice saying though the phone. "Ma'am? Are you still there?"

"Fine," Ty said finally. "Screw you." Then he looked me right in the eye. "Never call me again."

Like that was going to be an issue. I had a feeling that in some way, Ty really did love me. At least he thought he did. But his kind of love wasn't good enough. Not anymore. He walked out and slammed the door behind him.

"Yes," my mother said into the phone. "I'm still here." She gave my hand a squeeze, then walked into the kitchen, where we couldn't hear her.

"Are you okay?" Charlie asked me, running his hand gently down my arm. I stared down at my scarf on the floor, my bottom lip quivering.

"I'm fine," I said as one tear rolled down my cheek. "Except I feel like an idiot."

"You're not an idiot." He dipped down to pick up the scarf and held it gently with both hands. "I am."

"What do you mean? You just saved me." I glanced at the door. "How exactly did that happen, anyway?"

"Long story," Charlie said. "And I'm an idiot because there's something I've been wanting to tell you since the first time I saw you."

"What?" I asked.

"You deserve way better than that guy," he said, chucking a thumb over his shoulder.

I laughed and looked him in the eye, my throat tight. "I know."

Slowly Charlie smiled. He hooked his pinky around mine and

tugged me toward him. My heart caught, and I suddenly realized that I had dried tears under my eyes, that my nose was swollen, that my hair was sticking to my neck. Then he leaned in and pressed his lips against mine and I didn't care. I didn't care about anything other than him. And as he gently slipped my scarf around my shoulders, I somehow knew that he felt the same way about me.

CHAPTER FIFTY-TWO

True

"Now that is the kiss of true love," I said with a sigh.

Standing on the sidewalk a few steps down from the living room window was not the best vantage point, but I could see enough, and I knew. Charlie and Katrina were in love. I knew it in my swollen, pounding heart and the lightness within my lungs. A lightness that felt a lot like relief. When they parted, Charlie pulled Katrina to him, and she rested her cheek against his chest, her eyes closed, her lips curled into a sweet, contented smile.

"You about done now, voyeur?" Hephaestus asked, rubbing my back.

"Yeah. Let's go," I told him as Charlie and Katrina settled down on the couch together. "I have a feeling Charlie's going to stay a while."

Back home, I tore up the stairs and into my room. The timer had turned, the top filled once again with red sand. I squealed and twirled in the center of my room, tilting my head up to the sky.

"Thank you, thank you, thank you!"

In my mind I pictured Harmonia, knowing she was looking

down on me and doing a happy dance too. But if Zeus thought the gratitude was meant for him, even better. I was done being proud. After seeing that kiss between Charlie and Katrina, all I could think about was my first kiss with Orion, and what it would feel like to kiss him again.

I hovered among the trees outside the home we'd made for ourselves in Maine, cloaked from view, and watched Orion as he tore through the woods, his steps swift and silent, his eyes focused on his prey, a lone gray deer. Gripped in one hand was the bow I'd brought for him, the arrow poised, but not taut. He was waiting for his moment.

From time to time I returned to our island without him knowing, just so I could see him in his natural state—so I could make sure he really was improving and not just putting on a show for me. Today he was clearly feeling well, but still, I didn't want him to know I was there. He was so beautiful in the midst of a hunt. So alive and pure and strong. It had been about three thousand years since I'd seen him look so free.

And then Orion came to a clearing and tripped. A huge black bear let out a bloodcurdling roar and stood up on its hind legs. At full height, it was at least ten feet tall. It was the sight of the beast that had tripped Orion, but I hadn't seen it until it was too late.

It all happened in a millisecond. Orion lay prostrate on the ground, wisely frozen, his chest heaving as he stared up at the bear. I saw something flicker in the eyes of the predator, its primal instincts set to kill, and without even thinking, I slipped a silver-tipped arrow from my quiver, took aim, and pierced its heart. The bear let out an awful, wailing moan and dropped to the ground. Dead.

Orion sprang to his feet as I materialized in front of him. We stared into each other's eyes, both heaving in broken breaths, both charged with adrenaline. I took two steps, he took two steps, and suddenly we were in each other's arms. I kissed Orion for the first time, while still blinking back tears of terror, still trying to convince my heart that he'd survived. He kissed me for the first time, knowing I'd saved his life, realizing somewhere deep inside him that I was always there.

When he finally pulled away, his fingers were tangled up in my hair.

"I was sure I was dead," he said, searching my eyes.

"I will never let that happen," I promised him. "Not if I can help it."

"The timer's turned?" Hephaestus called up the stairs.

As I blinked myself back to the now, the timer came into focus. I raced out into the hallway and over to the landing, the echo of my promise to Orion still ringing in my ears. Hephaestus sat in front of the bottom step, smiling up at me.

"It's turned," I told him, my hair spilling over my shoulder. "Thank you, Hephaestus. I couldn't have done it without you."

"My pleasure," he said. "I'm gonna hit the sheets. Early day tomorrow at Gino's."

"I'm kind of tired too," I lied. I was far too shot through with adrenaline to sleep. "I'll see you in the morning."

"Congratulations, Eros," Hephaestus said sincerely. "You still got it. You just had to find it."

"Thanks," I replied.

I traipsed back to my room, light on my feet and in my heart. Hopefully, Hephaestus was right, and now that I had my matching mojo back, the next coupling would be that much easier. I twirled into my room and, just for fun, flicked my hand at the door.

It closed.

My heart hit my throat. I stared at my hand. That was just an illusion, right? I'd touched the door and hadn't realized it.

I turned to the window and flicked my hand again. The curtains fell over the panes, blocking out the lights on the street.

I stumbled back, startled. My fingertips tingled. I flicked them at my bed, and the blankets straightened themselves, the pillows plumping and lining up just as I'd imagined them in my mind.

My powers were back. My *powers* were *back*! But why? How? Perhaps Zeus had gifted them to me as a reward for finally succeeding with Charlie. But that wasn't exactly his style. He'd sent me here to watch me squirm. Sprouting zits, forming awful headaches, being mocked by my peers, and failing three times, but then succeeding under the wire . . . that wouldn't be enough for him, would it? Surely he would rather I continue on my mission in relative misery and not try to make it easier for me. But there was no denying what I'd just done. I stared at my warm fingers and could have sworn I saw a hazy glow beneath my skin.

A laugh bubbled up inside of me, burbling out and filling the room. I didn't care how my powers had returned. What mattered was they were back. And with their help, I'd be out of this place in a day.

"What are you about?"

I hadn't heard the door behind me open. Ever so slowly I turned around to face my mother, pushing my hands casually under my arms. She stood in the center of the threshold in her work outfit— black pencil skirt, white silk shirt—her beautiful face blank.

"I'm . . . nothing," I told her. "I just got home. How was work?"

Her steely-blue eyes flicked over me and narrowed. She leaned one shoulder against the doorjamb and crossed her arms at her waist.

"It was abysmally dull," she replied. "Were you aware that the majority of the populace is severely unhinged?"

"I can't argue with that," I said, my fingertips on fire.

"And they speak so . . . familiarly," she said, scrunching her nose. "Is there no decorum in this modern age?"

"It doesn't seem so, no," I replied.

At least she hadn't seen anything. I'd known my mother long enough to know her ways. If she'd seen me use my power, she wouldn't be acting cool. She'd be demanding I do it again and that I try out my other powers. Which was exactly what I needed to do.

"I see your timer has refreshed," my mother said casually. "Have you finally managed to form true love?"

I bit down on my tongue at the thinly veiled negative commentary. "Yes! I did. I'm one third of the way there."

"Thank the gods," my mother said, looking to the heavens.

"You know, you could be a tad more compassionate," I told her. "You *are* my mother, and I *am* working my butt off over here."

"Oh, daughter, dear. Must I remind you?" she sang, putting her hand on the doorknob.

"I know. I know. I'm the one who got us sent here," I replied.

She smirked as she closed the door, and I wondered if she'd ever forgive me for visiting this great shame upon her, for getting her banished to Earth like some criminal. I flicked my hand at it, and the lock turned with a click.

Sweet.

I waited until I heard my mother's door close, then raced over to the window, shoving the curtains aside. An elderly man strolled by, his shoulders curled, a dog leading him along by a leash. I focused all my energy on him and waited to hear his heart's desire.

Nothing.

I cursed under my breath and tried again, this time focusing on a young late-night jogger, her ponytail bouncing prettily as she passed my window.

Nothing.

With a groan, I turned my back on the street. So not all my powers were back. Not my soul reading and obviously not my golden arrows. Not the ones I could really use to complete my mission and return myself to Orion's arms.

But I wasn't about to look a gift horse in the mouth. Telekinesis was something. It would, at the very least, make daily life easier. Give me more time to concentrate on the task at hand. And it had other benefits as well.

I looked outside again. With a flick of my wrist, I raised a square of concrete up an inch, and the jogger tripped right into the arms of a young man toting a small bag of groceries. They both laughed, and as he righted her, she looked down at her feet and blushed. Even with the window closed I could hear the warmth in his voice as he asked if she was all right, and her girlish giggle in response.

I smiled and closed the curtains.

CHAPTER FIFTY-THREE

True

"I am pleased you suggested this activity, Eros," my mother said, sitting back on her heels on the front walk. She wiped her brow with the back of her hand, distracting a guy on a dirt bike so thoroughly that he slammed into the bus-stop sign and went sprawling. My mother giggled. "Fresh flowers soothe me."

"Did you just say something positive? To me?" I teased as I patted down the earth around the pink asters I'd just planted.

"This place will never be my home, but I've decided to approach our exile as an adventure," my mother said. "And besides, there are a few amusements to enjoy." She twiddled her fingers as the man righted his bike. He muttered something under his breath and rode off, his wheels wavering beneath him. My mother laughed.

I rolled my eyes. "Well, they say that gardening is therapeutic," I told her. "Plus, it's a good activity for mother-daughter bonding."

"From whence did you glean this knowledge?" my mother asked.

From the books in the library when I was up all night. After I'd tested out my power a few thousand more times, I'd been far too awake to sleep, so I'd wandered into the library downstairs and read. I had told myself it was research. That the more I knew about actual life on Earth, the better equipped I'd be to match couples. But really, I was trying to distract myself from the many questions crowding my brain. Like whether Zeus was responsible for my regained power. And if not, how had it happened? Did he even know about it? If he found out, would he punish me? Would I be able to regain my other powers as well?

Now, in the light of day and on no sleep, the questions exhausted me.

I lifted my shoulder. "It's just something I learned in school this week."

She sighed and looked down at the floral border we'd created. "Don't place the pink blooms alongside the peach," she scolded. "They clash."

"Hey, True."

We looked up to find Charlie strolling toward us on the walk. I pushed myself to my feet, my heart giving a *thunk* of dread.

"What is it?" I asked, tugging off the gardening gloves. "What's wrong?"

"Um, nothing," he replied, looking confused. He gestured at his bike, which was leaned up against the hedge. "I was just on my way to the library to visit Katrina and I saw you out here, so I . . ."

He trailed off as my mother stood up behind me. I recognized the look on his face. Harmonia and I called it "Aphro-dumbfounded."

"Wow," he said.

"Charlie, this is my mother. Mom, this is Charlie," I said flatly.

She reached out to shake his hand. "Charmed."

"I . . . um . . . sorry . . . I . . . wow."

He hardly touched her fingers, and his cheeks were on fire.

"Well, thank you!" my mother trilled, flipping her hair.

"Let's go inside."

I took Charlie by the hand and led him past my mother. He watched her over his shoulder until the heavy oak door was firmly closed between them. Inside, he cleared his throat and shoved his hands into his pockets.

"God, that was embarrassing," he said.

I waved a hand. "It happens all the time," I told him. "So . . . you're going to visit Katrina? Everything's good?"

He grinned. "Everything's great. I was there till one in the morning," he said. "We ordered pizza with her mom . . . it was really cool."

"That's great!" I said, relieved. "I had a feeling you guys would fall in love."

Charlie laughed. "I knew it!"

"Knew what?" I asked.

"It was you. You rigged our compatibility tests in econ somehow," he said with a grin. "That's why you and Heath didn't hand in tests when I *know* I saw you guys filling them out."

I tried to think of some way to refute this, but then I realized there was no reason to. "Guilty," I said, raising my hands.

"So we're not really compatible," Charlie said. "I mean, not that it matters. I'd never let a computer tell me who to go out with, but still. We wouldn't have been matched up, right?"

"Actually, you would have," I told him.

"Come on. Seriously?"

I smiled. "Come with me."

Upstairs, Charlie hovered at the door of my bedroom while I went over to the desk and pulled his answer sheet and Katrina's from the drawer just under the sand timer. I unfolded them and handed them to him. He scanned the answers and his eyes widened.

"Forty-six out of fifty match," he said incredulously.

"Yep. Not that I'm sure the opinions of the Sure Match Corporation matter, per se, but yep."

Charlie laughed and pulled me into a hug. I was so stunned it took me a second to realize what he was doing, but eventually I hugged him back. Instantly I felt calmer, when I hadn't even realized I'd been tense. I missed touching people, hugging, kissing, holding hands. It was a part of daily existence on Olympus, but people hardly ever seemed to do it on Earth.

"Thanks, True," Charlie said. "If I had to be the new kid again, I'm glad I got to do it with you."

· I grinned. "Same here."

Together we walked downstairs, and I watched from the porch as he pedaled off to his new love, the compatibility tests clutched in one hand. My mother shaded her eyes and watched him go. I noticed she had entirely rearranged my plantings, and they looked much prettier her way.

"Who was that lovely young man?" she asked with a familiar gleam in her eye.

"He's not for you," I replied. "He was my first match." I took a breath as Charlie lifted his hand, then dipped down the hill and out of sight. "And my first human friend."

CHAPTER FIFTY-FOUR
Charlie

Universal Truth had just come to the noisy climax of the Romantics' "What I Like About You" when the garage door rattled open. Fred shielded his eyes against the sun as the grille of my dad's truck slowly scrolled into view. My father started to hit the gas, but then slammed on the brakes when he saw us. His jaw hit the steering wheel.

"Here we go," I said under my breath.

This was it. I was about to have the dreaded conversation with my dad. And I was going to do it with an audience.

"Should we bail?" Noel asked. Noel Finkle was the real name of Steve Miller Band. His friend, Clean-Cut, was actually Tom Lipnicki. I'd found this out earlier when I'd texted Fred—whose last name was King—to see if they wanted to come over and jam.

"No. We're cool," I replied.

Then my dad unfolded his massive body from behind the wheel of his truck. He was wearing his SJP polo and baseball cap, his whistle still hanging around his neck and his playbook gripped in one hand. Tom whistled.

"We don't look cool," he said.

322 • kieran scott

"Charlie?" My father slammed the truck door so hard it reverberated in my bones. "What's all this?"

I cleared my throat. "This is my new band."

"We're Universal Truth," Fred said.

My father flicked his eyes over Fred's unruly hair and too-tight T-shirt like he was a toad.

"Your *band?*" The word dripped off his tongue like poison. "No one asked me if you could be in a band."

"It just sort of happened," I said, keeping my voice even.

My dad put his hands on his hips. "You're supposed to be concentrating on cross-country."

"I can do both," I told him, gripping my sticks in my sweaty hands.

"How exactly?" he asked. "How are you going to make time for your studies and the team and . . . this?"

"Practice is only an hour after school," I told him. "I can study at night and then we rehearse on the weekends. Besides, the season's over in two months. Then I'll have tons of time."

He shook his head. "I don't like this, Charlie. Look at your brothers. They dedicated themselves to one thing and one thing only, and look at how successful they've been."

I swallowed hard as that telltale resentful anger burbled up inside me. It was always about my brothers. Always about how perfect they were and how I should follow their lead. Well, not this time.

"Okay then," I said tersely. "I'll dedicate myself to the band."

My father paled. So did my new bandmates.

"You will not!" my father shouted, pointing at the floor. "You made a commitment to the team."

I stood up from my stool, shaking from head to toe. "I don't care about the team!" I shouted. "This is what I want to do, Dad. I want to play the drums. You want me to be on a team, so I am. But if you make me quit this, I'll quit that, too. I'll go back to sitting home doing nothing. Is that what you want?"

"Don't take that tone with me, son," my father said. "You sound like a petulant child."

"That's because you treat me like a child," I said. "I'm trying to make a mature decision here. I want to fulfill my commitments to the team, and to the band. I can do both. I know I can. But you don't even want to let me try. You just can't stand that I'm not exactly like you."

My words hung in the air, echoing through the lofty garage.

Tom unhooked his guitar strap. "Maybe we should go."

"Wait," my father said.

We all looked at him, surprised. I felt like my heart was about to burst out of my chest. My father looked at the floor, then took off his baseball cap and scratched the top of his head.

"You're right," he said.

"I am?"

"He is?" Fred, Noel, and Tom said.

"Yes," my father replied. "You are trying to make an adult decision. You're trying to live your life." He took a breath and blew it out. "You can play in your band and run cross-country. But if your grades start to slip one notch, we're having a conversation. Understood?"

I was so dumbfounded I couldn't move. But my heart was darting around my chest like a firework set off inside me.

"Understood," Fred whispered to me. "Say 'understood.'"

"Understood," I replied.

My father shook his head and clomped his way across the garage, avoiding wires and amps.

"Universal Truth," he said under his breath as he opened the door to the kitchen. "What the hell kind of band name is Universal Truth?"

Then the door slammed behind him, and the guys slapped hands and clapped me on the back. I stared after my father, feeling like I could cry and laugh and scream and then laugh some more.

It had actually happened. I'd finally stood up to my father and lived to talk about it. Not only that, it had worked. I grabbed my phone out of my bag and headed for the driveway.

"Hey! Dude! Where're you going? We still have two more songs to run through!" Fred called after me.

I turned around to walk backward, grinning from ear to ear. "Take five," I told him. "I gotta call my girlfriend."

CHAPTER FIFTY-FIVE

True

Monday morning. It was a new day, a new week. The sun shone and everyone outside Lake Carmody High seemed full of promise to me. Everyone a potential project.

"Looking for your next victim?" Hephaestus asked, staring up at me through mirrored sunglasses.

"Very funny." I took a breath and drew myself up straighter. "This time it's going to be much easier. I've learned from my mistakes."

Stacey and her friends snickered as they walked past me. Darla shot me a look of death from the top of the stairs. Darnell lifted his hand and rubbed his fingers together with a menacing stare. At least I had his money in my pocket after cashing my paycheck on Saturday. That was something.

"But you're still a weird loser with no friends," Hephaestus said, stating a fact that I couldn't ignore.

"I'm going to have to work on that, aren't I?" I replied. "I mean, I *am* going to have to work on it. I have to succeed. Orion's life depends on it."

Hephaestus tilted his head. "Maybe you and I should pretend to date. I *am* totally popular. I could up your stock like *that*."

He snapped his fingers just as a big white SUV pulled up to the curb. I was about to shoot down his ridiculous idea when the door of the SUV opened and out stepped a tall guy with dark hair pushed back from his face in waves. He wore a dark-blue cotton jacket over a white T-shirt, and perfectly snug jeans. Every girl around us started to drool. And then he turned his head.

"Orion!"

The word left my lips at a gasp. I dropped my bag on the ground next to Hephaestus's wheel and ran, my knees weak beneath me, my vision blurred. He turned into me and I flung my arms around his neck, my mind desperately trying to understand what my eyes were seeing, what my body was certainly feeling.

"I can't believe it's you!" I cried, pressing my hands against his familiar cheeks. Tears of joy spilled over, and I could scarcely breathe. "What are you doing here? No, wait. I don't care! This is the happiest day of my existence."

I pulled him to me for a kiss. His lips were exactly as I remembered them. Soft, warm, and just the tiniest hint of salt. It was a moment before I realized he wasn't kissing me back, and he suddenly, firmly, pushed me away, his hands cupping my shoulders.

"Orion?" I said, looking up into his eyes. They were confused and a little bit scared. Just as they had been on the day I'd returned him to Earth. The day I'd begun to fall. "What's wrong with you? Are you quite well?"

"I'm . . . fine," the love of my life mumbled, searching my face. "But who the hell are you?"